THE AMERICAN HEIRESS

By mid-morning the fog had dispersed and an hour later the Irish coast was sighted. The *Lusitania* seemed to be entirely alone on the now calm and dazzling blue sea.

Clemency suddenly jumped up and said she was going to take a turn on deck. She never reached the door. A sudden devastating explosion reverberated through the ship. Nothing was stable. The trunks were sliding about the floor and Clemency was shrieking, ''We've been torpedoed! Oh, Mother, what shall we do?''

Hetty urged Clemency and her mother forward to the boat deck where a great many people were attempting to clamber into the lifeboats. The horror of this made Hetty close her eyes; then she was tumbled into a lifeboat and a sudden rush downwards and a dizzy lilt as the doomed lifeboat upended and hit the water.

In seconds the sea, dark and cold and stifling, closed over everyone, and Hetty knew she was drowning.

Also by the same author,
and available in Coronet Books:

The American Heiress

Dorothy Eden

CORONET BOOKS
Hodder and Stoughton

Copyright © 1980 by Dorothy Eden

First published in Great Britain
1980 by Hodder and Stoughton Limited

Coronet edition 1981
Second impression 1982

British Library C.I.P.

Eden, Dorothy
   The American Heiress.
   I. Title
   823[F]   PR9639.3.E38

ISBN 0-340-26743-7

———————————————————

Printed and bound in Great Britain for
Hodder and Stoughton Paperbacks, a
division of Hodder and Stoughton Ltd.,
Mill Road, Dunton Green, Sevenoaks,
Kent (Editorial Office: 47 Bedford
Square, London, WC1 3DP) by
Richard Clay (The Chaucer Press), Ltd.,
Bungay, Suffolk

For Jack Geoghegan

I

The morning Mrs Jervis, her daughter Clemency, and Harriet Brown (known as Hetty to her friends) were to leave, New York was beautiful. It was the kind of day when the city was at its most magical. It had other moods, and well enough Hetty knew them. She hadn't always lived in a tall important house overlooking Central Park, with its view of the early unsullied green of the trees and shrubs, and the sweep of brilliant blue sky.

In the shadowed streets of her childhood there had been few glimpses of the sun, and none of passing carriages, or of welldressed children bowling hoops or tossing gaily-painted balls. The children Hetty had known had had no time to play. Thin and wizened, with eyes and noses running from the cold, they had either stumbled behind their mothers to sit all day, silent and sleepy from malnutrition, in sweat shops turning out endless garments for the Seventh Avenue warehouses, or had grown old enough to sweep the floor and fetch and carry for the drab tired workers in those badly-aired, badly-smelling rooms.

The background music to Hetty's young life had been the rattle and clatter of sewing machines. She had never forgotten it and, ten years later, awoke every morning to a sense of escape, a sense of the miraculous. The sweat shop was an evil dream of the past, her mother's worn pale face a sadder dream, and this rich house reality, although she still had as little life of her own as she had had as a child worker.

The sewing machines had rattled busily, making Clemency's trousseau and Mrs Jervis's extensive wardrobe of ruched silks and satins, but Hetty's wardrobe remained sparse and simple, and very unobtrusive, as befitted a lady's maid. Long before the trunks were packed Hetty's arms had ached. There was so much tissue paper, so many garments, morning dresses, afternoon dresses, tea gowns, dinner gowns, ball gowns, furs and feather boas and, most important of all, there was the wedding gown.

This was a truly beautiful creation made of heavy satin like thick cream, and embroidered with slightly yellowed old Chantilly lace. The veil was also made of Chantilly lace, an heirloom worn by both Clemency's mother and grandmother.

Hetty was not allowed to pack these two items. They were entrusted to the experienced hands of the couturière, Madame Natalia from the big Fifth Avenue store, Lord and Taylor. They occupied a trunk of their own, together with the long white kid gloves, the white and gold brocade shoes, the silk stockings and the hand-embroidered undergarments.

Of course, in London, Hetty would have to be trusted to unpack the precious garments and dress the bride. And wasn't she just too lucky for words, to have the chance to be there? Miss Clemency, the Fifth Avenue household said, would make the best-dressed bride in England.

And the prettiest, Mrs Jervis added complacently. Mrs Jervis was one of those mothers who fed on their daughters' lives. She was dictatorial, organising, possessive and overpowering. Only Clemency ever dared to oppose her, but that was over relatively trifling matters. Fortunately they both saw major issues in the same way, and had similar ambitions.

It was inconceivable, however, to imagine slim young Clemency ever growing to look like her big-bosomed mother, even though the arrogant confidence was already apparent. Clemency's green eyes, not yet protuberant and faded as were her mother's, could on occasion hold the same hard stare, the same will to be obeyed.

Hetty knew that well enough. But she also knew Clemency's youthful butterfly gaiety, her wilfulness which had a certain charm, her supreme selfishness contradicted every now and then by some spontaneous act of generosity, her continuing love of schoolgirl pranks, accompanied by paroxysms of giggles, and her quite unscrupulous flirtatiousness.

Clemency Jervis, twenty-one years old and a spoiled only child, had enough character and determination to succeed in her new life. She would not be meek and scared and incompetent in her role as mistress of an English great house. The title would not come amiss with her either. She had a cool practical streak, unusual in one so young. She was ambitious, above all. Of course she would like to be loved, and to be in love, but position was more important. The love could follow, in one way or another. She was longing to wear the long white gown with a train and her sparkling little tiara, and curtsey to the Queen of England.

Which all slightly shocked Hetty for she realised that Clemency was not yet in love with her English fiancé, Lord Hazzard of Loburn in the Cotswolds. Of course she had seen him only briefly on his visit to New York last summer, a visit he had had to curtail when the European war broke out, and he had to hasten home to rejoin his regiment. His proposal had been made perhaps earlier than he had intended, for he, too, Hetty had suspected, had not been entirely guided by love. Indeed, the thought of Clemency's dowry had probably been paramount in his mind. He was willing to give a pretty American girl a title, which naturally she would adore, a wedding in St Margaret's, Westminster, and the chance to show off a wantonly expensive trousseau to London society, in return for a plump injection into his bank account.

Hetty knew that if she were in Clemency's place she would not be thinking only of clothes and jewellery and being presented to the Queen, and becoming mistress of a famous old house. She would be thinking of the man whom she was to stand beside in church, and lie in bed with afterwards. And although she had been given little chance to observe Lord Hazzard, she had known that she found his blond good looks and his dazzling blue gaze very exciting. He had not, of course, noticed her. In her neat white cap and apron she was part of the background furniture. She was Harriet Brown, a lady's maid. And Clemency, who was not always too possessive of her suitors, was very jealous of this aristocratic one.

Clemency's grandfather had made some millions in various ways which could have been honest or dishonest, but which must have required skill and cool nerves. Perhaps Clemency, in the matrimonial stakes, had inherited his instinct for a profitable deal. She and Lord Hazzard no doubt would suit each other very well.

The outbreak of war had been both a disaster and a blessing. Even Mrs Jervis doubted if Lord Hazzard would have made such a speedy proposal if events had not precipitated him into a decision. There had been sundry hurried meetings with her brother, Jonas Middleton in Wall Street, consultations with lawyers, and a long private interview with Mrs Jervis. Then the intended marriage of Miss Clemency Millicent Jervis, only child of Mrs Millicent Jervis and the late Howard B. Jervis, Wall Street financier, to Major Lord Hazzard of the Coldstream Guards, and of Loburn near Cirencester, England, was announced.

Lord Hazzard had pressed for an early date. He was going home to go to war.

"He wants an heir," Hetty said.

"Of course," Clemency agreed.

"I think that's more important to him than having a bride."

"It always is with the English aristocracy. I'm not dumb, Brown."

"You don't love him, Miss Clemency."

"Oh, yes I do." Clemency sighed and stretched her arms voluptuously. "I love all good-looking men. Don't look so shocked, Brown. I think I could be happy with any of them. But Hugo is making me a lady. That's extra. I like it. So does Mother. Lord and Lady Hazzard are going to have fun."

Hetty was genuinely shocked.

"There'll hardly be balls and garden parties while the war's on."

"Oh, it will be over before we know it. Hugo says so. So does Uncle Jonas. He says three great cultured peoples like the English and the French and the Germans can't truly be trying to annihilate each other. They're all got too much sense."

"England isn't used to giving in, Miss Clemency. History shows that. Neither is Germany. And France is wanting revenge for the Franco-Prussian War. She's a proud nation. Besides, we don't really know what it's about, do we?"

"I certainly don't," Clemency said cheerfully. "I expect Hugo will explain. I hope he's being careful. I don't want a wounded hero. And you, by the way, are coming to England as a lady's maid, not as a history student."

"I always liked history."

Clemency gave her critical stare.

"Mother should never have let you have lessons with me. You'd be a better maid if you didn't try to be literary."

"I'm not literary, Miss Clemency. I wish I were."

"Well, you always did have your head in a book, at every opportunity. You won't have any time for that in future. And don't sulk. You're getting a trip to England. You never imagined that would happen, did you? That day when your mother brought you here as a starved little creature, with nits in your hair."

"I never did have nits!"

Clemency who could be a cruel tease, relented. She was too excited to indulge in the perennial amusement of tormenting Hetty, her poor, her extremely poor, relation, who was not expected to answer back.

"All right, no nits, but you had plenty of other things wrong. Your clothes had to be burnt."

And I never saw my mother again, Hetty thought silently, with a grief that had never healed.

She had been told, that day, to wait in the hall, a vast marble-floored place like a palace, while her mother was closeted with an alarmingly haughty lady, who was apparently the mistress of this grand house. She had sat motionless on a hard chair with a carved back that had pressed into her thin bones, and waited.

It was only after some time that the voices behind the tall closed doors became audible. That was because Mother had begun to sob, and the lady of the house had begun screaming at her. One hadn't known that ladies lost their tempers.

"It isn't true. It's a wicked lie. A fabrication. I will destroy these letters instantly, and you can leave my house and take your ba—— your child with you."

Then Mother had stopped sobbing and, with un-accustomed spirit had said, "Destroying them will do no good. They're only copies. I have the real ones at home. I know where to take them if you don't do as I ask. To a newspaperman on the *New York World*."

"You're blackmailing me!"

"I know. I apologise, ma'am. But I'm sick and my little girl —" Mother's voice wavered and faded, and the part of the conversation that Hetty desperately wanted to hear became inaudible.

She had begun trembling with apprehension. Something terrible was happening. She was going to be deserted, and by her own mother. If she could have found her way back to the Bowery she would have run off, there and then. But she was even more afraid of the alien streets than of this cold echoing hall. So she waited.

At least the double doors opened and the lady, her head high held and angrily, came out. She looked at Hetty with critical distaste.

"Eleven, you said? She's very undergrown."

"Undernourished, ma'am. She was a pretty baby."

"That's hardly the point. If she's to live here she must be thoroughly scrubbed and decently dressed. Can she read and write?"

"I've taught her as much as I could, and she's had a bit of schooling. She's very bright."

"Doesn't look it to me. I can't have an ignorant girl in my house, in any capacity. She can have lessons with my daughter's governess for a year or two. Then when she's fourteen she can learn to be a maid to my daughter. If Clemency likes her, of course. She will be known as Brown. Well, speak up, child. Would you like that?"

"Of course she would," Mother said, looking so unhappy that Hetty was completely without words.

"Child?" said the imperious voice.

"Yes, thank you, ma'am," she managed to whisper. "If Mother says I have to."

Mother's trembling but stubborn chin went up.

"Her name is Harriet, ma'am."

"So you told me. As a servant, she will be called Brown."

Hetty tried to meet this fashionable woman's long hard domineering stare, as she was to do many times later, on many different kinds of occasions.

"She knows nothing?"

"Nothing," Mother said. "I'm telling you the truth."

"Then I'll send for my housekeeper. She can bath her and find some place for her to sleep." She moved towards a bell rope, shrugging her shoulders fatalistically. "I believe I must be the most magnanimous woman in New York."

Before Hetty could beg in horror not to be left in this strange house with this alarming woman, Mother was saying fervently, "Thank you, ma'am. It's a great relief to me," and then adding, with some daring, "Life can be unfair to women, ma'am."

This was a sentiment to which the lady did not respond. She obviously hardly thought that she and someone like Mother with her shabby clothes and dark piteous eyes could be talking about life on the same planet.

Hetty only realised years later how extreme misery could toughen and harden and shape one's character. For good or evil.

She didn't think she had it in her to be evil, but neither could she go on for ever being a meek nonentity. She was told that as she came from a very poor and distant branch of the Jervis family she must expect to work for her board and lodging, her wearing apparel and her education. She could never presume to be the equal of Miss Clemency, the pampered and adored daughter of a widowed mother.

After the death of her husband at the age of only forty-five Mrs Jervis said she did not intend to remarry. She would devote herself entirely to her little girl's future. She would make it a glittering one, to compensate the poor child for being made fatherless so young.

In a way Hetty's arrival was a boon, for Clemency, over-protected and cosseted, had been lonely and bored with her life.

The two girls were not unalike in appearance, both being dark-haired and green-eyed with slim neat bodies. But they were totally unalike in character, Hetty's early austerity having made her introverted and wary, and with a love of beauty, and a greedy desire to learn about everything, books, pictures, manners, food. She was not unhappy, for the servants, hearing of her previous life, had made something of a pet of her, a thing that did not escape Mrs Jervis's notice. As a consequence she made it so evident that Hetty was an unwelcome outsider, taken in only by Mrs Jervis's Christian kindness, that Hetty never had the courage to demand more details of that distant family relationship.

Actually, her slum upbringing hadn't left her in much ignorance of the facts of life, and by the time she had reached puberty she had had an intuition about the true nature of her relationship with the Jervis family. Hints dropped below stairs and her own growing awareness of the opposite sex made her suspect what must have happened. When she was told by Cook, a fierce-tongued but kindly woman called Mrs Crampton, that her mother had briefly been an upstairs maid in the house shortly before Mr Jervis's marriage to Mrs Jervis, she was almost certain that, far from being a distant cousin of Clemency's, she was, in fact, her half sister.

The knowledge didn't shock her. She was only full of pity for what her mother must have suffered, and intensely admiring of her for having had the courage to enter into such an emotional and hopeless relationship.

She eventually discovered that her assumptions were correct when, one day, just after her sixteenth birthday, a rather grubby package addressed to her, Miss Harriet Brown, was delivered at the servants' entrance of the house.

"By a very sharp-looking fellow," said Cook disapprovingly. "What is it, Hetty, the family jools?"

They were not jewels, only a small package of letters tied with faded ribbon. A badly-spelled note accompanied them. It read:

Dear Hetty Brown, Your Mam intrusted me with these when she died. I promised to deliver them to you on your 16 birthday which she said was first May 1908. She said you would be old enuf to unnerstand, I hope

15

you are, dear. Your pal, Alf.

Whoever Alf was, he had kept his promise, and Hetty, shaking with emotion, had read the creased pages:

My darling girl,
    I hope life is not too hard for you. It is bad luck it must be like this. I trust you to understand, and enclose some money for your needs. I will send more after the baby is born, and continue to do so. Remembering all the sweetness we had.
                           Howard

More letters followed at infrequent intervals, mentioning money, and later, her, the baby. "Harriet is a good name, but I shall call her Hetty."
Then a final letter:

I seem to have developed a touch of heart trouble, nothing to worry about, but I have to take a vacation. Millicent and I are going to Florida for a few weeks. Don't worry if you don't hear from me for a while. Enclosed, enough to cover things for the next few months.

This letter ended with a touch of more open emotion. The signature was "Your own Howard".
It was the last letter, for it must have been soon after that Howard B. Jervis had died from his "Slight heart trouble". His younger daughter, aged five years, was an heiress, his elder, aged six years, was precipitated into her education in a Bowery sweat shop, beside her shocked and grieving mother.
Howard Jervis might genuinely have loved Hetty's mother, but he had been too dreamy and unpractical to provide permanently for her. He had certainly never set eyes on his illegitimate daughter. Wouldn't have wanted to, indeed.

Poor Mother must have nourished her bitterness for years, until she had become fatally ill, and took her sad and desperate revenge by depositing Hetty on the doorstep of the Fifth Avenue mansion.

After reading the letters Hetty felt as if she had attained maturity within a few hours. She wept a little then, drying her eyes and lifting her head proudly, had resolved never to stoop to using the letters as a weapon, as perhaps her mother had intended her to do. Clemency would never be told of their relationship and Mrs Jervis never reminded of it. All in all, Mrs Jervis had treated her well enough, considering how outraged she must have been, and an illegitimate child did not expect an inheritance. Clemency must be rich and she poor. That was the way of the world.

But she had learned a great deal in the Jervis household. She was no longer an illiterate Bowery child, but a reasonably educated young woman with natural good taste. The ways of the rich had easily enough rubbed off on her. She had inherited, too, her father's love of beauty and poetry but, fortunately for her, these qualities were leavened with a good deal of her mother's common sense and instinct for survival. She had no intention of remaining a lady's maid for the rest of her life.

She was a bastard.

When she had accepted that fact she knew that she had lost the last traces of her childish sentimentality, and began to think frequently and seriously about her future. After all, she was just as attractive as Clemency, and could easily adopt the same haughty air and the same sweet persuasive manners. Indeed, Clemency had occasionally extracted enormous fun from making Hetty dress in her clothes and receive the male callers whom she found too boring. Hetty had entertained these unfortunate rejects in the south drawing room, and none of them had discovered the truth. It had been a great lark. Clemency had giggled helplessly at the keyhole, and Hetty had had to

17

raise her voice vivaciously to drown the sound. Naturally she had not been permitted to play this game with Lord Hazzard, which she regretted. She would have enjoyed having those brilliant blue eyes fixed on her only, although she was not at all sure that he would not have seen through the disguise. She had wondered if he had a sense of humour.

That was something Clemency would have to discover. It didn't seem to be worrying her. She was totally involved in material plans. Besides, Hugo seemed a bit unreal, didn't he, on the other side of the Atlantic, and perhaps being a rather grim soldier.

But everything would settle down happily, wouldn't it? That was the only time Hetty detected any nervousness or uncertainty in Clemency. However, it was gone in a moment, and she was crying, "Brown, did you pack my Ascot dresses? We'll be in England just in time."

As soon as Hetty had been old enough to learn her duties as a lady's maid, the two girls' schoolroom friendship was over. Clemency must now be addressed respectfully as "Miss Clemency" and Hetty herself by her surname. It had been a difficult lesson to learn. But Hetty was becoming adept at adjusting to circumstances.

"I shouldn't think there'd be any Ascot this year, Miss Clemency."

"Oh, nonsense, it's an English institution. As soon say there'd be no Parliament. Or no King and Queen."

"And that's a stupid remark, if I may say so, Miss Clemency," Hetty said evenly. "You'll have to learn more about England than that. She's fighting a war that's getting worse each week."

"Brown, I forbid you to scare me! You'd just better stop reading the newspapers."

2

The Dodge motor car, of which Uncle Jonas was extremely proud, stood outside waiting to take them downtown to the Cunard pier.

But the ladies had been delayed over their breakfast by Uncle Jonas's arrival, and the alarming news he had brought them. He had come in flourishing a newspaper and asking if they had read the shipping notes in the *New York World* a week ago.

"Why, no," Mrs Jervis answered. "We have our time of sailing. What else do we need to know?"

"This," said Uncle Jonas, pointing at a column. "A damned odd notice put out by the German Embassy. Shall I read it to you?"

"Do. But we're not sailing on a German ship. I personally would have preferred the *Kronzprincessen Cecilie*. So many of my friends have said how wonderful she is. But under the circumstances we thought it diplomatic to choose a British ship bound for a British port. Didn't we, Clemency?"

"Let him read the notice, Mother."

Uncle Jonas cleared his throat and read in his most sonorous voice, "Travellers intending to embark on the Atlantic voyage are reminded that a state of war exists between Germany and her allies and Great Britain and her allies; that the zone of war includes the waters adjacent to the British Isles; that, in accordance with formal notice given by the Imperial German Government, vessels flying the flag of Great Britain or of any of her allies are liable to destruction in those waters and that travellers sailing in the war zone on ships of Great Britain or her allies do so at their own risk. Imperial German Embassy, Washington D.C. April 22, 1915.

"Now what do you make of that, Millicent?"

"I guess it's honourable behaviour by the Germans, but it doesn't mention the *Lusitania*."

"It's put right beside the advertisement for the *Lusitania* sailings. Don't you think that significant? I wish I'd seen it a week ago, but my clerk only brought it to my notice this morning. It's still not too late to cancel, Millicent."

"At the last minute like this! Why, all our trunks are on board. Clemency's wedding gown and all. What do you think, honey?"

Clemency answered her mother without hesitation.

"We can't cancel now. Hugo is getting leave so that he can meet us at Liverpool. Goodness, Uncle Jonas, we can't have Hugo thinking we're scared."

Uncle Jonas, who was Mrs Jervis's brother and much resembled her with his pale grey eyes and florid complexion, said in his downright manner, "Better to be scared and alive than brave and dead, my girl. Think about it, Millicent. There's an hour before we need to leave for the docks. You can telephone the Cunard people. I think they could be persuaded to get your trunks off. Even if they can't, I guess there are other wedding gowns to be had. And I can send a cable to freeze that million dollars in the Westminster bank. We can't have milord getting his hands on the marriage settlement before the marriage."

"Uncle Jonas, Hugo would never do that! He's absolutely honourable. Anyway, I don't suppose the bank would let him."

"Not if it conducts its business in a proper manner. We've given clear instructions. Credentials, including the marriage certificate, to be produced."

"And the bride, too?" Clemency asked. "I think this talk of money is a bit heartless when you should be worrying about German submarines."

"That's what I am worrying about," Uncle Jonas insisted, thumping his fist on the table, making the delicate china rattle. "Haven't I made that clear? Millicent, I know your hopes for your daughter, but it's my personal belief that the stakes have got too high. Is a title for Clemency worth a million dollars, and risking her life into the bargain?"

"Jonas, you're being an old woman. The Germans would never dare to sink a passenger ship, especially when there'll be so many Americans on board. They'd be mad. Think of the outcry. They're already accused of murdering babies in Belgium. This would be murdering them at sea. Why, it would just about make the United States declare war."

"Which would suit the British and the French nicely, wouldn't it? You've got to realise that devious things go on during a war. I've even been told this morning that there's a rumour the *Lusitania* is carrying munitions, though apparently the manifest doesn't say so. Now the British aren't naïve innocents. They'd never have got their Empire if they were. So if the *Lusitania* is armed she's a legitimate target for German submarines."

"I don't believe a word of it, and I think it's cruel of you to try to frighten us at the last minute. You're too cautious. I don't believe you ever took a risk in your life. I suppose that's being a banker." Millicent had put down her napkin. Except for her hat, gloves and furs, she was dressed for departure. "But I'm not entirely ignorant either. Isn't it the code that an enemy submarine surfaces and gives passengers time to leave a ship before it is sunk?"

"Take a mighty long time to disembark two thousand souls in mid-ocean. And I can't see any liner carrying enough lifeboats to accommodate so many. But there is that point, I grant you."

Clemency stood behind her uncle, bending over him and nuzzling his cheek.

"Darling Uncle, I have an important date in St Margaret's Church, Westminster, London, exactly two weeks from now, and I surely don't intend to miss it. Not even if the Kaiser himself warned us."

"This is the Kaiser's warning, through his spokesman. But I can see both I and the Kaiser are wasting our time."

"Goodness me, Jonas," Mrs Jervis broke in, "the *Lusitania* has the blue riband of the Atlantic. She can surely outsail any enemy ship. And I expect we'll have an escort when we enter dangerous waters. I'll personally get the Captain's reassurance. As soon as we go on board."

"You won't get to talk to the Captain until you're steaming outside the heads, and it'll be too late to turn back. Well, I've warned you, girls. And I'm bound to tell you that from what I hear not many people have cancelled. Not even young Alfred Vanderbilt."

"There you are then, Jonas."

"I know where I am, Millicent. Safe in New York City. Now shouldn't you be asking the maid you're taking how she feels?"

"Brown!" said Clemency. "She wouldn't miss it for anything. She knows she'll never have another chance like this."

"All the same, you ought to let the girl make up her own mind."

"But I couldn't possibly do without her. She has to dress me for my wedding."

"All the same," Uncle Jonas said stubbornly, "I think we Americans can call ourselves a compassionate people. We regard our servants as human beings."

"Jonas, you're just too interfering," Mrs Jervis said crossly. "If Clemency and I decide to risk all these dangers you talk about then so can Brown. I don't intend saying a word to her."

Most of this conversation was related to Hetty by Polly, the maid who had been waiting on the family at breakfast. Mrs Crampton, the cook, showed the most indignation. She was a motherly person who had taken Hetty under her wing from the day of her arrival, a scared little creature, grieving for her mother and utterly bewildered by the size and richness of the house.

Now she was exclaiming, "I think it's downright wicked not to give Hetty a choice. All Mr Jonas seems concerned about is the money in the Westminster bank. But Hetty's a person, not a slave, after all. Slavery went out last century. She ought to be allowed to decide whether she wants to put her life in danger. Hetty, show your spirit and refuse to go."

"But what would I do then, Mrs Crampton? I wouldn't have a job. You know what the mistress is if she doesn't get her own way. Miss Clemency, too. I'd be walking the streets."

Hetty was twisting her hands in deep agitation. She didn't want this exciting voyage to melt away like a mirage, yet she had a strong intuition that it would be dangerous. The Germans didn't play games. But they would prefer that the British ships they sank didn't carry Americans. They wouldn't want to antagonise the United States. In that, her conclusions were the same as Uncle Jonas's. She also knew it wasn't right that Mrs Jervis and Clemency should so carelessly decide her fate. Was that all they thought of her after all these years?

However, for what it was worth, she had made up her own mind. "I'll go, Mrs Crampton," she said definitely. "I have to look after Miss Clemency's wedding dress."

In the big kitchen they were all looking at her fondly, Mrs Crampton with moist eyes, Polly with admiration, Mr Banks, the butler, unbending enough to shake her hand, and Topsy, the smallest maid and as black as the polished stove, rolling her eyes fearfully.

"I declare," said Mrs Crampton aggressively, "Hetty will never drown. She'll bob up like a rubber ball. Won't you, honey? But always remember, we're all your friends."

"I'll always remember," Hetty said shakily.

The bell was ringing for her to go upstairs. She was dressed for travelling, except for her hat and cloak. Her hair was smoothly brushed, parted in the middle and twisted into a neat bob, while the small white collar of her dark stuff dress made her look meek and obedient. Yet there was something about her that made Mrs Crampton say, as she left the room, "That one will never stay a lady's maid. And good luck to her, I say."

So, three hours later, they waved to the rotund but diminishing figure of Uncle Jonas on the wharf, and sailed on the full tide. Mrs Jervis and Clemency were to occupy a spacious suite on the promenade deck. Hetty was to share a cabin in steerage with a young mother and two small children. She would spend most of the day and the night, of course, attending to her employers' wants. Naturally she couldn't eat in the first-class dining saloon. Anyway, Mrs Jervis and Clemency were at the Captain's table, along with the millionaire, Mr Alfred Vanderbilt, and several other important people who had not been afraid to sail on the famous Cunard liner.

Mrs Jervis was sure that on such a fine ship the food would be acceptable, wherever it was eaten. Not that she would have worried too much about Hetty's menu. So Hetty was to descend to the bowels of the ship three times a day. It was aggravating that she could not be rung for. Mrs Jervis overcame this difficulty by drawing up a list of the hours she would be required in the first-class suite.

Hetty saw that she was not going to be spending a great deal of time in steerage, either having meals or getting to know people, or even indulging in seasickness. Mrs Jervis would certainly regard that last as an indulgence.

She was perfectly sure that Mrs Jervis was getting a final vindictive pleasure out of the situation that had been forced on her twelve years ago. Where else should the daughter of her late husband's mistress travel but in steerage?

"And what are you going to England for?" Mrs Drummond, the woman who was sharing her cabin, asked.

"I'm a lady's maid. To Miss Clemency Jervis. She's to be married in St Margaret's, Westminster. To a Lord."

"Isn't that romantic?" Mrs Drummond said. She had a harassed face, and her two small children, aged one and two, constantly tired her out. She was seasick as well. At least the thought of a grand wedding cheered her up. Hetty helped her as much as possible, but the ladies in the first-class suite, with all their frills and furbelows, allowed her very little free time. It was a pity, because she felt an affinity with Mary Drummond. She reminded Hetty of the faces of her childhood.

"You don't look like a lady's maid, love."

"Don't I?"

"You look like a lady yourself."

"Apeing my betters?"

"But you don't think they're your betters, do you? I'm sure you're right. I'm sure they'd never be kind to my Alfie and Benny like you are."

The little boys were bewildered pale-faced creatures who clung to Hetty when their mother was laid low with seasickness. She spent more time feeding them than herself. Mrs Drummond's husband was a Canadian who had enlisted in the Royal Navy and sailed some weeks previously. She was following him to England with the children. They would live in lodgings in Portsmouth. No, she wasn't nervous on such a big ship. Having so many rich and important Americans on board the Germans would never dare to touch it, would they?

But she wanted to hear all about the high life on the upper decks, and looked to Hetty for this information.

Inevitably Clemency was soon conducting several flirtations at once. Her mother looked on blandly, as always delighted by her daughter's social success. Her dear child had such high spirits, she told various passengers to whom she had already boasted about the noble fiancé waiting in England. Wasn't it well known that sea voyages always turned young girls' heads? It would be dear Clemency's last fling before settling down as a wife, so who could blame the girl. She was only twenty-one years old. And to tell the truth, Mrs Jervis confided to Mr Vanderbilt (who had been divorced and remarried and was therefore extremely worldly and sophisticated) Clemency didn't really know her intended husband that well. Did any bride, if it came to that? So let her have some shipboard fun. Besides, it took her mind off the thought of submarines.

They were not yet in dangerous waters, the Captain said. The Irish sea would be the place where the most strict look-out would be kept. But that was still three days' steaming away. If they wanted to get nervous, the Captain added, and he wasn't a joking man, let them wait until then.

Impervious, the two ladies, Mrs Jervis and her daughter, perfumed and bejewelled, sallied forth each evening. They were having a tremendous time. Imagine if they had listened to that old woman, Uncle Jonas, and cancelled the trip!

I despise Clemency, Hetty thought, getting out yet another of the dinner gowns and spending an hour or more ironing the soft silk folds. These gowns were part of Clemency's trousseau. They should have been kept for her husband, that tall blond blue-eyed Englishman, who was surely expecting a bride who loved him.

Hetty climbed down to steerage for her evening meal, helped Mary Drummond put the children to bed, and talked to Mrs Drummond and other passengers, until it was time to go up again to undress her ladies. Mrs Drummond found the whole business fascinating but unbelievable. Two grown women who couldn't undress themselves.

"But I don't intend doing it for ever," Hetty said. "I've been talking to those nice girls who want to be Red Cross nurses. I think that's what I'll do, too, when I've got Miss Clemency married. If the war's still on, and they'll have me."

"They'd be lucky to get you, dear," said Mrs Drummond.

On the last night at sea there was to be a concert in the first-class saloon and several parties in the cabins of the more famous passengers. Wasn't it exciting, Mrs Jervis said, Mr Vanderbilt was going to buy horses, and he had been persuaded to come to Clemency's wedding. There was also a party in steerage, where some amateur musicians were going to play dance music, but the dress there would be informal.

It was only stipulated that strict black-out rules must be observed, and wandering on the decks in the moonlight was not to be encouraged. Even pale dresses and the gentlemen's white shirt-fronts could be detected from the sea if the moon was shining brightly enough.

Apart from that there was no reason not to celebrate the closing stages of an uneventful voyage. Tomorrow morning the Irish coast would be in sight, and an escort vessel would be waiting to shepherd the great ship through the more hazardous waters. In a few hours, when the tide was full, they would sail into the refuge of the Mersey channel.

Clemency was in a state bordering on hysteria. She had just received a wireless message from Lord Hazzard saying that he would be waiting at Liverpool to meet her. "Marriage arranged for the twentieth May," the wireless ended. "Not too soon I hope. Stop. Time is of the essence. Stop. Love Hugo."

Clemency crumpled the paper in her hands. She seemed to be on the verge of tears.

"But that's wonderful, honey," Mrs Jervis said. "What are you upset about?"

"It seems – kind of cold. Kind of businesslike."

"Nonsense. You have to be economical with words in wireless messages. And he sends his love. Saying time is of the essence probably means he's not got very long leave."

"Or that I've got to get immediately pregnant," Clemency muttered.

"Maybe," said Mrs Jervis serenely. "That's no bad thing. Give him his heir and then have fun. That's how the nobility do it."

"I'm having fun now, Mother. I think I'm in love with Bobby Merrit."

"That young man you've been flirting with? Nonsense!"

"Don't keep on saying nonsense, Mother. It's the truth."

"Clemency! You haven't gone too far, have you?"

"No, but I'd like to. We did climb into a lifeboat last night, but the look-out saw us and got us out. Pity!" Clemency giggled faintly. "Only it was rather cold."

Mrs Jervis sighed deeply. "It's the sea voyage. It always goes to young girls' heads. You're being very naïve and naughty. Now the moment you see Hugo waiting for you, you'll forget all about this and get your sense back."

Clemency pouted.

"Bobby and I are going to have tonight, whatever you say, Mother."

"Of course. But don't lead the young man on. And don't keep poor Brown up too late. I want you here in bed before dawn, or I shall be angry."

"Poor Brown." Hetty was only referred to in this way when it suited Mrs Jervis's purpose. She didn't relish the thought of staying up until dawn to divest Clemency of her finery. All her jewellery, too, for both ladies had been to the purser that afternoon and had taken their valuables

28

out of the ship's strongroom. Mrs Jervis intended to wear her diamond choker, her pendant diamond ear-rings and several rings. Clemency would wear her double rope of pearls, two gold bracelets, and a diamond clip in her hair. And, of course, the charming antique engagement ring Hugo had given her.

The jewellery would not be returned to the purser for safekeeping, for they would be packing tomorrow and it would be Hetty's responsibility never to let the jewelcase out of her sight.

"Have you had an enjoyable trip, Brown?" Clemency thought to ask."

"Yes, thank you.. I've met some nice people."

"In steerage!"

"Why not? We're having a party tonight. When am I to come up to undress you?"

"Oh, I daresay I could manage myself."

"No, you could not," interrupted her mother. "Brown, be here at one a.m. and I'm sure Clemency will have the courtesy not to keep you waiting."

"Oh, Mother! You're just spying on me."

"And I should think so. For your own good.'

They had cleared the dining saloon in steerage, an Irishman returning to his native Galway played the fiddle, and everybody, even the oldest, danced in lively fashion.

Hetty was partnered by a young man from Toronto. He was going to England to join the Flying Corps, he said. He had always wanted to fly, and under the pressure of war the British were making great strides with their airplanes.

"That's if we arrive safely in England," he said.

"But we're nearly there."

"Don't you believe it. The most dangerous bit of ocean is still to come. And I don't go for all that stuff about the Germans being too honourable to sink a passenger ship carrying neutrals. Why, even if this ship flew the

American flag, she'd be a target, and a legitimate one."

"What do you mean?"

"Because she's carrying guns beneath her forward decks. They've only to be rolled into position ready for firing. Don't ask me how I know. But I do know."

"Then, if it's secret, you shouldn't have told me," Hetty burst out in alarm.

"Suppose I shouldn't have. I haven't told anyone else. But it's better to be forewarned. It might just give you that much more chance if we're torpedoed."

Hetty caught her breath. She wasn't so brave after all.

"Do you think we will be?"

"Well, it's always on the cards that the Huns may miss." He threw back his head, laughing. He was attractive and reckless. He would make a good airman – if he lived.

If any of them lived.

"What's your name?"

"Hetty Brown."

"Now I've spoiled your evening, Hetty. Anyway, what's a nice girl like you doing travelling alone? You are alone, aren't you? I've watched you."

"I'm not exactly alone. I'm a lady's maid. My mistresses are in first class. I keep going up and down stairs. I have to go up later tonight to get them out of their finery."

"No! I can't believe it! You mean two grown women can't undress themselves!" He was virtually repeating Mrs Drummond's words.

Hetty found his astonishment amusing.

"I can see you don't know much about the ways of the rich."

"And nor do I want to if that's the way they go on. You're too good for that, Hetty. Let the bitches wait on themselves."

"Actually, I intend to." Now she was getting reckless, too. It wasn't only Clemency feeling the alchemy of a sea voyage. "As soon as Clemency is married. She's to have a grand society wedding, you should see her trousseau. But after that I thought of joining the Red Cross, or doing something useful while the war's on. Will it go on for long, do you think?"

"Much longer than they say. I was a history student. I known the megalomaniac dreams of the Germans. They want to be world conquerors."

"I liked history, too," Hetty was pleased to have something else in common. "Although I never had a proper teacher. But I read a lot. I read everything."

"I think that's cute, a blue-stocking lady's maid." He was holding her more closely. "Say, Hetty, couldn't we meet in London?"

"If you like. When you're not up above the clouds."

"Actually that's where I am right now." His cheek lay lightly against hers. She was amazed at the softness of his skin. She hadn't ever before felt a man's skin. Or looked into a man's eyes at such close range. She felt a moment of intense promise, like great happiness. And she didn't even know the young man's name.

"Give me an address where I can find you, Hetty."

"We're staying at the Ritz hotel until the twentieth, when Clemency gets married. You'd have to write to me care of Mrs Howard B. Jervis. What's your name?"

"Donald Newman, and I can't give you an address until I get posted." He tickled her ear. "But we'll be seeing each other, Hetty. Gosh, I feel like a bird tonight. And that's nothing to do with flying in airplanes."

The fiddler was playing an Irish folksong, "The Kerry Dancers". Someone began singing, mournfully, *Loving voices of old companions*" . . . The steady hum of the ship's engines accompanied the reedy voice. Few eyes were dry, Hetty noticed. She wanted to cry herself. But for joy, for excitement, for hope. It had turned into a wonderful voyage.

3

It was disappointing, in the morning, to find that fog
shrouded both the sea and the distant tip of Ireland's
coastline, which should have been visible. The fog horn
was blaring. Passengers came on deck wrapped in overcoats, and found the scene extemely depressing. Most of
them were a little jaded from the parties of the previous
evening. They had hoped for a bright spring morning
and the green hump of Ireland in the far distance to raise
their spirits.

Speed had had to be slackened. A rumour that the
Captain had had a wireless message to say that submarines
had been sighted off Fastnet Rock was being whispered.
However, the fog that hampered the *Lusitania*'s speed
would also hamper visiblity for lurking submarines.
There was no sign of anxiety among the ship's officers,
although in the early morning lifeboat drill had been
carried out. The ropes had rasped as the lifeboats were
swung out, twenty-two on the starboard side, eleven on
the port side.

Clemency had put her hand in Bobby Merrit's as they
strolled on the deck. She told Hetty when she returned
that she and Bobby were probably the only passengers
who had had any practice in climbing in and out of lifeboats. She was laughing but her eyes were strained. Not
only enemy submarines, but the Liverpool docks, were
imminent. There would have to be farewells. And greet-
ings . . .

After breakfast Mrs Jervis kept Hetty busy packing the

trunks. Such a profusion of garments had been taken out for use on board. They must all now be carefully folded in tissue paper and repacked. There would be no dressing for dinner that night, the last on board. She and Clemency would wear the coats and skirts in which they would go on shore the following morning, Mrs Jervis's bottle-green worsted, Clemency's grey flannel with a ruffled white cravat.

Clemency's lower lip was developing a tendency to tremble. Hetty was genuinely sorry for her, for she was having similar trouble.

She hoped that evening to see Donald Newman again and make sure that he meant what he had said about their meeting in London. She couldn't see him at luncheon because Mrs Jervis had ordered a meal to be sent to her stateroom. Hetty would share it, since there was too much to be done to allow her to leave, even for an hour. Garments to be ironed, buttons to be sewn on (even those that showed no signs of coming adrift), the sacred wedding dress to be checked.

Hetty suspected that Mrs Jervis was deliberately inventing tasks because she didn't want to be left alone. She felt much safer when the two girls were with her. Hetty felt a further twinge of pity. It was strange to see that demanding woman with uncertainty in her eyes. Surely it was the fog that was making people nervous.

The fog also must be the cause of the absence of an escort vessel. No one suggested that it might not have been sent. Some people thought, more alarmingly, that it might have been sunk.

By mid-morning the fog had dispersed and an hour later there were sporadic cheers on the decks as land was at last sighted. They were heading up the coast towards Queenstown. The Irish coast was becoming clearer, trees, grey rooftops, a church spire. But there was still no sign of any other ship to shepherd this monster of the ocean safely home. The *Lusitania* seemed to be entirely alone on the now calm and dazzlingly blue sea.

But she was within sight of land. Surely there was little to fear, although, once that familiar landmark of mariners, the Old Head of Kinsale, was sighted, the passengers were alarmed that the ship had altered course and seemed to be heading again for the open sea.

The steward who had come for the luncheon trays assured Mrs Jervis and the girls that there was nothing to worry about. The Captain knew what he was doing. He must stay in deep water. He wouldn't want to run aground on the Saltes Islands, would he?

Hetty looked at the time and wondered if Mrs Drummond had managed to get the little boys down for their afternoon nap. Clemency suddenly jumped up and said she wasn't going to stay indoors another minute. It was ten minutes past two. She would take a turn on the deck and come back and report what was happening.

She never reached the door. A sudden devastating explosion reverberated through the ship. Immediately the floor seemed to slide away beneath the three women's feet.

Mrs Jervis screamed and clutched at a table which tipped over, then at the wardrobe which was nodding sideways in the strangest manner. Nothing was stable. The trunks were sliding about the floor, and Clemency was shrieking, "We've been torpedoed! Oh, Mother! What shall we do?"

Hetty, balancing against an upturned trunk, tried to keep calm, for in a minute Mrs Jervis was going to faint, and Clemency have a full-scale attack of hysterics.

She managed to edge her way to the hook where the lifebelts hung and, getting them down, threw one to Mrs Jervis and the other to Clemency. There were only two. Her own was in the cabin in steerage.

"We have to get on deck," she gasped. "Put on your lifebelts. Come on, Mrs Jervis."

"No, wait a minute!" Mrs Jervis had regained a measure of her self-control. "Get the jewellery."

"Mrs Jervis, we haven't got time."

"The case is right there. Clemency, open it."

The ship seemed to be tilting more sharply, and Hetty was sure she had heard the distant thud of another explosion. A stewardess, her cap crooked, put her head inside the door crying, "Get out to the boat decks, ladies. Hurry!" and vanished.

"Mrs Jervis, we can't carry a jewel case," Hetty cried despairingly. Damn this vain woman. Were they all to drown for the sake of baubles?

"We'll wear everything," Mrs Jervis answered, grabbing at the contents of the velvet-lined case. She had her diamond choker round her neck in a flash, and was fumbling with ear-rings. Clemency, catching her greed, had flung on her pearls and all the rings she could cram on her fingers. She thrust a heavy gold bracelet and a couple of rings at Hetty.

"Here, wear these."

Hetty dropped the rings and they went skittering away across the sloping floor. But, simply to placate the two crazy women, she put the bracelet on to her wrist.

"Oh, do come!" she begged them. "I'll take you to the boat deck and then I must go down and help Mrs Drummond with the children."

"I don't know who Mrs Drummond is," Mrs Jervis declared hoarsely, "but I forbid you to leave us, Hetty."

"I have to get my lifebelt. I haven't got a lifebelt," Hetty was nearly sobbing. "And little Alfie and Benny – oh, come on!"

The sounds of pandemonium outside were growing, shuffling steps, a woman crying, someone shouting orders. Clinging to the handrail on the almost vertical deck, Hetty urged the two women ahead of her. She didn't think what a strange sight they must make with their lifebelts and their glittering jewels. Other people were carrying all kinds of belongings; several clutched small infants. Exactly like a shipwreck, Hetty thought dazedly, and said aloud, "It is a shipwreck, God help us."

Where was Mrs Drummond and her babies? And where was her daring young aviator?

There was a desperate crush on the boat deck where a great many people were attempting to clamber into the lifeboats. One boat had been launched safely. It looked very small and frail down in the shining sea. The next one, lowered too clumsily because the list had become more acute, swung in against the ship's side, and spilled all of its occupants, like a scattered harvest of fruit, into the water far below.

The horror of this made Hetty close her eyes. When she opened them she saw forms struggling in the water, some of them clambering on to the upturned boat. People were sobbing. A woman was holding her baby so tightly that it looked as if it had been suffocated. There were a lot of babies in steerage and in third class as well. She *must* get down to Mrs Drummond. The ship was going to sink, there was no doubt about that, for the doom-like cry, "Abandon ship", was echoing all about. But surely it couldn't happen too quickly. Hadn't the *Titanic* stayed afloat for some hours?

"Hetty! Hetty!"

She saw that Mrs Jervis and Clemency were being pushed into a lifeboat, and someone was pushing her, too. A brawny seaman with a face bright red from terror.

"Come along, miss. Don't waste time. She's going. We'll all be jumping for it."

"But I have to go down to steerage —"

"No hope there, miss. The sea's flooded it."

It was no use to protest. The very list of the ship toppled her towards the boat. She saw Mrs Jervis and Clemency ahead of her, mid-way down the boat, clinging to one another, the sunlight catching fire on Mrs Jervis's diamond choker. Then she was tumbled in like a sack of

36

potatoes, a plump woman falling heavily on top of her.

Someone was shouting, "That's enough. Lower away. Careful now, lads. No more spills."

The fat woman was almost suffocating Hetty. She was aware of a floating sensation, a sudden rush downwards, and then a crash, and a dizzy tilt as the doomed lifeboat upended and hit the water, precisely as its predecessor had done.

In seconds the sea, dark and cold and stifling, closed over everyone, and Hetty knew that she was drowning.

It was just twelve minutes since the torpedo had struck. No one had really known, or would ever clearly remember, what had happened.

Drowning people did come to the surface once, often twice, Hetty remembered hazily some time later. For without knowing how she had managed to do it, she found herself clinging to a floating lifebelt, her arms stiff with strain, her lungs half-choked, her body frozen.

But alive. So far.

She was dimly beginning to realise the miracle of it when something bumped gently and persistently against her. An arm, a wild white face.

Hetty began paddling away in horror. A dead body. She saw that all the sea around her was full of floating debris. There was no sign of the ship. It was as if it had never existed.

She began to shout, "Mrs Jervis! Clemency! Clemency!" At least she thought she was shouting, but the sea water lapped into her mouth and silenced her. Then she tried to loosen her arms from the lifebelt so that she could sink into darkness. Away from the nightmare. But she had no strength. Her arms were locked round the slippery rubber.

"This one seems to be alive." It might have been hours, or days, later that she heard voices, and felt herself being tugged. "Get her on board. Jesus! She's young. How many are we now?"

"Twenty-one."

"Well, that's better than twenty. Twenty-one out of two thousand. Jesus!"

"There must be other boats afloat. Is she going to be all right?"

"Looks pretty far gone to me. It's getting dark. If we're not picked up soon we're all goners." The voice cracked. "Damn those bloody Germans! Damn them, damn them, damn them!"

Someone was saying the Lord's Prayer. A woman's soft Irish voice. "Our Father who art in heaven. Hallowed be Thy name . . ."

"Cold!" Hetty muttered between chattering teeth. "Cold!"

"Ah, dear child, are you waking up? Thanks be to God. Sister! Sister! This one's coming round. There, I'll put another blanket on you." There were fingers holding her wrist, counting her pulses. Then the voice again, "Do you think now you could take a sip of hot soup? It'll put some heart in you. You just close your eyes. I'll be back in a minute."

Other voices floated about.

"Who is she? Anything on her to identify her?"

"She'll tell us herself soon enough. She's a young one, poor soul. She was brought in practically naked. Wrapped in a seaman's jersey . . ."

And then, "Here I am again, little one. Try a sip of this. It's Mrs O'Brogan's best broth. That's better than sea water, isn't it?"

"T-thank you," Hetty tried to say. She was deep in the nightmare. She didn't think Mrs O'Brogan's hot broth had any place in that.

She wanted to drink a little, and be warm, and sleep That was all she ever asked again.

"Do you see, she's got a bracelet on her wrist. A fine gold one. Let's be having a look at it. Do you see, now." The soft voice was excited. "It has initials on it. Now then, wake up, my dear. It's morning, didn't you know? Can you tell us your name? I have your initials here. C.M.J. What do they stand for?"

"Clemency Millicent Jervis," murmured Hetty, the faces shadowy above her.

"Ah, then, that's another one we know, thanks be to God. Rose will bring you a nice hot cup of tea and then we'll talk some more."

Rose, with her bright cheeks and awed dark eyes, looked scarcely more than a schoolgirl.

"Can you be sitting up then, Clemency?"

"I'm not –" She was too tired to explain. Mrs Jervis would come presently and sort things out in her confident manner. Mrs Jervis with the sun glinting on her diamonds. As if she were dressed up for entering heaven.

"Oh, yes, you can, I think, if I help you. There now, don't be struggling like that."

"Where are they?" Hetty asked hoarsely.

"And who would you be meaning, dear?"

"Mrs J-Jervis."

"Your mother? I can't be telling you that, dear. They're still bringing bod— people in. Wait until you're stronger and then you can look for her. Or perhaps she'll be coming looking for you."

"I'm sure she's dead. I saw her fall out of the boat. Clemency, too."

"But that's you. You're alive, thanks be to God. Did you not know it? Come along now. Drink up your tea."

Hetty lifted her leaden eyelids, and saw that she was in a hospital ward. It was terribly crowded. The nurses, most of them nuns, could scarcely move between the beds. There were supine forms on either side of her, grey-headed and unconscious. Neither of them was Mrs Jervis or Clemency. She tried to lift her head higher to observe other beds, but the white plastered walls and ceilings, the narrow windows, the dark crucifix hanging at one end of the room, swung dizzily.

"Now, love, you're not going to faint. You're doing nicely. We'll have you moved up to the hotel before long. It's a bit sad in here." The rosy-cheeked child had tears in her eyes. "Mother of God, we've never seen anything like it in this town. It's a terrible war."

Her hand trembled and it was Hetty who had to steady it. The small action helped to revive her. She gulped at the lukewarm tea thirstily and asked if she could have another cup.

Rose cheered up immediately.

"It's the salt water. You'd swallowed gallons. You must have wanted to live, Sister said, or you never would have. It's all in your own will. I'll get you some more tea."

It was all right when Rose, young and healthy and sympathetic, was beside her. But when she had gone and Hetty was aware of the moans and stirrings and difficult breathing all about her, the nightmare returned.

The suffocating black water, the screams growing weaker, the horrible debris, a dead baby tied to a lifebelt, a struggling baldheaded man gulping and sinking, a table – was it a table? – draped with a young couple clinging desperately together in death. And the empty innocent sea where the great ship had been.

But she had survived. It was in her will, Rose had said.

She remembered herself as a terrified child being abandoned in the big house on Fifth Avenue. "Because it's your rightful place," Mother had said. She remembered Mrs Jervis keeping her so reluctantly, and then owning her. Giving her no choice as to whether she would sail on a doomed ship. Believing she was a second-class human being and in this world merely to do what she was told.

But her spirit had survived, she had remained hopeful and ambitious. And now her body had survived as well.

She was a survivor.

They thought she was Clemency Millicent Jervis. Presently they would ask her what she meant to do, and she would say, "I mean to go to London to meet my fiancé."

Ah, no, she was having delusions. She had to get out of this narrow bed and go and look for Mrs Jervis and Clemency. Perhaps they were at the other end of the ward. Or at that hotel Rose had mentioned.

Rose was returning with the second cup of tea.

"Rose –"

"You remembered my name. That's fine."

"Rose, how many drowned?"

"Now, I can't be telling you that, Clemency, because I don't know."

"Many?"

"It's been a terrible awful thing, and that's the truth."

"Where are – the drowned?"

"They're still bringing them in, up and down the coast as far as Queenstown. There can't be many living ones now. But don't be thinking of it."

"I have to find Mrs Jervis."

"Of course, dear. That's natural. Your own mother."

"She was wearing a diamond necklace. You couldn't miss that."

"Glory be to God!"

"And Clemency had – a gold bracelet."

"Sister's put that away safely, dear. Don't you be worrying. And you'll be told as soon as your mother's found."

But if she were Clemency, Hetty, as well, had still to be found.

"Were there just the two of you, dear?"

"We had – a maid." The treacherous words were coming out of her mouth again.

"Now, now, don't cry, love. Don't cry."

Hetty was sinking, drowning, strangled with ropes of

pearls. Clemency was the survivor, with a tall blond Englishman waiting to marry her.

Because the young aviator from Toronto would never be seen again. He had been in steerage, the worst place of all, where the sea had flooded in through the ship's torn plates. She hoped he had tried to help Mrs Drummond and Alfie and Benny. But she mustn't go on thinking about it. A glimmer of happiness had been instantly snuffed out. It was past. Past and dead.

She must have fallen asleep again for she opened her eyes to see a priest with a kindly wrinkled face bending over her.

"I'm Father Neely, my child. How are you feeling now?"

She realised that she felt better, stronger, and said so.

"That's good, because I have some sad news for you. We think we have found your mother."

"A-alive?"

"Alas, no. The fishermen brought her in. The fishing boats are going up and down the coastline looking for survivors, you understand. You told us your mother was wearing a diamond necklace. That's why we think it's her."

"She was alone? There wasn't a dark-haired young lady –"

"Just herself. May God have mercy on her soul."

Hetty sat up. "I have to see her."

"That's what I was about to ask. Are you up to it? I'll be blunt. We need an identification apart from that bauble she was wearing. Then we can send messages to your family, and to whoever was expecting you in England. The American Ambassador has sent us instructions from London. Mr Walter Page, would you be knowing him?"

Hetty shook her head.

"Ah, he's a good man. He wants all American nationals looked after, and that includes yourself. Now I doubt you'll be able to walk as far as the school. But here's what we'll do. I'll get Rose to put you in a chair and push you. She's a strong young girl. That way you can get the shock over as soon as possible. Rose. Rose! Can Sister spare you for half an hour? And get a warm wrap to put round Miss Jervis."

Rose came hurrying up.

"Father, isn't it a bit soon for the poor young lady?"

"Yes, it is soon, but it's a terrible tragedy and we have to deal with it as we can. There are a great many identifications to be made and the authorities have to act as fast as they can. There'll be funeral instructions, and a coroner's inquest."

The simple barren little schoolhouse stood a short way up a gentle hillside, near to the grey weathered church. Why hadn't Mrs Jervis been laid in the church?

Because it was full, Father Neely said briefly.

Hetty shivered.

"Are there so many dead?"

"This is only a small town. Its name is Kinsale. I hear that a lot of bodies are being taken to Queenstown. They say several hundreds altogether. Ah, a big shipwreck is a terrible thing."

It was a terrible thing, too, to look down on poor Mrs Jervis's drowned face, the unmistakable choker, its diamonds sparkling brilliantly from their immersion in sea water, cutting into her swollen throat. She looked grey and quite lifeless. But someone had mercifully closed her eyes and folded her pudgy hands on her breast. She would never again shout "Brown!" in her commanding voice.

It was hard to believe. So dreadful that Hetty couldn't speak. She only nodded in response to Father's Neely's unspoken enquiry. Then she clutched her throat, feeling she couldn't breathe, and Father Neely, misunderstanding, said, "She won't be buried with her jewellery unless you specifically request it."

43

"I wasn't thinking of that. Anyway, it must go back to New York."

"Surely. That's what we'll talk about. Let us get out of here. We can do nothing for any of these poor souls," he indicated the rows of sheeted bodies, "except pray for them."

Hetty had collapsed by the time they got her back to the hospital. So they left her alone for the rest of the day, except to bring her a plate of bread and milk in the evening. Then she was afraid to sleep because sleep would bring back the nightmares, dominated by Mrs Jervis's face, so still and yet somehow so full of reproach. "How dare you be alive, Brown, when Clemency and I are dead!"

But where was Clemency? Hetty had asked to be told if a dark-haired young girl were found.

"Ah, the maid," said Father Neely. "Yes, we'll look for her. You may find she's still alive. But don't be building up your hopes."

"If she was alive she'd be asking for –" Hetty had been going to say "her mother" – "for us."

But so far no one answering to the description had been found. They had telephoned to Queenstown to make enquiries.

Hetty did eventually sleep and dreamed that she was holding Clemency's head under the water. It was an appalling dream, and she woke sobbing in horror. The night sister came to her bedside, the gentle shadowed face looking down at her. "Hush, child. You're disturbing the others. I'll bring you some hot milk. Then you'll sleep more soundly."

Surprisingly enough, after drinking the milk, she did sleep, and in the morning found herself starving. She could eat everything they brought her. She wanted to live. She was so hungry to live now that she had laid the way to becoming an impostor and seizing Clemency's golden opportunities. She was Clemency Jervis, an insistent voice within her repeated over and over.

She was ready to leave the hospital, she told the tired sister on duty.

"That's grand, dear. But don't go until Father Neely comes. He wants to ask you some questions."

Was he going to accuse her?

"We have discovered that you are impersonating a dead girl, Harriet Brown. Aren't you troubled for your immortal soul?"

Far from any such thing, Father Neely, who came at mid-morning looking serene and harassed at the same time, asked her whom she wanted to notify of her escape from death.

"We didn't want to disturb you yesterday. But I'm sure your family will be very worried."

"Is there any news of the girl I asked about?"

"None at all. What did you say her name was?"

"Harriet Brown." So there, in a second, she had killed poor Brown, although she could have sworn she had no intention of speaking the fatal words. But, "This is your rightful place," Mother had said, looking up at the rich house. And she had known it was.

"Is there any chance still of her being found alive?"

"Well, now, she might be found wandering lost somewhere, but I doubt it. We have so many searchers out. We believe we have found all the survivors. But I do hear there's a great search going on for an important American gentleman, Mr Vanderbilt. He hasn't yet been found. He must have gone down with the ship. A fine gentleman. They say he was last seen tying lifebelts to babies in their baskets. God rest his soul"

Hetty breathed deeply, the pain too bad to be born. Alfie and Benny, Seaman Drummond waiting for news of his wife. Poor Donald Newman who was never going to fly above the clouds.

But she had been given the chance to live. She was going to live and live and live.

45

"Could you send a cable to my Uncle Jonas in New York?" she heard herself asking calmly. "He is Jonas Middleton of the Middleton Bank, Wall Street."

"And what am I to say?"

"Just say, 'Clemency has survived'."

"Is that all?"

"Yes. No. No, it isn't. Would you also send a message to England. To Lord Hazzard of Loburn near Cirencester. Say, 'Will be arriving London with survivors *Lusitania*. Longing to see you, Clemency.' "

"And this gentleman?" Father Neely was at last able to produce a twinkle in his eyes.

"He's the man I'm going to marry."

4

The ferry boat nudged into Holyhead, and its passengers, a wan-faced collection of exhausted people, still dazed and haunted by what they had seen and endured, went ashore. They were dressed, by courtesy of the Cunard line, in a motley collection of Irish garments, tweed overcoats, tweed skirts, thick Irish sweaters, woollen stockings. Some of them talked too much, still hysterical and afraid of silence. Some seemed to be in the grip of permanent nightmare.

Hetty had stayed on deck for the whole of the four-hour crossing. She had shivered in the sea wind, and closed her eyes so as not to see the rising and falling waves. It was cold and lonely on deck, but the claustrophobic atmosphere of the saloon or the over-crowded cabins would have been worse. She would have been looking for Clemency all the time, as she had been doing ever since leaving the little Kinsale hospital and travelling to Queenstown, where the majority of the living and the dead from the disaster had been brought ashore.

She had seen so many corpses that she had become numbed. They were so much debris, untidy, ugly, anonymous, and ready to be shovelled out of sight. As a kind of necessary penance she had chosen to stay for the mass funeral of the victims, the coffins carried on waggons drawn by horses gathered from all over County Cork. They had rattled over the cobblestones in a seemingly endless procession, past the little grey Irish houses with their shuttered windows and along the long winding

47

road out of the town. The cemetery was on a headland. The Atlantic winds swept over it day and night. The dead would never be out of the sound of the sea.

Hetty, in her role of daughter, had decided that Mrs Jervis should be buried there. She had sent another cable to Uncle Jonas telling him of her intention and he had cabled back, "Perhaps wisest decision. Stop. It would be sensible to go ahead with your wedding plans. Stop. Put flowers on poor Millicent's grave for me. Stop. Uncle Jonas."

He hadn't made any more enquiries about the presumably missing Harriet Brown. This was typical of the lack of personal interest the Jervis family took in their servants. She resolved there and then never to behave in that way herself, when she was Lady Hazzard of Loburn.

Lady Hazzard: she was living in a dream, and hoped she would never wake up.

She guessed that Uncle Jonas didn't want to be too disturbed by the tragedy. His headstrong sister had brought it on herself, acting as she had done in defiance of his advice. Insulated by distance, snug in his rich surroundings, he must have regarded the whole thing as the kind of sensational newspaper headline that occurred constantly during a major war. Anyway, he and his sister had not got on particularly well. He would be relieved to hear of Clemency's wedding, so that he could retire from responsibility for her.

Hetty had been trying to remember Clemency's handwriting. She thought it had been large and bold and rather stylised and probably not difficult to imitate. When she wrote to Uncle Jonas, as she would have to do shortly, or to any of Clemency's friends – fortunately Clemency hadn't much cared for her own sex, and had not had a best friend, or even a particularly intimate one – she imagined she would be able to perform quite satisfactorily. She could even use the old ruse of apologising for using her left hand, having damaged her right.

On the train journey from Liverpool to London in the early dawn, her brain buzzed with plans. But as the train slackened speed, and slipped through the smoke-shrouded suburbs, her heart began to thump so violently that she thought she would faint.

The discomfort served to remind her sharply that she was alive, and that fact alone gave her ineffable pleasure. Compared to surviving a desperate shipwreck, meeting a strange Englishman and making a pretence of loving him was simplicity itself.

She intended eventually to love him, even if she had not quite achieved that felicitous state by the time she became his wife.

At one end of the station platform a small official group stood waiting. Someone nudged Hetty and told her the American ambassador was there. If she were an American she should go and be greeted by him.

Anything to postpone the moment of meeting Lord Hazzard, Hetty thought, her heart renewing its hard thumping. She stood before Mr Walter H. Page, looked into his worn, troubled face, and allowed her hand to be taken. She told him her name in a low voice.

"Have you friends in London, Miss Jervis?"

"Yes, I have. My fiancé. I think he is to be here to meet me." Her tongue hadn't tripped at all. But she was suddenly overcome by the thought of her first mistake. Clemency had always done her hair in an elaborate coiffure of curls. She had completely forgotten to make some attempt at that elegant style. In her clumsy makeshift clothes she must look like an Irish waif. Hugo would never recognise her.

"Can I have him located for you, Miss Jervis?" Mr Page was asking in his courteous concerned voice.

"I think he'll be in uniform. He's on leave. Oh –" she gave an audible gasp. "I do believe I can see him."

The sight of that tall broad-shouldered figure in khaki, standing apart from the crowd, perhaps not particularly wanting to be part of it, since this drama was not something he had expected, made Hetty want to sink into the ground, or disappear into thin air. Whatever had she embarked on? She was appalled at the extent of her audaciousness. But how was she to retrace her steps? She couldn't. She had set out on a course that could not be altered unless Clemency suddenly materialised in front of her and condemned her duplicity.

She felt a slight push in her back. She realised that the Ambassador was paternally guiding her in the right direction. And then Hugo saw her and came swiftly forward, his face full of unmistakable relief. So she was recognisable as Clemency, she thought dazedly, and smiling uncertainly she made the final step into her future.

"Hugo!" Her voice was completely spontaneous, as was her action of throwing her arms round him. But then she was distinctly aware of his wince. Oh, God, he knew! It was all over. He had realised her deception. Her panic, and she suspected she would have many moments of panic in the next few days, passed when she saw that he had been leaning on a cane, and her impulsive embrace had nearly unbalanced him.

"You've been wounded!" she cried.

He nodded. "Just out of hospital. Damned lucky, actually. I have a month's leave. Poor girl, have you had a ghastly time?"

"Worse than that. I can't talk about it yet." She breathed deeply. "But I'm alive."

"Your mother? Has there been a funeral?"

"She's buried with the others. I thought it best. So did Uncle Jonas. Hugo, I have nothing. Even these comic clothes aren't mine." Surely that was what Clemency would have said, caring as she did about her appearance. "Do I look terrible?"

Now she was making him study her, challenging him to discover her lie. He did look at her hard, and she had the courage to return his stare, her first face to face encounter with the man she had decided was to be hers.

Did he look as attractive as he had done in New York, glimpsed when entering the house, or leaving with Clemency on his arm? She had thought his blue eyes so sunny, his fair skin and blond hair so English. Now she saw that his face was florid and a little puffy, his eyes paler and colder than she had imagined. She had only seen him in the distance, after all, she herself invisible in her neat maid's uniform, for he was not the kind of person who noticed servants.

She hadn't remembered his neat straw-coloured moustache over full, rather pouting lips. He must have grown that since his visit to New York. But he was agreeably tall and erect, broad-shouldered and wide-chested, as she remembered, the epitome of a handsome British army officer. She was sure she could love his body well enough, but his mind, his intellect, his sense of humour? Those qualities she had yet to discover.

"Stop staring at me," he said, a trifle sharply. "I'm not at my best. And you certainly do look rather awful."

Hetty's hands went guiltily to her wan face, her pulled-back hair. Clemency would never have permitted herself to look like this, even after a shipwreck.

She made an attempt at perkiness.

"It's partly because I'm starving. We've been travelling all night."

"Of course you must be famished." He seemed relieved by this practical explanation. "We'll have breakfast at the Berkeley before driving down to Loburn. Pimm's outside with the Rolls."

From Clemency's avid study of fashionable London Hetty had picked up a good deal of useful information, including that the Berkeley Hotel was much favoured by debutantes and smart country people.

"Hugo, I can't go to the Berkeley dressed like this."

"Nonsense, of course you can." His voice was supremely confident. "You'll be with me."

51

He limped slightly as he walked, but even so she had to hurry to keep up with him. It was clear that he hated the sad scene on the station platform: he had probably seen too many scenes of scarecrow refugees in France and Belgium. She understood that. She was beginning to understand war. It was far from the picture Clemency had had of gay young officers home on leave, drinking champagne, being fêted by beautiful women.

Poor Hugo! He had a painful wound, and his beautiful woman had been dragged out of the sea, limp-haired and bedevilled by ghosts. But they were both survivors. Reminding herself of that miracle Hetty quickened her step and came abreast of the man who was to be her husband. Surely he didn't think her rightful place was two steps behind him.

A grey-haired chauffeur in uniform was standing beside a highly-polished motor car.

"This is Pimm," said Hugo laconically to Hetty. "All the young men are joining up nowadays. We had to bring Pimm back out of retirement. The Berkeley, Pimm. We'll have some breakfast before we set out. Miss Jervis is starving."

The elderly man's face remained impassive, not giving any intimation of what he thought of the waif his master was bringing home.

"Very well, m'lord. I expect the young lady has had a bad time."

"Terrible. In you get, Clemency."

Clemency. The name was like a stone thrown in her face. It made her shudder. She couldn't be faced with her guilt day after day, besides taking the risk of absent-mindedly not recognising when she was spoken to. She would have to make a decision about it, and very soon.

"Well, take a look at London now you've finally arrived."

Sitting beside her in the back of the car, Hugo had suddenly taken her hand in his, an abrupt gesture that

52

had made her jump. Now his voice was gently teasing, a fact that reassured her. Surely then he did have a lighter side. Shortly they would be able to smile and joke together.

"It looks awfully grey," she ventured.

"Not when the sun comes out. It is spring, you know. Loburn's marvellous in the spring." Now there was some warmth in his voice. He cared about Loburn. Rather more, probably, than the American girl whom he had asked to be his wife. She had heard that Englishmen who were fortunate enough to own old family estates were passionate about them. She found this fact curious and interesting. She would like to experience such a passion herself. After all, Loburn was to be hers, too. She had, metaphorically, dragged it up out of the Atlantic.

"Where's your ring, darling?"

Oh, heavens, she had forgotten the emerald and diamond engagement ring still adorning Clemency's hand at the bottom of the sea.

"I lost it," she said steadily. "It must have come off in the sea. I was holding on to a lifebelt for hours. Nearly all my clothes were washed off. I only had this bracelet," she fingered the heavy gold circlet that she was never going to wear again after today, "to be identified by. Some people," she continued dispassionately, "were completely naked."

"Were they really? Just like being caught in a shell blast," said Hugo. "Damned unpleasant."

Hetty seized on the new subject.

"How did you get your wound?"

"Hit by a shell fragment. Made a nasty gash. Didn't damage my riding muscles, thank God."

"It must be pretty awful in the trenches."

"It's not exactly a picnic. Unless you like bully beef. Still, I can get a bit of riding when we're behind the lines, if we're camped near a cavalry outfit. We even managed a race one day, my company and another. But a

Hun aeroplane came over and frightened the horses. We had to dismount and take pot shots at it with revolvers. The pilot crashed later in some woods. I don't think we potted him; I rather gather it was engine trouble. He was practically skimming the ground."

Dear Donald Newman, would you have found the aeroplanes you longed to fly more dangerous than enemy torpedoes if you had lived?

"Serve him right," Hugo was saying. "He shouldn't have frightened the horses."

Was Hugo only eloquent when he talked of horses? That was going to be a little boring. She had hoped to develop all the interests she had had to suppress in the Jervis household – music, books, paintings, talk about many things. She knew that her father had been an accomplished conversationalist. Her mother had used to say so. "He knew everything, and he talked as easily as a bird sang," she had said.

"I'll get you another ring," Hugo was saying, patting her hand. "Do you think emeralds are unlucky?"

Hetty made herself laugh.

"I hardly think it was an emerald that sank the *Lusitania*."

"We'll find another stone, to be on the safe side. You can make the choice." And she was suddenly wondering how different her finger might be from Clemency's, bigger, smaller, longer? Offhand, she just didn't know. But already she had decided that Hugo wasn't particularly observant. He probably carried no sharp memory in his mind of Clemency's slim young hand.

Over breakfast in a fairly deserted restaurant, Hetty felt her spirits rising. The coffee was good, the poached eggs and thin slices of toast, generously buttered, tasted better than anything she had ever eaten. She couldn't resist some hot muffins.

Hugo watched her with an amused smile.

"Food not much good in County Cork?"

"You're teasing. At first I was full of sea water, and then –" her face sobered, "the circumstances weren't right for enjoying eating."

He looked at her more attentively.

"I don't remember you talking like that, in that precise way."

She lowered her head.

"We didn't really know each other that well, Hugo. Did we? It was for such a short time." She added deliberately, "I only knew I wanted to marry you. And you said you wanted to marry me."

"By jove, yes, of course I did."

She knew that the warm food had brought colour back to her cheeks, and that she was looking prettier.

"And still do? Now I'm a waif from the sea?"

He laughed again, obviously relieved that they were getting on better, and that she was not going to be nervous and hysterical about her near drowning.

"Now you're looking more like yourself. I'd say more a mermaid than a waif."

"Hugo, how gallant." It was rather fun being coquettish. Now she knew why Clemency had enjoyed it so much.

"Wait till we've got you a new wardrobe. But I told you they wouldn't raise an eyebrow in here."

It was true that they hadn't. The doorman had said, "Good morning, my lord. Good morning, miss," his expression just as much in control as Pimm's had been. And the elderly waitresses had clucked over them both in a maternal way, not showing any surprise that Lord Hazzard should bring in someone looking like a peasant. It would be amusing to come back here one day when she was Lady Hazzard and dressed by Worth or Patou.

She watched the attentive waitress refilling her cup with the delicious hot coffee, and suddenly an immense surge of gladness went through her. It was so unexpected and dazzling that she could have stood up and shouted, for the bliss of being vividly alive, past horrors suppressed, future difficulties not thought about. She was taking nothing from Clemency who was dead. She would eagerly repay Hugo for her deceit. He would find her an amenable and loving wife, and would never know that he had been cheated. The past was finished with. From now on, beginning with this charming room, the agreeable attention, and the handsome young officer sitting opposite her, she was going to be head over heels with delight in everything.

"What are you smiling about?" Hugo asked.

"I guess I was just feeling happy to be alive and here with you."

"Well, that's a good beginning." His face had softened and he had lost a little of his stiff army-officer look. She was doing splendidly.

"Can we start soon, Hugo? I'm longing to see Loburn."

"At once, darling. But it's a long drive. Do you feel up to it?"

"Of course I'm up to it. I'm absolutely rejuvenated by this marvellous breakfast."

"Capital. We'll be there in time for luncheon. They're expecting us. By the way though, Clemency, there's one thing I'd like to mention away from old Pimm's attentive ears. The money."

"The money?"

"You know what I'm referring to. The marriage settlement. We threshed it out in New York, your Uncle Jonas and I. He's a hard business man."

"Oh, that. Oh, yes, I guess he has to be."

She couldn't look at Hugo. The thought of Clemency's money shocked her too deeply. How much was the marriage settlement? She had no idea. She had stepped into Clemency's shoes with little thought of them being gold-lined or diamond-studded. She had truly overlooked the fact that by becoming Clemency she had become an

56

heiress. For not only was there the marriage settlement, but she would now presumably inherit Mrs Jervis's considerable fortune. She had even had to accept the grisly diamond necklace, thrust into her hands by an embarrassed Mother Superior, and hidden at the bottom of her makeshift travelling bag.

"It's all in order, I hope. No hitches?"

Hugo was embarrassed, too. His blue eyes had gone stony. The suspicion that he had been much more in love with Clemency's fortune than herself became a certainty. Clemency must have known this. But, with her cool calculating little head, she had happily settled for the advantages of this particular marriage of convenience. So why was Hetty feeling momentarily daunted?

She searched her memory for snippets of information.

"I think it was to be lodged in the Westminster bank." Someone had told her that. Polly, the parlour maid, who had overheard the conversation at that last breakfast in New York. "Didn't Uncle Jonas tell you?"

"He did. But communications haven't been simple since the war. I haven't had confirmation. The drill was to present credentials, our marriage certificate being top of the list."

"That will be easy enough, Hugo. When we're married."

Supposing the money hadn't arrived, would she then be jilted? She – no, Clemency – had been dispatched like a bundle of goods. But that was the way things were done.

"What's the money for?"

"To save Loburn, of course. My father left a lot of debts when he died, and I confess I've some hefty ones myself."

Hetty found she didn't care much for this conversation. She guessed too that Clemency would have slid over it merrily.

"People like you value your homes very much, don't you?"

"Naturally." His voice had a distinct arrogance. "After all, you Americans haven't anything comparable, have you?"

Being in love with the past: was that a good thing? But she was going to love Loburn. And it was going to be hers as well as Hugo's when it was repaired with her money.

Her money. Good. Now she was getting into the part. Except for one thing. She was making a spontaneous decision no matter what the risk. She was going to have to be bold about risks.

"Hugo, could I persuade you not to call me Clemency?"

"Why not?" He was surprised. "You never said anything in New York."

"Then I was at home. Mother, and the servants, called me Clemency. But I've always hated the name. It's so puritan. I was only given it because it was Mother's name, too."

"Don't care for it much myself, to tell the truth. What do you want to be called? Did you have a pet name?"

"Yes. It was Hetty. My father called me that." (*I will call her Hetty . . .*) She longed to keep some small part of herself. Perhaps it wasn't a significant risk. Now that Mrs Jervis was dead the Fifth Avenue house would be shut up, the servants dispersed. She was unlikely to see any of them again, and Uncle Jonas had known her only as Brown.

"I rather like Hetty. It's neat. Better than Clemency, as you say." He was being kind, if a little patronising. "Everything's going to be capital. I want to buy a couple of hunters if I can find any decent ones. Most of the good stock has gone to the front. You do ride, don't you?"

That was one of the questions she had been dreading. Clemency had ridden very well at the Jervis's summer place on Long Island. She herself had never attempted to

58

mount a horse. She had never had the opportunity.

"I don't, actually."

He looked surprised. "I thought you did. I thought you told me so. Well, never mind. I'll teach you. It will be the first thing I do when my leg's better. Now, shall we go?"

The countryside soothed and enchanted her. She was going to love those low green hills dotted with sheep and crying lambs, the farm buildings nestling like tabby cats in the hollows, the clumps of elms and beeches, the streams glinting sharply in the hazy sunshine. It was a green and grey landscape, infinitely peaceful, a quiet dream.

"Like a Corot painting," Hetty murmured.

"Is it? Didn't know you cared about pictures."

"Oh, I do." She was emphatic. "Having been so near to death I care passionately about everything. Did you think I was just a party girl?"

"I'm getting to know you better by the minute. You're not going to turn out to be a blue stocking, are you?"

He sounded slightly alarmed. She must remember to be more Clemency, less Hetty, at the beginning at least. Hetty the bookworm who had made herself invisible for hours in the library whenever she had had the opportunity.

"I'm not a blue stocking, I just look awful," she murmured, leaning her head against his shoulder.

He gave his short bark of laughter. He appreciated that kind of wit. "Don't worry. Kitty will fix you up."

"Who's Kitty?"

"My sister-in-law. My brother's wife. They have a son, Freddie. Bit of a milksop." He squeezed her hand again, painfully. "We'll do better than that."

His thoughts were so transparent. As head of the family it was his duty to save Loburn. It followed logically that he then wanted an heir. Failing that, one supposed the property and the title would revert to the younger brother

59

and then to the milksop, Frederick. An eventuality that must be absolutely avoided.

Well, I'd like a son, too, Hetty told herself stoutly.

"Who else will be there, Hugo?"

"My mother. She's waiting to meet you."

"Does she approve of an American daughter-in-law?"

"Not entirely. But I daresay you can convert her, if you try. Don't be deceived by her delicate look. She's a strong-minded lady. Look, this is the beginning of Loburn land. We ride to hounds over those hills. It's marvellous hunting country. If my leg stopped me hunting I'd rather have had a fatal wound, I can tell you."

The low mounded hills, the patches of bluebells which were the same hazy blue as the sky, rooks squabbling noisily in a tall elm, a farmer following two horses and a plough, carving his slow sculpture over the hill's breast and down to the hollow.

The cold waves and the cries of the drowning were receding in her mind, were surely nothing but a nightmare. The little village they motored through, a narrow street bordered by the rock-grey houses, a church steeple at the end, was infinite peace.

"Oh, Hugo! I love it!"

He was pleased.

"Capital, old girl. Capital."

His vocabulary was a bit stereotyped. But she would improve it. As she would persuade his strong-minded mother to approve of her. And as she would become pregnant as soon as possible to give Hugo his heir. For who knew how long the war would last, and how many young men like Hugo, and presumably his brother, too, would be killed.

That fear was the only cloud over this miraculous day of rebirth.

5

The stairs seemed endless. Suddenly Hetty had been seized by an overpowering tiredness. The euphoria of meeting Hugo and the pleasure of the drive to Loburn had left her. She was not only tired but extremely nervous, an actress waiting to go on stage for her first big role.

Loburn, the weather-worn grey stone house at the end of a winding drive, was not as large as she had expected it to be, although who knew what warren of rooms there was behind the austere façade. Worn stone steps up to a pedimented doorway, a butler swinging the door open, and then the sun-splashed gloom of a black and white tile hall, a long curve of staircase, a smell of pot-pourri, of generations of beeswax, a bowl of plum blossom on an almost black polished oak table, some chairs with faded needlework covers and curly legs, like spirals of candy. What were they called? She must learn about furniture. A fire that had almost gone out in a wide stone fireplace, two Labrador dogs making a rush at her.

And a plump woman whose mouth looked a bit pinched. Hugo's mother?

"This is Mrs Evans, our housekeeper," Hugo said. "She'll show you your room."

Only a housekeeper to welcome her? Considering the circumstances of her arrival, she had hardly expected a contingent of servants to be lined up on either side of the hall, but she was sure Clemency would have expected this, and been deeply disappointed, slightly insulted, too, at being greeted only by such a disapproving matron. What would Clemency have done? Treated the matter flippantly?

It seemed nothing was expected of her, for Hugo was saying, "Miss Jervis has no luggage, Mrs Evans. I hope someone has thought to put some things out for her."

"I believe Mrs Lionel has," Mrs Evans answered primly.

"Where is Mrs Lionel?"

"At the hospital. She was on duty from eight o'clock. But she'll be home for luncheon. And Lady Hazzard is feeling poorly, but hopes to be down later." Mrs Evans turned to the stairs, "Will you follow me, miss."

Hetty cast a slightly panic-stricken look at Hugo, but he was already making off in another direction, leaning on his cane, the two big dogs following him. One flight of curving stairs, then another, much steeper. Hetty's tiredness made her stumble. Mrs Evans looked round.

"We've put you in the grey room, miss. We thought you'd like to be quiet after that terrible shipwreck. Are you quite recovered, miss?"

"I don't think I'll ever truly recover," Hetty answered, knowing she spoke the truth.

"Yes, it was dreadful, but worse things are happening in France. Perhaps you don't know, being American."

"I guess I don't."

"Then you'll soon learn. All our fine young men are being killed. The master has been lucky so far, with only an injured leg. Mr Lionel is leaving for the Dardanelles. We'd never heard of such places before." Mrs Evans's anxiety was making her more friendly. But she still had difficulty in accepting this dishevelled white-faced young woman as the new bride for Loburn. Or was it that she didn't care for Hetty being an American?

"Funny you arriving without any trousseau. We had expected great things."

"I did have a lovely trousseau. It's at the bottom of the sea."

62

Mrs Evans gazed at Hetty for a moment with unguarded sympathy, then said briskly, "Never mind, you're here and alive. That's the main thing, isn't it?"

It was the only thing, Hetty reflected, nodding vehemently, and wondering what Clemency would have thought of the sad room into which she was shown.

A four-poster bed with grey brocade hangings, grey walls, a beamed ceiling. Cold. A room for a second-class guests? Who had decided she should be put here until she occupied the Master's bedroom? Hugo hadn't yet said anything about wedding plans. Supposing he decided that after all he didn't want to marry her, and packed her off back to New York? But no, the money in the bank was too great an attraction. That was her insurance.

"Nothing will disturb you up here," said Mrs Evans, "except the rooks squabbling, and the wind. You'll want to rest. Luncheon is in half an hour, but Mrs Lionel said if you didn't want to come down you could ring for a tray."

"Oh, I'll come down," said Hetty. The grey room. A meal alone. It was too melancholy. Her lip trembled, but she was determined not to begin weeping. "I'll just wash and change. You said there were some clothes?"

"In the wardrobe, miss. Shall I send Effie?"

Send Brown to button up Miss Clemency. She heard an echo of Mrs Jervis's autocratic voice . . .

"No, I'll manage. Thank you, Mrs Evans."

"The bathroom's just across the passage. You do look peaky, miss."

When Mrs Evans had gone, Hetty began to shiver violently. Oh, God, what had she done? Was this the rich, pampered life Clemency had talked of so gaily? No welcome, a sad-coloured room, an unknown array of faces at luncheon, a cool, if not positively reluctant bridegroom.

She could end it all this minute by going downstairs and confessing what she had done. She could say she had been suffering from delusions after the terrible nightmare of the *Lusitania*. She could humbly ask to be sent home.

But where was home? Uncle Jonas would never forgive her for her monstrous deception, the Fifth Avenue house would be shut up empty or possibly with a caretaker, there would be no mistress in residence to need a lady's maid or any other kind of help. She would never never go back to the misery of the Bowery.

Sitting on the edge of the bed in the quiet room, in a suspension of will, strained and bleak and unbelievably tired, Hetty had a sudden startling vision of her mother's face on the day she had taken her daughter to the Jervis household. It had been sharp-boned, pale and lined, a skeletal face, dominated by the dark eyes that had burned with such intensity. Sick as she was, Mother would not have accepted any capitulation, any going back. "You must grasp the big opportunities in life, Hetty. Do you know what I mean?" "No, Mother." "You will, in time. When there's something important, seize it. Don't run away from a challenge. Girls like you can't afford to. I want you to be something. It's your right."

It was strange how clearly those words came back, as if Mother were in the room and speaking aloud. Poor pretty Mother who had loved so unwisely and paid so dearly. But had refused to harbour regrets and had never lost her courage. She would thoroughly approve of the challenge facing her daughter now. It was, she would have said, Hetty's right. Hetty would like to think that her unknown father would also have agreed. He had been a cultured man, sensitive, romantic, unorthodox. But not unorthodox enough to do something about his bastard daughter. Would he approve of the gamble she had taken?

Hetty got slowly to her feet and went to the wardrobe.

Yes, there were some rather nice clothes, though no doubt Clemency wouldn't have thought too much of them. A cardigan and a plaid skirt, a cream silk blouse, an afternoon dress in a soft green material, and a long dark blue taffeta, cut low and rather straight, in the new fashion. That must be for dinner. To whom had it belonged?

There was also a warm wool dressing gown, a white cotton nightdress with lace trimming, and in a drawer underclothing, stockings, handkerchiefs. They couldn't be new clothes, Hetty surmised, so whose were they? The sizes looked fairly accurate. Someone must have sent over Clemency's measurements. All the same, it was unfortunate having to go down to meet her new family in borrowed clothes.

She went into the cavernous bathroom and washed, then changed into the silk blouse and plaid skirt. Whoever had stocked the wardrobe had forgotten shoes. She would have to wear her sturdy Irish brogues, courtesy of the Cunard shipping line. But she could brush her hair and twist it up a bit more elegantly, and pinch some colour into her cheeks and lips. She couldn't do anything about the look of strain and horror that lingered in her eyes.

Nevertheless, she looked passable enough. She guessed she could get through luncheon. Mustn't let them think that an American lacked courage.

No one had told her where she would find the family assembled. In the dining room, she supposed, but where was the dining room?

It wasn't fair. She felt like an employee, a governess perhaps, newly arrived and insufficiently briefed. In the hall, looking about for someone to guide her, she wasn't prepared for the very clear feminine voice coming through a half-open door. She listened in shock.

"Can you possibly go through with it, Hugo?" And Hugo's answer, "I have to. Thank God she survived."

"Does she look like a drowned rat?"

"She's had plenty of time to dry out. Actually, she's behaving rather splendidly, poor girl. She lost her mother, you know."

"We're all losing somebody these days, aren't we?"

Afraid of what else she might hear, something too cruel, Hetty boldly pushed open the door and walked into a room lined with books, a dark cosy room with leather-covered furniture and turkey-red rugs. And two people standing before the fireplace, the fair-haired young woman moving abruptly away from Hugo. Was it her imagination, or had they been embracing?

"I'm sorry. No one told me where to find the dining room. Or anything, really." Her voice was firm and composed, with just a hint of reproach. I won't let them walk over me . . .

Hugo began talking rather quickly, "Oh, Clem – I mean, Hetty. My fiancée prefers to be called Hetty, Julia, and I agree. The other was a damned awful name, it suggested whole colonies of Puritans. You two haven't met. Julia, Hetty, Hetty, Julia."

Hetty shook a narrow ringless hand. She was too confused to take in the young woman's appearance clearly. A delicate-skinned aristocratic face, pale blue eyes, blonde hair. Rather like Hugo, in a strange way. Could they be relatives?

"You're not Hugo's sister-in-law? He said her name was Kitty. He didn't tell me about anyone else."

"Well, I'm only staff. Aren't I, Hug?"

Hug? Staff? She was mighty familiar.

"Julia is my mother's companion. She –"

"Fell on hard times," Julia interposed flippantly.

"Shut up, Julia, and let me explain to Hetty. Julia's mother was one of my mother's closest friends. When she died, Julia was left in rather straitened circumstances and Mother invited her here to live. Since then Mother has become a bit invalidish, and Kitty's occupied with her brat. So it has all worked out very well."

Except that Hugo and this elegant flat-bosomed creature were perhaps a little more than just good friends. Or Julia would wish them to be so. Hetty was good at recognising hostility, even so politely veiled. Julia, moneyless, and she the rich usurper.

It was too soon to work out these complications.

But Hetty saw that it would have been better if she could have arrived here as a bride. A *fait accompli*, so to speak. The sinking of the *Lusitania* had so nearly prevented the marriage. Julia must have been cherishing hopes.

The awkward conversation came to an end as Hugo took Hetty's arm and marched her out of the room.

"The gong went ten minutes ago. Mother isn't coming down, Hetty. She wants you to go and see her when you have rested. Although I must say you're looking better already. More like yourself. Loburn suiting you?"

It was absurd to imagine that the house felt friendlier than its inmates. She knew already that she would fall in love with these winding passages and uneven floors and old brocades and faded carpets, and the gleam of picture frames enclosing dark pictures on dark walls. Everything was muted, like a dream. It would be something just to love the house.

"I think very well," she answered Hugo. "I have so much to explore."

"Which room have they put you in?"

Who were "they"? Julia answered for her.

"Your mother and I thought the grey one. It's the quietest room in the house. You must admit Freddie can make quite a noise when he's being difficult. I'm sure Miss Jervis will appreciate quiet after her ordeal."

"Will you find it a bit lonely, Hetty?" asked Hugo. "Never mind, it isn't for long." He laid his arm heavily and possessively across Hetty's shoulders. "We've got a lot to discuss. But food first. Ah, here's Kitty."

A lumpish figure in shapeless clothes was hurrying down the stairs.

"Hugo, I'm terribly sorry I wasn't here to welcome Miss Jervis. How are you, Miss Jervis? I'm Kitty,

Lionel's wife – Hugo's sister-in-law." A warm hand was wrapped round Hetty's, the handshake firm and friendly. "I had to do my shift at the hospital this morning. I'm doing V.A.D. work at the military hospital in Cirencester. We're getting busier all the time, I'm sorry to say."

"You've heard from Lionel?" Hugo asked.

"Yes. He hinted heavily that they'll be sailing in the next few days for the Dardanelles. Oh, God! I do think the First Lord has some reckless ideas. I expect he'll pull one of them off one day. Do you know, it's even being suggested he might have had something to do with the sinking of the *Lusitania*. To have America outraged enough to come into the war. Did you hear that rumour, Miss Jervis? After all, you were one of the innocent civilian passengers. Your mother was drowned. As a neutral American you have every right to be highly outraged with the Germans."

"I don't think I know who you're talking about."

"Winston Churchill. First Lord of the Admiralty. Too clever by half. Anyway, Lionel's gone."

Her outburst seemed to have been made to cover her grief at her husband's departure. Her face was flushed and aggressive. She had bright dark eyes and a wide mouth. She wasn't good-looking, not even pretty. But she was alive. She must look well when she was dressed up, Hetty thought. Just now she was wearing a loose sweater and a shapeless tweed skirt. Her hair was inclined to tumble down. Hetty liked her.

There were just the four of them at the long dining table, Hugo and the three women. There was an abundance of silver and crystal, and an abundance of food, too. So it wasn't true that England was in danger of starving because of the blockade by German submarines. Certainly the inmates of Loburn were not starving. Hetty swallowed her soup, and then toyed with some fish. She found she was too tired to eat. Too tired to join in the conversation, too, although it concerned her so vitally.

"I do think Lady Flora might have made an effort and come down," Kitty said. "Doesn't she want to hear about the wedding plans? What are they, anyway, Hugo? Now that the grand affair in St Margaret's is off. Do you mind that, Hetty?"

"Not now that I've lost my trousseau." Some animation was expected from her. Some regret too. "I had a lovely wedding dress. And my grandmother's wedding veil. I haven't anything of my own now. Everything's borrowed. Thank you for leaving some things in my room."

"That's a small thing," said Kitty. "But we'll have to get you outfitted. There's quite a decent shop in Cirencester that I could take you to. If you don't insist on something grand from Fortnum and Mason's or Harrods."

"I don't want anything grand. Oh, unless Hugo insists."

"Under the circumstances," said Hugo, who was eating heartily, "the less fuss the better. I thought next week in the village church. Just a quiet ceremony. I have a medical board in a couple of weeks, and then I'll be off back to France. So the sooner the better. What do you say, Hetty?"

"Yes," said Hetty, in a strained voice. "Yes, of course."

"Must say you're taking it well, darling. You'd set a lot of store on a grand wedding, hadn't you? I know your mother had."

"It's different now. There's nothing I want less. After all, I'm in mourning. But I suppose I won't be the first bride ever to be in that position."

She made herself look up and meet the three pairs of eyes, Kitty's interested and sympathetic, Hugo's excited – was he thinking of being in bed with her, or of the money? – Julia's blank, surely refusing to believe what she was hearing.

"I've got to get my affairs straightened out before I go to France," Hugo said, proving that her guess about the money was the correct one. "Got a lot of debts to settle, and I do want a couple of hunters. Thought you might have a look around, Julia. Julia's a magnificent horse-woman, Hetty. She keeps my horses exercised when I'm away."

That Hetty could have guessed, too. That flat upright disciplined body, the long narrow hands.

"Where shall I look, Hug?"

Don't call him Hug in that familiar way. You're only his mother's companion.

"You might get Pimm to drive you over to Newmarket. But I don't want any cavalry rejects, mind."

"Would you like to come up to the nursery and see Freddie after luncheon?" Kitty asked.

"He's a spoiled brat," grumbled Hugo.

"He isn't spoiled. He's just an original. An eccentric. I adore him. But he's rather delicate, and at the present time –" Kitty's voice was tinged with apprehension – "he's the only heir Loburn has. What with you and Lionel in the thick of the fray, Hugo, he may remain the only one."

"I'd like very much to see him," said Hetty. "But could it be later? I'm so tired –"

The table, the floor, seemed to be rising and falling dizzily, almost as if she were back on board ship. She had to prop up her eyelids with her fingers. She had a terrible desire to weep. It was the calculated way these old English families talked of heirs as if they were some special privilege created only for them, and all she could see were those helpless babies, strapped into their wicker baskets, ready to be flung into the hungry sea, heirs to nothing but the fishes. She had a scared feeling that the nightmare of the *Lusitania* would come over her at unguarded moments for the rest of her life.

Kitty sprang up. "Come upstairs, Hetty. Excuse us,

everybody. You should have seen this poor girl wasn't ready for social life yet, Hugo. Honestly – men! I believe all Hugo truly cares about are his horses, and Lionel his books. Well, we women must survive. We always have."

Helped by Kitty, Hetty was out of the room and it was safe to let her lip tremble, her eyes go blind with tears.

"Go on," said Kitty kindly. "Cry. Have hysterics if you want to. Most women would. You've been holding yourself in too long, haven't you?"

"I had to. One does."

"I know. I see the boys in hospital, letting go when there's no one to shout orders at them. I'm going to put you to bed and give you a couple of pills to make you sleep. Tomorrow we'll pretend we're meeting for the first time."

"Hugo's mother –"

"Lady Flora can wait. Selfish old thing. Julia pampers her too much. And Hugo's just as selfish. You'll have to keep him in check."

"I thought – was he pleased? . . ." The words stumbled on her tongue.

"That you'd survived? Oh yes. He was terribly pleased and grateful."

"Because of the money? The marriage settlement?"

"That, too, to be honest. He's in a bit of a fix. There are a lot of estate debts and he gambles too much. And he does have this thing about Loburn that all the Hazzards have. Lionel has it, too, though less, since he's the younger son. But I can tell you, Hetty, Hugo does care about you a lot. He came back from America cock-a-hoop about this beautiful girl he'd persuaded to marry him. He couldn't wait to see you again."

"And then I arrive looking like a drowned cat."

"Well, let's say not quite the lovely creature he expected. But that's only temporary. Wait until we've got you fixed up. You lost your maid, too, didn't you?"

Hetty nodded, unable to speak.

71

"That's easily fixed. You can have Effie. She's wasted on me. I work in the hospital, and in the garden here, and scarcely ever have time to dress up. But you must have a shopping spree and give my stupid brother-in-law a surprise. You two got on all right in London this morning, didn't you?"

"Yes. He was – nice."

"There you are. What are you scared about?"

Hetty made no reply, but the question stayed with her. What *was* scaring her? The pampered invalid, Lady Flora, upstairs? Julia? No, I'm not scared of anybody, Hetty told herself. Not after all I've been through. Hugo might not love me, I might never love him. But I'm going to be Lady Hazzard. I'm going to be mistress of Loburn. That will be enough. For the hungry child from the Bowery it would be more than enough.

6

The nightmare was so vivid that she cried out, and woke
to see an unfriendly English face bending over her. Not
Clemency's as she had dreamed, nor Mrs Jervis, magis-
terial with rage and declaiming, "You have stolen my
diamonds, Brown, and now you're planning to steal
Clemency's husband!" In her dream she had been protesting frantically, "You don't need your diamonds now,
and Clemency doesn't need Hugo, either!"

And there was the bright light in her face, and Julia
Pemberton watching her.

Had she said those words aloud?

"It's nine o'clock, Miss Jervis. Lady Flora sent me to
see how you are."

Hetty sat up. The bright light was morning sunshine
streaming in through the windows. She must have slept
through yesterday afternoon and all through the night.
She felt rested and sanguine, even the dark nightmare
receding.

"I was dreaming about the *Lusitania*. Did I call out?"

"You were mumbling something. Better not do that
when you're married. Hugo won't care for it."

In her new mood of optimism Hetty felt almost sorry
for this cool haughty young woman who obviously had
hoped to marry Hugo. Perhaps she still thought such a
thing possible. But it wasn't. Hetty had lived long enough
in a rich household to know the power of money.

Nevertheless, Julia might be troublesome. She couldn't
marry Hugo, but she could stop him falling in love with

his bride. It would be better if she were not at Loburn.

Feel your way at present, Hetty said to herself. Make friends with Lady Flora. Learn about things. Be subtle.

"I guess I won't have nightmares for long. Anyway, I guess Hugo could have them about the trenches. We may have to comfort each other."

"The best way to comfort Hugo is to go on early morning gallops with him. I believe you don't ride."

"It's nice of you to worry about my deficiences, Julia. But I'll correct them."

She had the satisfaction of seeing the slight scowl on Julia's smooth brow, and knew she had made her first point. It was bad luck for Julia that she imagined her adversary to be a spoiled rich girl, naïve and unused to criticism, not the tough child that Hetty had been. A child used to fighting for her rights.

"Tell me when Lady Flora would like me to visit her. I'm looking forward to meeting her. I hope she's looking forward to meeting me."

"She suggested eleven o'clock in her sitting room. She doesn't like unpunctuality."

"Don't worry, I've always been trained to be punctual," Hetty said truthfully. She had been trained to take orders, too. This was an order.

And she was just about to give one herself. A plump rosy-cheeked maid answered her bell, bobbing and then stealing curious glances at Hetty. There would have been a lot of speculation about her. Hetty knew all about kitchen gossip.

"What's your name?"

"Annie, miss."

"Then, Annie, tomorrow I'll come down for breakfast, but this morning I slept in. Could you bring me some coffee and – say, what do you have for breakfast in this country?"

"Bacon and egg, miss. Grilled kidneys. Sausages. Kedgeree. Toasts and marmalade. Hot muffins."

74

"Do you really have all that food in wartime?"

"There's plenty to eat. So far, anyway. Although Bates – he's the butler – says if the German submarines go on sinking merchant ships – Oh, I'm sorry, I didn't mean to mention submarines, miss."

"It doesn't matter, Annie. We didn't see the submarine. We just heard a great explosion." We. Mrs Jervis, Clemency, herself. Mrs Drummond and her babies, Donald Newman and all those unfortunates trapped in steerage.

"It must have been horrible, miss."

"Yes, it was, but I don't want to talk of it now. I'd like bacon and eggs, toast and marmalade, and lots of hot coffee. And quickly, Annie, before I starve to death."

Annie giggled behind her hand. She bustled off, ready to report in the kitchen that the new mistress was ever so nice and jolly.

So there was a friend made. She might need friendship among the servants in this house.

Breakfast, a bath in the huge marble bath with gold taps shaped like dolphins, and then dressing in the borrowed silk blouse and skirt. Perhaps Kitty would take her shopping this afternoon.

It was still only ten o'clock. Repressing her eagerness to go and explore, Hetty decided to do something much less agreeable, but very necessary. She must compose a letter to Uncle Jonas, and, for safety write it with her left hand. She wasn't sure how familiar Uncle Jonas was with Clemency's handwriting. At this early stage she couldn't take risks.

Dear Uncle Jonas,

Please forgive wobbly writing, my right hand was hurt when I was dragged aboard the Irish fishing boat, and it is still troubling me. But I am well otherwise, and so grateful to be alive. Poor, poor Mummy. And Brown I never saw again. She was in steerage, which was the worst place.

Mr Walter Page, the American Ambassador, met us (the American survivors) at the railway station in London yesterday, and Hugo was there, too. He (Hugo) took me to breakfast at the Berkeley Hotel and then we drove to Loburn.

Everyone is being kind considering that they had been expecting an American heiress, not a drowned cat without a single possession to her name.

The war is much worse than we, or I anyway, realised. Hugo has to go back to France very soon – he is recovering from a wound – but he wants to be married first. I have quite given up the idea of a grand wedding. It would be wrong and tragic without dear Mummy. Hugo doesn't want it, either. So we are to be married next week in the little village church.

I already love Loburn. Now that Mother has gone, I expect Father's money comes to me. Will you advise me what I should do? I think some of it should be put in trusts for my children. I have changed since the disaster. I no longer want balls and parties, but only quiet and safety. I realise how lucky I am to be alive.

When you write to me you must address your letter to Lady Hazzard for that is who I will be then. Dear Uncle, you are my only remaining relation,

Your loving niece,
Clemency

There. Apart from the difficulty of using her left hand, the letter had written itself. She thought it was the way the new subdued Clemency would have expressed herself, slightly garrulous, slightly excited, but mostly over-awed by her brush with death.

Anyway, Uncle Jonas, a bachelor, would not know too much about the way a young woman's mind worked. He would give her good advice about investments, but none on how to cope with loneliness, grieving, guilt. Nor show any personal interest in her marriage beyond seeing that her aristocratic husband didn't make off with all her fortune.

Lady Flora's sitting room was a large light room overlooking a charming vista of lawns and blossoming trees, an avenue of limes and a fountain. The room itself, with its apple green and white colours and its orderly clutter, innumerable small tables covered with silver-framed photographs, bowls of flowers, china and glass objects, was a perfect setting for the slim grey-haired woman sitting with poker-back spine in a handsomely carved chair at the window. The room told the story of Lady Flora's well-ordered privileged life.

She extended a regal hand to Hetty. The dowager duchess, Hetty thought, straightening her own spine. Instinct told her to play this encounter with great caution. Lady Flora was almost certainly opposed to an American daughter-in-law, rich or otherwise. Her wide faded blue eyes, an older version of Hugo's, were deceptively innocent, her high-bridged nose, long narrow face and strong chin, the opposite. She could change her expression, but not the shape of her features. They spoke for her, even when her gaze was completely seductive. Hetty had heard of these strong-minded autocratic supremely confident English women. She was dismayed to find that her future mother-in-law was one of them.

Even so, her blood stirred to the challenge. She was twenty-two, good-looking, healthy and clever. This woman was sixty at least, and tired. Her tiredness showed in the fragility of her skin, the smoky tinge round her eyes, the thinness of her hands and wrists.

So it's an unfair contest between us, Hetty told herself. But when I'm pregnant with your grandson you will accept me, Lady Flora.

She made herself smile with the dimpled charm she knew she was able to produce.

"I'm so glad to meet you, Lady Hazzard."

"You must call me Lady Flora. You, I imagine, are going to be Lady Hazzard."

"I guess so. Well, I guess that's Hugo's intention."

"I apologise for not being downstairs yesterday to greet you. I understand you had a rather poor welcome. I had one of my bad mornings. I have a tiresome heart. And then, in the afternoon, they said you had gone to your room to rest. You were in a distressed state, Kitty said."

"Yes, I was. That nightmare comes over me – about the ship, and everything."

"It must have been a terrible experience."

Hetty nodded. "I hope I'll forget it in time. I'm just learning how appalling war can be. We didn't know so much in New York. We were – cushioned I suppose is the word."

"But it isn't your war, is it?"

"It is from now on," Hetty said with some vehemence. "Especially when I'm married to Hugo."

"That's so. One will expect that." Lady Flora's eyes narrowed. "Where's your engagement ring?" The question came out sharply and suspiciously.

"I lost it. In the sea. It was a little too big for my finger. I meant to get it altered."

"What a pity. That was Hugo's grandmother's ring. A very fine emerald. It can never be replaced."

"I lost my grandmother's wedding veil, too," Hetty said. "That can't be replaced, either."

"Yes, I realise that family heirlooms give one an identity. Without them how does one know who one is?"

The mildness of her tone was deceptive. Hetty was aware of the trap.

"Hugo recognised me without his ring on my finger, Lady Flora. Are you suggesting he might have made a mistake?"

Had those wide blue eyes become a shade more chilly?

"You sound rather aggressive, my dear. Hugo told me you were a charming butterfly, very bright and amusing.

78

Just the kind of girl he admired. He never said you were clever."

Hetty refused to be discomfited. "I'm not clever. But if I were, maybe I would have concealed it. Men don't like clever women, do they? At least, Mother always told me so."

"I can see you've had a conventional upbringing. Personally, I think it's quite wrong for a young girl to have to hide her intelligence. We're surely growing out of those repressive ways. But if you aren't as clever as I think, you do have a determined look. As if you are one of those fortunate people who know what they want."

Hetty made her voice flippant, as Clemency would have done.

"I do know what I want. Your son Hugo, first. And then this lovely, lovely old house."

"You're a New Yorker, used to modern things. How can you love a house like this, creaking with age?"

"Just because it is old, I think. We don't have houses that go back this far in history. It's fascinating. But it does need a great deal of money spent on it, doesn't it?"

She had the satisfaction of seeing a flicker in the stern face. Was it an acknowledgment of defeat? She wasn't sure, for Lady Flora had begun another ploy. And now she was less tactful.

"I believe a title has a quite irresistible lure for ambitious American girls. There have been several marriages of this kind in England. I'm not sure how successful they've been."

Hetty attempted a look of complete honesty. She didn't know how long she could deceive this sharp-witted woman.

"I admit it will be kind of fun being Lady Hazzard. I'll have to get used to it. But it wasn't for that reason I came to England." Now she was speaking the truth far more than Lady Flora would ever know. "I'll make Hugo a good wife, and give him a son or two sons, or maybe three."

"Do you love my son?" the question was clipped and abrupt.

"I did, in New York. I wanted him terribly." Hetty knew this answer was important and had to be convincing. "Since the shipwreck I've felt kind of stunned and I just know I want not only Hugo, but everything. Everything!"

Lady Flora's eyes were narrowed.

"A close escape from death seems to have made you remarkably greedy."

"I was always greedy. For all manner of things. To see life almost vanishing made me want to grab just everything."

"Yes, I believe I understand that. Well, I suppose that attitude has made you a survivor. Hugo's one, too, so far. It's terrible at the front. All our good young men are dying."

Now Hetty was aware of the grief behind Lady Flora's composure.

"He'll need to care a great deal about staying alive. That's up to you. And he must have a son. Otherwise there's only Freddie, and he's delicate. His mother barely survived his birth, so there won't be any more from that quarter. I know Kitty looks strong, but she isn't."

"I'm very strong," Hetty murmured.

"You've already proved that. So shall we agree on this? If you give Hugo a son I may forgive you about the money."

"Forgive me!"

"It is an unfair weapon, isn't it?"

And one that her favourite, Julia, hadn't got?

"I can't help that, Lady Flora. And I'd never expected to inherit poor Mummy's estate so soon. But I'd rather not talk about that yet. Uncle Jonas will write to me and explain things."

"Your Uncle Jonas is your nearest relation?"

"My only one – except for some distant cousins we never saw."

"Then we must cable him about the wedding. Hugo and I decided perhaps next Wednesday. Depending on what your uncle says."

Hetty's eyes flew open wide.

"You've discussed this without me!"

"Last evening. My dear child, you were fast asleep and we wouldn't disturb you. It had to be planned, hadn't it? Hugo is due for a discharge from his medical board, and then he'll go back to France, poor boy. Lionel, unfortunately, won't be here. We will just have to make the best of things, won't we, we women?"

She seemed amused at Hetty's indignation.

"In a war such as this one is turning out to be, one makes compromises. I never thought it was right to have a big society wedding at this time, anyway. There would be too many gaps among the guests, apart from anything else. Hugo has lost several of his closest friends already. One could hardly have a church full of widows. I know you had set your heart on a grand affair –"

Hetty shook her head vehemently. "Not any more."

"Then perhaps we understand each other. On this point, anyway."

Lady Flora sighed and leaned back, at last relaxing her upright spine. She looked white and tired.

"So we'll wait for a reply from your Uncle Jonas, and then Hugo will see the vicar. I believe Kitty has undertaken to take you shopping. You'll find some quite decent clothes in Cirencester. Now, if you would be good enough to ring that bell, Annie will bring us some hot chocolate. And tap at the next door down the hall and ask Julia to join us. Did they tell you her mother was my best friend? Poor Julia has had some miserable bad fortune. You must promise to be friends."

"Can we be friends?" Hetty asked daringly.

Lady Flora sighed. "Yes, you are clever. But just remember, even with that terrible tragedy the other night, you've been able to realise your dream. Julia hasn't.

81

But she stays here because I love her and need her."

And me? Hetty wanted to ask. Will you love me?

No, you never will. I will always be the usurper. And I don't want your love, you cold proud old woman.

Uncle Jonas's answer came expeditiously.

"By all means arrange marriage soonest possible. Stop. Should be no problems with transfer of funds in bank. Stop. Wish you both happiness. Stop. Uncle Jonas."

What with that prompt, almost relieved answer, and the test she seemed to have passed successfully with Lady Flora, Hetty was able to relax and feel more sanguine.

She had to remember to sign the church register "Clemency Millicent Hazzard". Supposing she had a lapse of memory? She had also to get a clear picture in her mind of Clemency's thick up and down strokes, since no doubt Hugo had had frequent letters from her.

Ah, there was the solution. If Hugo had kept Clemency's letters she could study the handwriting at leisure. But this could not be done until she and Hugo shared the same bedroom, and she had access to his writing desk and his personal papers.

He would certainly not keep love letters in the library, a room everyone used. If he was sentimental enough to keep love letters at all.

When would it be safe to stop being Clemency, and become entirely herself? Not until she had a wedding ring on her finger, and even then with caution.

But things were going better. Hugo, in his curiously abrupt way, was paying her more attention. He was delighted with the result of her and Kitty's shopping expedition to Cirencester, a stone grey town with medieval buildings and ancient parkland. Now there, he said with satisfaction when Hetty came down to dinner in a new dinner gown, was the girl he remembered. Chic and sophisticated and saucy. Not the drowned kitten he had rescued on Paddington railway station. She realised he must have felt some dismay at that apparition and credited him with what had been a display of excellent manners.

He became noisy and high-spirited that evening, and after drinking a good deal of wine and brandy he tore up all his dunning letters, making them into a funeral pyre.

Hetty was shocked at how many of these unpleasant missives there were.

"Hugo, what are all these debts?"

"Mostly estate expenses. I've never been able to get clear since my father died. Death duties and all that. And I confess I've been going rather too often to gaming clubs. I mean to reform when I am married, and, I promise you, I will. Anyway, there won't be much opportunity to play while I'm spending most of my time in stinking trenches, so perhaps you could call the war a blessing in disguise."

"Is all of that million dollars going to be used in this way?"

"Most of it, I'm afraid."

"Then didn't you make your price too low?"

"My price?"

"For marrying me."

He roared with laughter, not in the least abashed.

"It was a decent settlement. Considering that I was getting such a charming bride. It wasn't only the money, you know. Surely I never gave you that impression? You haven't got a suspicious mind, have you?"

She found she liked his arrogance, his absolute certainty of rightness. It had a sexual quality. An excitement stirred deep in her stomach. She suddenly wanted to see him without his clothes on. She had never seen a naked man, although she was not ignorant about the mechanics of sex. One couldn't work in a servants' hall without learning rather too explicit details.

She had thought herself fairly impervious to desire, not

vulnerable as her mother had been. Even that poor young Canadian airman, Donald Newman, had stirred only a pleasant curiosity in her.

This leaping excitement was tremendous, if only because it blotted out nervousness and guilt. Perhaps they could have a happy marriage, after all, she and Hugo. It would justify everything.

She made a thick black generously rounded C, and carefully finished the names "Clemency Millicent". The nib of the pen scratched and made a tiny spray of blots. She wrote the name Hazzard with less intensity, breathing deeply.

There it was on paper, her new identity.

Hugo's signature followed in a fairly unintelligible scrawl. He grinned at her, and she saw that he, too, was relieved. He must have found it hard to believe that he was actually going to be rid of that mountain of debt.

The vestry of the small church was chilly and smelled of mould. The vicar was old and just short of senility, from the way he had fumbled the service. This, too, had given Hetty a feeling of relief. He wasn't likely to be around if the time ever came for awkward questions to be asked.

"Clemency Millicent, do you take Hugo Edward John Clarence to be your lawful wedded husband?"

Even if he were not dead, the vicar would have forgotten her clear aggressive "I do", which could have suggested a suspicious eagerness, and must have differed a great deal from the average response of modestly whispering brides.

The church had been sparsely occupied. Lady Flora, elegant in stiff grey silk, with violets tucked in her waistband, Kitty, scarcely more tidy than when she was working in the garden, and the little boy Freddie with his meagre delicate body. The vicar's wife, nearly as infirm as her husband, a young Captain in khaki, an army friend of Hugo's, and some of the staff from the great house, modestly at the back of the church.

No one belonging to Hetty. But now she had a family. Standing at Hugo's side, she was expecting the ache of loneliness to leave her for ever.

The singing and responses had been pitifully thin. It didn't matter. She was married. She was reborn. A female Lazarus.

It was not something that happened to many people.

Julia Pemberton had not been in the church. Lady Flora had spared her for a few days to visit some distant cousins. She would be back shortly. There was no rebirth for Julia. But one was now in the position to be kind to her and dispense favours. And make very sure that Hugo lost interest in her.

As they came out of the church a sprinkling of villagers stared. There was none of the gaiety and laughter of the usual wedding crowd. They were disappointed, of course, that Lord Hazzard of the great house, their lord of the manor, was having such a modest ceremony. They tut-tutted at Hugo's limp, and stared at Hetty. One or two of the women smiled in a friendly way. Then a child darted forward and thrust a nosegay at the new bride, and at the same moment an aeroplane roared overhead, flying low, almost touching the treetops. An abrupt memory of Donald Newman, the young Canadian aviator, flashed through Hetty's mind. She winced, and as the rattle of the engine died away Hugo leaned down to say, "There's a flying field near here. But that pilot's a bit off course. I don't know how those contraptions stay in the air. Tied together with wire."

That ghost from the past upset Hetty and the chill of the vestry seemed to have followed her, for as she entered the house a drenching cold enveloped her. Like drowning.

She dropped her spray of yellow rosebuds and maidenhair fern and the tight posy the child had given her, on the dark oak table, shivering uncontrollably.

"What's the matter, my lady?" asked Mrs Evans. "Are you ill?"

"N-no!" My lady. It made her want to laugh. And to cry. "It's only – the church was so c-cold."

"Bates, the champagne," Hugo ordered. "That's what we need." He put his arm round Hetty, holding her close. "Shuts out the nightmares," he said. "I have them, too."

Her gratitude for his unexpected understanding diminished her trembling. Warmth slowly returned to her body. What miraculous stuff champagne was. No wonder it was the favoured drink of the rich.

That night there was another bottle in an ice-filled bucket on the bedside table, but Hugo, when he came out of his dressing room, found that it wasn't necessary. His bride seemed to be pliant and ready.

At least this was what Hetty guessed he judged, for he discarded his dressing gown and got into bed quickly. She didn't have an opportunity to study his naked body, but only felt it, solid and warm beside her, and then heavy on top of her. He breathed heavily, too, and in his excitement disjointed words came out.

"You and me, darling. Got to make the best of it now." He was parting her legs. "By God, you have a nice body."

And then he was too impatient to wait at all.

It hurt. She was sure it would have hurt less if Hugo had taken more time. But she liked his ardent haste. She suspected that the next time she would be impatient, too. And that would be wonderful. But just now she could only hold her breath at the stinging pain and wait for him to finish. When he did he cried out, and then collapsed with his head on her breast.

His cry had given her that strange shaft of acutely exciting pain in her stomach. It was sexual, she realised.

"Hugo," she said tenderly, after a little while.

"Yes, darling. Are you all right?"

"I will be. Next time."

"Afraid I was clumsy."

"Just being a man, I guess."

He raised his head to look at her closely.

"You keep surprising me, Clem – Hetty."

"How do I do that?"

"In New York you were bubbly, like champagne. Sometimes girls like that go a bit flat – I mean, when one gets down to basic things."

"I won't, Hugo. I promise."

"I don't believe you will."

She couldn't resist a sly question.

"Are you getting a higher return on your investment than you expected?"

He gave his roar of laughter.

"You little devil! Now don't bring money into bed with us. But how is it with you, Lady Hazzard? How's your side of the arrangement?"

"Feels fine, from here."

"You won't be too dull when I go away? I thought you'd be wanting parties."

"They can wait. I'll be happy getting to know Loburn, and everybody. And having them get to know me. And doing some war work, too."

"Yes, that will be expected of you."

The lady of the manor. Hetty turned the strange thought over in her mind.

"Hugo. What about Julia?"

"How do you mean?" His voice had become guarded.

"She's jealous of me."

"Well, yes. I suppose she would be."

"Would you have married her if you hadn't had all those debts. Or if she'd had money?"

"Perhaps."

"In preference to me?"

"I didn't know you then. Shut up, will you, darling.

87

You're asking too many questions."

"But is she to stay here?"

"Afraid so. Mother needs her. I need her, too, in the stables now my best grooms are joining up. She's damned good with horses. She's going to give you some riding lessons as soon as I've gone."

Can I trust her? Hetty wondered silently. Hugo seemed a bit naïve about the possible malevolence of a jealous woman.

Hugo was regarding her closely.

"Why are you looking like that?" he asked. "I admit I was fond of Julia. Yes, I would have married her if she'd been an heiress. But she wasn't, and I married you. And I believe you're a little temptress. I'd like to – no, better wait a bit. Let's crack that bottle of champagne, and then see what the weather's like."

He wasn't very subtle with the language of love, but he was thoughtful in his way, and she found the strength of his body immensely exciting.

Oh yes, that fateful decision after the *Lusitania* disaster had been the right one, no doubt about it. Mother would have approved. Father too, she was sure.

Lady Hazzard of Loburn.

Be good, she whispered to herself superstitiously. Be good.

7

Her intuition that being Hugo's wife, becoming at ease
with him in the day, and going to bed with him at night,
would get better proved accurate. They established a
friendly, almost comfortable, relationship.

Hetty decided that his brusqueness came from shyness
rather than the limited interests of riding and hunting.
He could be drawn out on other things, particularly on
Loburn and his ancestors, and she eagerly planned to do
this when there was more time. At present the nights
were the best, when they didn't talk at all, but sought
solace and forgetfulness in the warmth and excitement of
each other's body.

By the end of the ten short days of their married life,
when Hugo had to leave to rejoin his battalion, Hetty was
convinced that she had conceived a child. She longed for
this to be so. It was one thing to make her husband happy,
as she had done her best to do, but to give him a son
would surely absolve her from her persistent guilt.

They said goodbye on a June morning, at the little railway station two miles from Loburn. There was sweet
briar blooming in the hedges, and climbing roses over the
modest station buildings.

Pimm waited outside in the Rolls. Hugo hadn't permitted anyone else to come. His goodbyes, even to his
mother, had been casual. Hetty herself had accompanied
him to the railway station for the simple reason that she
had refused to be left behind. Hugo had looked put out at
first; he was accustomed to being obeyed. But then he

had seemed to be pleased, his blue eyes momentarily as brilliant as she had remembered them in New York. She realised that suddenly they were both alive in a peculiarly heightened way. Death had been too close to them; they would probably have these moments of acute perception for the rest of their lives.

All the same, as they waited on the almost empty platform for the train to arrive, the scent of roses and the sweet June morning became too poignant.

"I say, darling, have a day or two in London. Take Kitty or Julia. Enjoy yourself in the shops."

Hetty shook her head.

"I don't think I want to."

"Aren't you extravagant by nature? I was sure you were."

"Oh, yes, I am. At least I was."

"Well, I've opened a bank account for you in Cirencester. All you have to do is to go and make yourself known and give them a specimen signature."

"That's nice of you, Hugo."

"It's your money."

She curled her hand inside his and spoke pleadingly, "But it's more than money, being your wife? Isn't it?"

"Of course it is. Always was," he added, a little belatedly.

The train was coming, smoking down the long green track, its whistle screaming. Darkness was blowing over her.

"Hugo?"

"Yes, darling."

She was speaking instinctively, "Are you afraid, in the trenches?"

His eyes went cold, as if something had pinched out their light.

"What an odd thing to say."

"But anyone would be. I mean, I know what deadly fear is. No matter how brave one tries to be."

The train had come to a halt. Hugo grabbed a door handle and pulled open the door.

"Sorry, darling. No time for intense conversation. Can't stand it, anyway. Goodbye. Take care."

He looked back, smiling jauntily. He looked very smart and debonair in his uniform. The friendliness had not come back to his eyes. He had been deeply offended by her remark. She must remember his touchiness. But what a pity they couldn't talk about fear; they both knew what it was.

She returned to Loburn, driven by a silent but sympathetic Pimm, and entered the house to the sound of piano music. Very expert music, too. The delicate notes of a Chopin nocturne rippled and sighed in harmony with the bereaved mood of the house.

"It's Lady Flora, my lady," said Effie, noticing Hetty's questioning glance. "She always plays the pianner when she's upset, like."

"Where?"

"In the music room, my lady."

This was a charming room which seemed to be seldom used. It had a collection of early English porcelain in glass-fronted cabinets, some low comfortable chairs, long windows that opened on to a terrace smelling of honeysuckle and wallflowers, and a grand piano which Hetty had not previously heard played.

Hetty had had private ideas about making this room her personal sitting room. After all, she was the mistress, wasn't she? She didn't feel at ease in the morning room or in either of the two drawing rooms, the summer one which was in constant use and the winter one which seemed to be mostly shut up, or even in the library – which was Hugo's, anyway. She wanted a room where she could be alone to read, to do needlework, to plan the running of the house, to dream of her hopeful future.

But now she found that again she was a usurper. The

music room was Lady Flora's, and Lady Flora was an accomplished pianist.

"Miss Pemberton's arrived back," Effie said, giving Hetty a sideways glance.

"Has she?"

"She was ever so upset she had missed seeing the master, to say goodbye. She got Lady Flora to come down because playing the pianner calms her most of all. It seems to suit, doesn't it, that sort of sad sound? Are you going in to listen, my lady?"

"No."

Effie nodded sympathetically. "It does make you a bit tearful, don't it?"

No, it didn't make her tearful, it made her angry. She wasn't going into that lovely room to see it possessed by the two elegant women who so emphasised that she was the outsider.

So they were four women at dinner that night, and this state of affairs could be expected to go on for a long time.

In spite of Julia's well-disciplined composure she couldn't hide the fact that she had been crying. The candlelight was kind to her pale face and reddened eyelids. It made her look forlorn and fragile. Had she wept because she thought she had lost Hugo for ever, if not to war, then to his new wife?

Lady Flora wore black velvet and several loops of lustrous pearls with immense dignity. Kitty, with her air of distrait cheerfulness, had her usual put-together look, hair inclined to tumble, blouse and skirt carelessly matched. But who wanted to dress up when there were no men present? What was Lionel like, Hetty wondered suddenly. Did he mind having an untidy wife? She had been so absorbed in Hugo that she had no time to find out anything about his brother. Could Lionel talk of fear?

"We'll have to get used to being a household of women," Lady Flora was saying, speaking Hetty's own thoughts. "Fortunately, Bates and Pimm are too old to join up, and we have one elderly groom, haven't we, Julia?"

"Yes, Lady Flora. Jackson. But that's all right because I'm exercising Hugo's horses."

"And I'm taking over the garden," said Kitty cheerfully. "The gardener's boy is staying and Pimm can help. No one will be needing the Rolls much, will they?"

She looked at Hetty questioningly, silently reminding her that she was the mistress.

"I need to go into Cirencester tomorrow," Hetty said. "Hugo tells me I must give the bank a specimen signature." How should she write it? Had they checked with their London branch? Had they seen any signature of Clemency's? She must search for letters now that Hugo had gone, and she could do what she liked alone in that big bedroom at night.

"I thought you would want to be off to London, Hetty." Lady Flora's face was long and dim at the other end of the table. But Hetty knew now that her remote look was misleading. She was deeply aware of everything that was happening, or was likely to happen. "Haven't you any American friends you want to look up?"

"Not at present, Lady Flora."

"Not even at the Embassy? I thought, for such a socially prominent young woman –"

"Oh, I had letters of introduction, of course. But since they were all lost when the ship sank I've decided not to do anything at present." She looked steadily at the long pale face watching her. "I'd have had friends in London for my wedding in peacetime, naturally. But with the war raging, they decided not to come. Fortunately for them, as it turned out."

"Did you know that the list of American dead and missing from the *Lusitania* has been published?"

The dreaded drenching cold was pouring over her again.

She gripped her hands together under the table.

"No. Has it? When?"

"In *The Times* yesterday. We decided not to show it to you until Hugo had gone."

"It mentions – my mother?"

"Your mother, Mrs Millicent Jervis. And maid."

Hetty took a long steadying breath.

"That was Brown. Poor Brown. She'd spent that morning on board ironing, and packing. We were expecting to disembark in a few hours."

"You haven't mentioned her before."

"Haven't I? I thought you knew we were travelling with a maid. She was lost. I – there were so many dead . . ."

"There are other maids and valets mentioned," said Kitty. "None of them by name. I expect everything will be documented in time."

None of them important enough to be named.

"Brown was a good maid," Hetty made herself say. "She thought my wedding dress was the most beautiful –" Now she genuinely couldn't go on. Her mouth was dry. She was desperate to ask the one question that couldn't be asked. Had Clemency's body been found and assumed to be the maid's? It was safer to change the subject at once.

"Speaking of lady's maids," she said, her voice again under control. "I can manage without one, especially while Hugo's away. So Effie can do other things, if she will."

"Oh, that's a good thing," Kitty said. "Because Annie wants to go into munitions. That's how she describes working in a factory in Gloucester. So perhaps Effie could be persuaded to be parlour maid. Thank goodness Cook is past the age for thinking she has to be patriotic. The other problem is that Mrs Evans probably has to go and look after her old mother, since the mother's nurse wants to join the Red Cross. It's like a sort of crazy musical chairs, isn't it?"

"I can run the house," Hetty said calmly. "In New York, I knew – I mean, my mother insisted I should know how to do things like that. She was very practical."

"Could you really do it?" asked Kitty. "We'd been wondering. We thought you rather young."

"I'm very capable." Hetty's voice was confident. At last she was on firm ground. It was quite an asset to know from the opposite side how a big house functioned. She had learned enough from the lectures, scoldings and instructions that took place below stairs to be able to assemble and manage a staff for the largest and grandest place.

And Loburn was neither large nor grand. It was shabby and under-staffed, and there was a war on. It couldn't be restored quickly, but in her lifetime she was determined to see it regain its one-time beauty.

"You surprise us all, my dear," said Lady Flora, after a moment.

My dear. Well, that was a beginning. When she caught Julia's swift hostile glance she knew it really was a beginning: Julia had hoped to run the house.

"Hugo said I could have the pictures cleaned," Hetty went on. "I want to get new drapes and new covers for the furniture, too. Everything's awfully shabby, isn't it? And I'm going to find someone to look at the roof. I guess other things can wait, but Hugo said the roof needed urgent repairs."

"It does," Kitty agreed. "We've had to shut off part of the west wing. It's full of mould, and infested with bats. Freddie hates them."

"You'll never get these things done while the war's on," Julia said in her cool precise voice. "You won't find the workmen."

"Oh, I expect to. After all," Hetty added slyly, "I was brought up on the theory that money can do anything."

"Don't put that to too many tests," Julia snapped. "This is England."

"Stop it, Julia," said Kitty briskly. "Don't be so high-minded. We have a healthy regard for money, too. I think Hetty's ideas are first rate. There are plenty of tradesmen left who are over-age or under-age, and not working in factories. Otherwise the country would come to a stand-still."

"I want to surpirse Hugo," Hetty said, knowing that sentiment would bring approval from Lady Flora, at least.

"Don't forget Lionel, too," Kitty said. "He cares just as much as Hugo does for Loburn."

"You've never told me much about Lionel," Hetty said.

"You haven't asked. Oh, I don't blame you. You've been wrapped up with a new husband. Lionel's quite different from Hugo. Isn't he, Lady Flora? Bookish, dreamy, sensitive, brilliant." Kitty's amiable face contorted. "And now he's expected to swelter on those awful Gallipoli headlands that not even a goat can climb. There's nothing but rocks and thorns and sand and flies and god-awful *rot*!"

"It's just as bad in Belgium," Julia said. "Except that they have mud instead of sand. Didn't Hugo tell you about the trenches there?" Her strained eyes went de-liberately from Kitty to Hetty. "He did me."

Hetty was sure she was lying. Hugo had said very little to anybody. She remembered how he had winced when she had mentioned the forbidden word, fear. He had shut the horror inside himself, and talked lightly of riding horses behind the lines when he could get a decent mount, of improvised concerts in small estaminets, of the solid pleasures of bully beef.

Julia was simply enjoying these small pin-pricks.

"I'm sure Hugo didn't alarm you, dear," Lady Flora said quietly. "He wouldn't. Lionel won't either. They'll both pretend its better than it is. But of course we women know the truth. So we all play a game. You're doing the

96

same yourself, Hetty, I think. You've said very little about your terrible shipwreck."

Hetty pressed her hands to her cheeks. "I can't talk of it," she whispered.

"I didn't want to distress you, my dear. But you must talk of it one day. No one can shut a nightmare inside herself for ever."

Was that a challenge? No, she was too suspicious. Lady Flora's voice had been quiet and matter-of-fact, her face dim and sad – a white blur in the wavering candlelight.

But if every dinner was going to be like this, full of undercurrents, she was going to long and pray for effective diversions.

Although not the one Julia suddenly produced.

"Hugo has asked me to teach you to ride, Hetty."

"Can't Hetty ride? Good gracious!" That was Lady Flora, startled out of her sadness, not quite believing her ears.

"You can't keep horses on Fifth Avenue," Hetty said flippantly.

"But didn't you have a country place?"

"Oh yes, on Long Island." Hetty saw that something more was expected of her. "I once had a bad fall off my pony. I didn't care for riding after that."

"Oh, you must overcome those things. Julia would have remounted at once. Wouldn't you, dear?"

Instead of answering the question, Julia said, "Hugo suggested beginning on Patsy."

"That old rocking horse," Kitty exclaimed. "Don't worry, Hetty. Even Freddie wouldn't fall off Patsy."

"Do you want me to teach Freddie, too?" Julia asked.

"He's only five. And rather timid. Lionel said he wasn't to be hurried. Still, it might give him confidence to see a grown-up learning at the same time."

Had that been another suggestion of Julia's to ridicule her? Hetty wondered. The grown woman and the little boy taking it in turns to mount the safe old rocking horse.

"What fun," Hetty murmured satirically.

Freddie was a peaky child, scarcely ever out of the company of Nanny Grainger. He had come up to her once in the garden and, raising his small moony face, had asked, "Who are you?"

"You know me, Freddie. You came to my wedding. I'm your new aunt."

"No, you're not my *aunt*."

Even from so small a person the disbelief came as a shock.

"Why do you say that?"

"Because I know you're not."

"Master Freddie," admonished Nanny Grainger. "That's very rude. I don't know what made him say it, my lady. He knows very well who you are. You must apologise, Master Freddie."

Freddie remained stubborn.

"But if she was pulled out of the sea she must be a mermaid. Only she's got feet. I can see her feet. Look."

"You get too many fancies, Master Freddie." Nanny Grainger was plainly not a fanciful woman. Which was bad luck for Freddie who obviously had a splendid imagination. He was a strange little boy. Difficult to rear, Kitty had said, and she had added that she was unable to have any more children. So Freddie would eventually be the heir to Loburn, unless Hugo had a son. No wonder Hugo was eager for his wife to have a quick pregnancy and a male child.

But if this happened, Hetty wouldn't have Freddie shut out. He had a wistful, if slightly bizarre, appeal. She knew all too well the hurt of being shut out, listening to laughter behind closed doors, lonely, longing to be part of the warm gay scene of comfort and privilege which was her right. Freddie obviously took after his father, who was clever and bookish. Hetty was curious to meet Lionel. But not over-impatient.

Dinner that night finally ended with Lady Flora saying she was a little tired and would like to have her coffee upstairs. Julia obediently sprang up, putting a wrap round the fragile shoulders and helping her from the room. So proud a young woman in the role of nurse was decidedly incongruous, and would have been sad had Hetty any pity to give. But pity in this situation was dangerous and she guarded against it.

Kitty excused herself, saying she wanted to write to Lionel.

"You'll find us dreadfully quiet in the evenings, Hetty, now the men are gone."

"I don't mind that."

"But didn't you have a very glittering social life in New York? Hugo says you did."

"I've changed. I don't think I'll ever be dancing all night again. At present I just want to be quiet. And anyway I'm going upstairs to write to Hugo, too."

In spite of that explanation Kitty seemed to give her a sceptical look, as if she knew Hetty's real intention, which was to search among Hugo's papers for letters from Clemency. She had to get that handwriting familiarised before writing to Hugo, and before going to the bank.

It was very quiet in the big bedroom where so many Hazzards had been born, loved and died. The lingering daylight – for it was almost June – showed the view of the yew walk, a famous view, Hugo had told her. But even in broad daylight she had found it dark and sad, with the small pointed yews, like sharpened pencils, leading to an ornamental lake which always seemed black no matter the time of day. She had shivered on seeing it the first time, and now she was still haunted by the sight and memory of water. She hastily put on all the lights, but the room still seemed dim and shadowy. The curtains moved slightly with a sound like the rustling of heavy silk skirts, and a thin chill came into the air. Hetty checked to see if a window was open, but this was not so. There didn't seem to be any wind. The trees were black against the pale sky, no leaves stirring.

Hetty shrugged. It must be the ancestors protesting about the little usurper. If she could hold her own with the living Hazzards, she was more than a match for the ancestors.

But the room was undoubtedly ghostly. It wasn't meant to be occupied by a woman alone. The bed, which had seemed only relatively capacious when Hugo lay beside her, now looked enormous, an uninhabited country. A shape seemed to move in the silver-framed mirror on the dressing table. No, that was surely only a reflection of herself, caught by chance. Though it would not be surprising if phantom images of other women, brushing long ropes of hair, undressing, climbing into the big bed nervously or eagerly, drawing the bed curtains, waiting for their husbands or their lovers, lingered in that bland gleaming surface.

She thought of her own husband. She had enjoyed being in bed with Hugo. At first his injured leg had pained him. Then he had forgotten it as she had forgotten the initial pain of her virginity. Eventually she had found making love a delightful occupation. She thought she must have inherited her mother's generous and sensuous nature. The memory of those nights with Hugo stirred in her body, and she longed for him to be here with her now. He was not going to get a bad bargain. Eventually he would love her. Or was it more important that she should love him?

She was allowing herself to dream, and deliberately postponing her first act of desecration in this house.

For it was desecration to go through a man's private belongings, even though the man was one's husband. Bought and paid for. Though legitimate only by virtue of a false signature on a marriage certificate . . .

Hetty discovered a locked drawer in Hugo's bureau

and, after a search, the key that opened it.

Inside was an untidy collection of papers, bills, business letters, documents, and, carelessly among this mish-mash, two letters on thick expensive writing paper. One from Clemency, the other from Julia.

She read Clemency's first because she was curious to study the handwriting and the style of the letter. To her relief, the handwriting was distinctly similar to her own, the careful script their governess, Miss Ashford, had taught them. So that was another problem solved.

Clemency wrote:

My darling husband-to-be,

The time is getting short now. Everything is arranged and we sail early in May on the Cunard liner, the *Lusitania*. It is all so exciting I can scarcely eat or sleep, and Mother says I am getting pale and skinny and you won't care for that. Will you mind how I look, Hugo? I hope you will. After the sea voyage you will find me with red cheeks like a country girl. I have got the most fabulous trousseau. I can't wait to show you everything, and I promise you you will be proud of your Yankee bride. You will be there when the *Lusitania* docks at Liverpool, won't you? And you don't need to wear a red carnation because I will recognise you instantly! As you had better recognise your so-nearly wife! I promise to love you very much, and I send you hugs and kisses now.

Clemency

It wasn't a grave that had opened, rather a chilly chasm through which cold winds blew, and Clemency's light-hearted laughter echoed, though growing fainter and fainter.

Hetty hugged her arms round herself, shivering miserably. Eavesdroppers, she had always heard, and similarly people burrowing into private matters, found nothing to comfort them. Was she to be haunted all her life by the memory of the gay extrovert girl whom poor Hugo had thought he was getting for his wife? Had he been terribly disappointed? He hadn't showed it, and she had been too nervous to try to explain her quietness and pallidness, other than attributing it to the shipwreck.

. On his next leave she would make it up to him. She would have some exciting clothes, and put colour on her cheeks, and chatter vivaciously. Or would she? Perhaps he hadn't been too discontented with the sea-changed wife he had got. After all, grave and terrible events were shadowing his life, too. There wouldn't have been much of a place for party-loving young women in the England she had come to. Hugo might have been apprehensive as to how he could have kept that kind of girl happy, and therefore had been grateful for her change in character.

Anyway, there was no use in sitting here pondering over things to which there was no answer. Only living would provide the answer.

And she must remind herself for the thousandth time that she hadn't been responsible for Clemency's death. There was no need to feel this weight of guilt.

Julia's letter was another matter. Hetty struggled with her conscience. It was loathsome reading private letters. But curiosity, and her instinct for survival in the future, overcame her qualms, and she read,

My dearest,

I simply cannot and will not accept what you told me last night, that you intend putting Loburn first, and saving it for your family. You expect me to understand that because I come from an old home, too. But mine has broken up and vanished and the world hasn't come to an end.

I know you think of your mother and your brother, and the prospect of having an heir yourself who will be stronger than poor little Freddie. And of course of your horses, and your staff, and your debts. But me, me, me, I am alive and I deserve something. If you really mean to marry this American you can't expect me ever to be a friend of hers. I will stay here and make her suffer. That is the kind of woman I am. Your kind. We could have a marvellous life together, even without money. Whatever you do, I will never give you up. Never, never, never.

Your Julia

Across the bottom of this passionate outpouring Hugo had written in his slashing handwriting, "Answered in the negative. Not practical. How could we live without money?"

But for some reason he had kept the letter. Hetty regretted that. Her fingers were poised to tear the missive in fragments, then she desisted. Old families preserved letters, they were part of their history and made interesting reading for generations to come. She was a member of an old family now. She must live by the rules.

Anyway, she was not afraid of a vengeful Julia who in spite of her threat had had to give Hugo up. And she could make certain that Hugo never had any desire to reread old love letters. It was all up to her. One day Hugo might add a further comment to his practical answer to Julia. "The American marriage turned out splendidly . . ."

It was comforting to dream like that. But even as she did so the curtains blew inward again with a long shushing sigh. Suddenly the room was distinctly chilly.

8

Although she was able to shake off the effects later in the morning, Hetty found that waking up in a state of apprehension was becoming a habit. For the first few days after Hugo's departure she couldn't even decide where she was. The big square room with the panelled walls and carved ceiling was strange and unidentifiable as her own. What right had she to be in this wide bed with its rich faded hangings suggesting a century or more of loved and legitimate brides? In the shadowy dawn, half awake, half drugged by nightmare, she developed a phobia that there was something menacing in the big mahogany wardrobe, something that moved. Sometimes it was an empty army officer's uniform swaying on its hanger, sometimes a naked newly-born baby, sometimes, worst of all, a woman soaked with sea water who never turned her face. But if she had done so it would have been Clemency's.

Even when she became fully awake, with the first sunshine of a soft English summer day touching the windows, and the garden alive with birdsong, it wasn't until Effie knocked gently at the door and came in with her early morning tea in a silver teapot on a carefully-laid tray that she was able to sit up and begin the day with any kind of composure.

She had begun to enjoy the custom of taking tea before breakfast. By the time she had drunk the second cup out of the delicate fluted porcelain, the last shreds of nightmare, like trails of evil fog, had dispersed and she was beginning to relish once again her new identity.

Effie had a routine. She would say "Good morning, my lady," with just the right amount of deference. Then she would put the tray on the bedside table, draw back the curtains and lay out the heavy cream silk robe that Hetty could still not quite believe was hers. Kitty had persuaded her to buy it that day in Cirencester when she had also found the simple well-cut coat and skirt in which to be married, and the lacy tea gown and the crimson silk dinner gown, and a little feathered hat for church on Sundays. After all, someone always had to sit in the Hazzard pew, and it ought, as often as not, to be the mistress.

The thought of all these things made her mood change from apprehension to an almost wild euphoria. She was becoming subject to bewildering swoops of spirits, from high to low, and then to high again.

The clothes were all that hung in the big wardrobe. There were only those innocent things, nothing sinister at all. And to sit at the window in the silk robe sipping her tea was the most delicious luxury. Although it would be more enjoyable when Hugo was home again.

What richness lay in the future. The only anxiety she must inevitably have was about Hugo's safe return.

There was no worry over letters from New York, for instance. Two came together, both addressed to Lady Hazzard, and at first Hetty was scared out of her wits.

"But, Hetty, aren't you pleased? They must be from your family," Kitty said.

They were at breakfast. The letters were beside her plate. Hetty knew that Kitty had seen her wince, even if Julia had not. Lady Flora rarely came down to breakfast, luckily, for those big pale blue eyes, deceptively vague, in reality saw a great deal.

I haven't got any family, Hetty could have answered. But officially she had. Uncle Jonas. The first letter was from him:

My dear Clemency,

By the time you receive this I assume you will be married, so I am addressing you by your new name. But I am waiting for your confirmation of your marriage, and may I dare to hope you will give it in more legible handwriting. It took me and my secretary a long while to decipher your last letter.

I now have the melancholy details of the coroner's inquest, following the *Lusitania* disaster, and the proof of your poor mother's death, so I am losing no time in filing Probate. I am the sole executor under her will, and you the sole beneficiary. You are going to be, indeed are at this moment, a rich young lady.

Mr Richard Colton, the family lawyer, will be writing to you with full details of your inheritance, and no doubt with some sensible advice. I would like to add my own advice. The two houses, on Fifth Avenue and Long Island respectively, have been closed, the servants paid and dismissed. There is no need to keep a batch of idle servants eating their heads off, but I recommend you retain both properties, even though shut up and empty, for they can only appreciate in value. It's possible your husband won't survive the war, and you will want to come home. *But I am home, Uncle Jonas, you insensitive old man. This is my home* ... On the other hand, if he survives, he has had a very handsome settlement, and I suggest you see how your marriage wears before you make over any more funds to him. As an elderly man, and your only living relative, I feel free to speak plainly, and I can tell you I have always thought this marriage to be one of Millicent's more flighty schemes with which you went along all too willingly. But you are a Jervis and should have a good business head, though I admit I hadn't seen any trace of it until now. No doubt that terrible shipwreck has made you grow up more quickly than you would otherwise have done, for you did wisely mention trusts in your letter. I would strongly advise you to set these up for your children, or, supposing you have none, yourself.

Don't let all this money, for which your grandfather laboured so hard, be eaten up by a perhaps romantic but nevertheless impoverished English estate.

Think this over, although I recommend that you don't discuss it with your husband until you have made up your own mind. And when you have made a decision, stick to it.

I write these things to protect you. I have a troublesome heart and may not live to see what happens to you in that high-flown marriage. Seems almost that the Almighty tried to prevent it! Just develop some good hard sense, because you will need it. Seems to me the world has gone crazy. There are people here saying that after the Germans sinking the *Lusitania* with all those neutrals on board, America ought to get into the war. I don't agree, but I'm an old man with a weak heart. I remember the agonies of the Civil War. War is agony, you can forget the glory they talk about it.

Your affec. Uncle Jonas

P.S. I've had enquiries about you from one or two of your friends, the Hayes girl and Amy Parsons. I've told them they'll no doubt hear from you when you're good and ready to write . . .

That letter definitely could not be shown to Hugo. Unless one day she wanted a weapon against him. Being financially independent was a weapon, in its way. She would follow Uncle Jonas's advice and set up a trust for her unborn children, one of which she had a distinct conviction was already conceived. How long before she was completely sure – two weeks, three?

But she wouldn't be writing to those giggly friends of Clemency's, Bessie Hayes and Amy Parsons.

"Hetty, was that bad news? You look awfully glum,"

Kitty was saying.

"Not exactly. Just my Uncle Jonas writing about my mother. Shutting up the houses. Things like that."

Kitty was sympathetic.

"Then read your other letter. Perhaps that's more cheerful."

It wasn't, of course. It brought that drenching shock of coldness over her again.

Dear Miss Clemency,

Pardon the liberty I take in writing to you, but I wanted to before we leave the house. Your uncle is packing us all off, though with characters and wages, of course. But I did want to know what happened to poor Hetty, I mean Brown. We never did hear a word, and wondered if you saw her drowning, or her body, even. Although, since there wasn't a mention of her name in the list of dead, I am clinging to the hope that she is still alive somewhere. Could this be possible? She could lose her memory, couldn't she? I was ever so fond of her, she was such a bright clever good girl.

I would be glad of a line. I'll be with my sister at 1315 Rodmell Street, New Jersey, until I find another position.

You must be very sad about your poor mother. I wish you happiness in your marriage. You at least are lucky and have life before you.

Your obedient servant,
Myrtle Crampton (Cook)

Could Clemency be wandering about with a lost memory? Would one ever know? The prospect of months, perhaps years of suspense slid into Hetty's consciousness and terrified her. Would she always have to be looking over her shoulder?

"You look as if you've seen a ghost, Hetty," Julia said in her crisp way.

Hetty steadied herself. "My life is a bit full of ghosts at present. I guess they'll fade away in their own good time. Will you excuse me? I think I'd like to be out in the sunshine."

"You've got to get over that disaster," Julia said briskly. "People do, you know. They get over much worse things."

How much worse? Hetty asked herself in angry misery. Julia didn't know what she was talking about. She hadn't heard the cries of the drowning, or seen the rows of bleached bodies. She was living safely in a comfortable country house looking after one old lady who pampered her.

And fretting for the man she loved.

She had to answer Mrs Crampton's letter and lay that particular ghost.

Dear Mrs Crampton,

It was kind of you to write. Forgive this answer for being brief. I can still scarcely bear to think of that dreadful night. Yes, poor Brown was lost. She followed Mother and me into the lifeboat, at least we thought she did and then she was never seen again. As many others were not. Even Mr Vanderbilt. I am now married, as I expect my uncle has told you, and I thank God every day for being one of the fortunate ones. I hope you get a good position. I will tell my uncle to give you a good reference, but I expect he has done so already.

She signed the letter firmly "Clemency Hazzard" and that was done.

The letters they all wanted, of course, were ones from the front.

Kitty looked wistfully every day for one from Lionel. It was more likely that Hugo's from France would come first, since that country was uncomfortably near. On the east coast on a still day the guns could be heard thudding across the channel. Lionel was somewhere in the blue Aegean, or more likely crouched in a shallow sun-scorched fly-ridden dugout waiting to wrest another painful yard of rocky cliff from the Turks. No one, said Kitty, had thought the Turks would be such a stubborn enemy. Gallipoli was supposed to have been a campaign that would be successfully completed in a month or so, the gateway to the Middle East and the oilfields firmly closed to the Germans. But then the Germans were supposed to have been retreating in France and Flanders, too. Those hopeful rumours hadn't been true. The war was going on and on.

Hetty sat across the table from Mr Edmonds, the grey-haired bank manager. He had asked to see her, and once more her heart had jumped with apprehension. Why did he want to see her? Couldn't he have trusted his head clerk to deal with such a simple matter as a specimen signature?

But it seemed he merely wanted to meet her. His gesture was part friendliness, part curiosity, part good business relations.

"It's the first opportunity I have had to welcome you, Lady Hazzard. It's a difficult time to be in England, but I hope you're managing to enjoy it."

"I enjoy being at Loburn." Hetty made her voice animated and enthusiastic, as Clemency's would have been. But did that matter, since Mr Edmonds had never met Clemency? "I think the house is wonderful. I even love its shabbiness, because it's going to be great fun fixing it up. And I don't need to beat about the bush with you, Mr Edmonds, that's what my money is for. It would be much more fun if Hugo were home, though."

Mr Edmonds didn't seem in the least suspicious about either her or her plans. He smiled indulgently, as if she were exactly what he had expected her to be, a vivacious fashionable young New Yorker.

"We all hope your husband won't be away too long, Lady Hazzard. His brother, too. You've met his brother?"

"No. Only his wife and little boy."

"Pray God both young men come home safely," Mr Edmonds said piously. "Now I believe we need a specimen signature. If you'll sign on this line here. Then we'll give you a cheque book and you'll be an independent woman."

"How do you want me to sign?" Hetty asked tensely.

"Just your usual signature. What's your first name?"

"Clemency."

"Then Clemency Hazzard will do. So long as you always sign cheques the same way. But I'm sure you know that."

What she did know was that every time she spent money she would be sharply reminded that it was not hers, but Clemency's. A dead woman's.

She wrote in the careful upright script she had practised, and after all it was easy. Euphoria rose in her again.

"The first thing I want to do while my husband is away is have the roof at Loburn thoroughly examined, and the necessary repairs done. Kitty says there are bad leaks in some of the rooms. But I'm told that all the reliable builders are in the army."

"Not all of them. I know just the man. Tom Grubb. In his fifties, too old to join up, and an excellent craftsman. Would you like me to get in touch with him, Lady Hazzard?"

"Oh, yes, please. That is good news. Send him up to Loburn to see me, if he will come. I do want to have achieved something for Hugo when he comes home."

Her delight must have showed in her face, for Mr Edmonds's gaze was admiring.

"If you look like that, Lady Hazzard –" he began and paused.

Hetty was amused by the stiff English embarrassment. "What were you going to say, Mr Edmonds?"

"I was going to say your husband wouldn't make the roof repairs his first priority."

Hetty laughed, transparently delighted. She had been finding out that she had the ability to charm men, not just susceptible young ones like Donald Newman on board the *Lusitania*, but older and staider ones, like bank managers, solicitors, clergymen. It was going to be a useful talent to have. If she could extend it to women it would be even better. But Lady Flora remained cool and aloof, refusing to be won over by an American daughter-in-law. And Julia, apart from the morning riding lessons, which were a bit nerve-racking, made no overtures of friendship.

It would be a long time before she could ride with the grace and elegance of Julia. Probably she never would. But she had graduated from the slow old rocking horse, Patsy, to a lively but good-tempered grey mare, Bessie, in foal. The irony of that hadn't escaped Hetty since every day was confirming her own hopes. She was almost certain she had heard that riding was safe in the early stages of pregnancy, and she so wanted to be adept when Hugo came home. If she were, she suspected that Julia would have lost a good deal of her power over him.

So she took a calculated risk, and resolved that if she still had symptoms of pregnancy in another two or three weeks, she would see a doctor. In the meantime she rode very carefully, at a walk or a gentle canter.

"I've told Hugo I'm teaching you," Julia said.

So she was writing to Hugo. Was he answering? When at last Hetty had a letter from him it was only a brief scrawled note written in a hurry because he was about to go up the line.

He addressed her as, "My dear Hetty", not dearest, not my beloved wife. But then she hadn't yet been able to address him as her beloved husband because some remnants of honesty in her wanted it to be true when she wrote it.

Safely back [he wrote]. The men seemed pleased to see me. Familiar faces are at a premium these days. They've had a bad time, but after a few days in a rest camp they have pulled themselves together and look pretty fit again. We're in a little place with a church with a drunken steeple, and some badly knocked about houses. Only a few villagers have stayed on. I think of something like this happening to our village, but find it beyond my imagination. Hope you have settled down and got over your miserable introduction to England. Have you been to the bank and fixed things up? I'm writing to Mother. Has Kitty heard from Lionel? My leg's fine and I'm passed as fit to go up the line. I'd a million times rather be having a good gallop over the Four Hills. Julia tells me you are coming along nicely. You can't do better than emulate her style. No more time now. Your loving husband, Hugo.

A love letter? Hardly. She might have been a respected friend. But it was friendly enough in Hugo's clipped fashion. Perhaps his letters to Julia were even more formal. She would never know that, for Julia was much too secretive, and always took possession of the mail bag, and the distribution of its contents, when it arrived in the morning. Although she was vocal enough when at last letters arrived from Lionel.

"Kitty! Kitty, a letter for you. One for Lady Flora, too, and one – oh, it must be for you, Hetty."

The letter was addressed to Lady Hazzard. Which undoubtedly was her. There had been no need for Julia to pretend confusion.

"Lionel's written to me!" she murmured with pleasure. "Why, he's never met me."

"He's a literary chap, didn't I tell you? Never happy

without a pen in his hand." And Kitty, pressing her own letter to her bosom, left her breakfast uneaten and disappeared to read it in privacy.

Something prompted Hetty to keep hers to read in privacy, too. She didn't care for Julia's large forlorn eyes on her. To start feeling sympathy for that young woman could be dangerous. It would let down her guard.

My dear Sister-in-law,

I hear that my son, to his disappointment, has discovered that you are not a mermaid. I was relieved to hear it. Cold slippery creatures, mermaids, singing false songs to foolish sailors. No one has told me much about you. Mother says you are neat and pretty, which makes you sound like a new parlour maid, but Mother, for various reasons, has her prejudices. Kitty, who has no prejudices, thinks you are charming, and will do old Hugo no end of good. If the present grotesque hostilities ever allow happy spouses to get together.

I am perched in a dugout two thirds up the side of a veritable mountain, high enough for the sea below to look idyllically blue and bright as stained glass. There is an occasional ambrosial scent of thyme wafting on the warm air, delicately overlaying much less pleasant smells. When the guns stop one can hear larks singing. Aegean larks, think of that. They make me feel like Zeus sitting on his mountain top, "turning his shining eyes into the distance" away from Homer's "lamentable war". I would I could in reality turn my eyes away.

I will tell you all about it when I come home. In the meantime, be happy, dear sister-in-law, life is short,
                                        Lionel

"Where are the Four Hills?" Hetty asked Julia.
"At the other side of the Loburn woods. They're a succession of low hills. They make rather a long ride."

"When can I do it?"

Julia gave her a dispassionate assessing look. "Oh, I'd say in a month or so. You need stamina."

"I've got stamina."

"Well – if you take a tumble, Hug isn't going to thank me."

"I want to, one day soon," Hetty said stubbornly.

"When I decide you're ready. Allow me my professional pride." Julia seemed to be finding something hard to say. "Are you all right, Hetty?"

(Are you pregnant, Hetty?)

"Of course I'm all right."

"Well, do say if you're not. I don't want the blame for any accident."

Unexpectedly from then on, time began to pass pleasantly. It was because Hetty's love for the old house and garden was growing absorbing enough to be a passion. Not the stables and the acres of woodland, and the sheepfolds and the Four Hills Hugo spoke of. She could regard those things dispassionately. But the shadowy house with its dim corners and sudden glimpses of colour and light, and the garden, even the dark yew walk and the sombre lake that looked like a mirror smoky with age no matter how bright the day, became infinitely precious to her.

By June the roses were beginning to bloom. Hetty decided the white rose garden, situated in a secluded part of the garden against an ancient brick wall smothered with pearly climbers, was her favourite spot of all. No one else seemed to come there although one day, as a gust of wind swayed the rich blossom, she thought she had seen a pale figure move and seem to dance across the grass. For one frozen moment she had had the fantastic notion that it had been Clemency. She had sprung up and swayed with dizziness and fright. Kitty, in leather apron and gardening gloves, ambling across the lawn, had seen her distress and come running.

"What's the matter, Hetty? Seen a ghost?"

"No, no, of course not. But I did see something. It must have been one of the maids in her white apron. Going to get vegetables for lunch, I guess."

"This isn't the way to the kitchen garden. You *have* seen the ghost."

"*The* ghost? What do you mean?"

"An unhappy lady who is rumoured to haunt the rose garden. She was supposed to have drowned, I believe."

"D-drowned!"

"Sorry, Hetty, I didn't think ... That's an emotive word for you. But this was about two hundred years ago. We can't still weep for her. Besides, even if she was unhappy, she has chosen the best part of the garden as her bit of paradise. Hetty, are you all right?"

"It must have been a trick of the light. I was half asleep."

"At eleven o'clock in the morning? Then you're not all right." Kitty's eyes were shrewd. "You're going to have a baby, aren't you?"

Hetty nodded. "Perhaps. I'm not sure. I think so."

"Aren't you going to see a doctor?"

"I was waiting. What can a doctor do? If the baby's there it will grow."

"True. Well, it's your secret. I won't give it away if you don't want me to. Are you going to tell Hugo?"

"No," Hetty said sharply. "Not until it's absolutely certain. I've thought about it all, Kitty, over and over. I could just be out of sorts after all those emotional things that have happened. Women's rhythms do get out of order."

"In spite of putting that so politely, you do think it's a baby, don't you?"

"Yes. I do think so."

"Well, jolly good luck," said Kitty generously. "If it's a boy it will put Freddie's nose out of joint. Poor little frog. Not that he'll care at this stage in his life, but one day he'll loathe not getting Loburn. All the Hazzards are the same about that. Well, Hetty, if that's the condition you're in, don't let me see you climbing ladders after Tom Grubb as I did yesterday."

"No. That was foolish of me. I won't do it again. I'm only so passionately interested in what's going on. I do want the roof finished before Hugo comes home on leave. Tom says it will be by the end of the summer, provided he can get enough help. Before the winter rain, anyway. So all that damage will stop happening. And then I'm going to find the most beautiful chintzes and brocades in London, and oh, Kitty, I'm getting fascinated by needlework. I'm going to spend the next ten years covering the worst worn chairs, beginning with the music room –" (which will be mine, surely, by then, Lady Flora having given up the piano and other earthly pursuits). "I'm planning an azure blue background, with corals and creams and grass greens. Subtle colours, mellowed already."

"Well," said Kitty, "for a graft to a strange tree, you seem to have taken pretty well."

"Did you think I would be a social climbing New Yorker?"

"Yes. We all did."

"I'm not," said Hetty. "And I won't ever be an unhappy ghost, either."

"That's an odd thing to say. Are you tempting fate?"

"No, I'm challenging it. Hugo's got to come back safely. So has Lionel. To justify –" But she stopped there. She was getting careless. She had been going to say, "To justify what I have done."

All the same, one couldn't be flippant about ghosts, or dismiss them lightly.

An eerie thing, that afterwards Hetty put down to the fancies of pregnancy, happened. She was in the picture gallery on the first floor of the house. She often walked there. It was quiet, and nobody interrupted her examination of the portraits and her meditations. One portrait in

117

particular fascinated her, that of a young woman in a yellow dress. The colours were faded, the eyes dim, the face long and pointed and delicate. She had meekly clasped long-fingered hands and meekly closed lips. Yet the depredations of time had not quite taken away a wilful, even wanton look in eyes that must once have been very bright. The clothes suggested the late seventeenth century.

A fancy came over Hetty that this was the lady who haunted the garden.

"Who were you?" Hetty asked aloud, and a quick brittle voice answered, "Why do you care? You won't be here long enough for it to matter."

No one had spoken. The voice had not come from the long dead lady. Nor even, more chillingly, from Clemency. The silence had never been disturbed.

9

The Dardanelles campaign was going badly, judging by the lengthening casualty lists. Lionel wrote that he had had what used to be called "putrid fever" and that that description was particularly apt. "It is pretty prevalent and I am lucky to have had only a mild dose. We consort with too many flies, that's the trouble. They're worse than the Turk himself. But I'm well again."

"Thank goodness," Kitty cried thankfully. "I don't care what happens to that campaign, and I don't care if you call me unpatriotic. So long as my husband comes home."

Hugo wrote one of his increasingly formal letters, as if the very composition of the sentences were an effort, or as if his so new and only slightly-known wife was already half-forgotten.

"I hear you have begun on the repairs to the house. What a practical person you are, you surprise me all the time. And generous, too, since I believe the money is coming out of your own coffers. When I see all the empty and destroyed châteaux in this country, I self-ishly like to think of my own home being preserved, and I am glad you appear to have the same feeling for it. At least a war like this has never been fought on English soil, which is about the only thing one can find in its favour. How is the riding going? Julia tells me the horses are in good shape. We will have a gallop when I am next home . . ."

We? Did he mean Julia or herself?

Hetty had at last gone to see Doctor Bailey in Cirencester, the Hazzard family doctor, not because she needed her pregnancy confirmed, but because those two strange ghostly experiences still haunted her.

"Would a woman in my condition have fancies, doctor?"

"Indeed, yes. Particularly about food."

"No, I mean tricks of the imagination. I sometimes think I hear things that simply can't be there."

The doctor smiled indulgently.

"You mean ghostly voices?"

"Sort of."

"Ah well, I'd put that down to your dreadful experience on the *Lusitania*. You're suffering from the delayed shock, I expect. How do you like Loburn, by the way? The house?"

"Oh, I simply adore it. I feel as if I utterly belong there. If that doesn't sound presumptuous."

"Well, there you are, my dear. You're an American accustomed to much more modern houses, and you obviously have a keen imagination. You've responded too well and you think the old house has been talking to you. You'll forget it all when your husband is home and your baby born. By the way, have you told Hugo about the baby?"

Hetty shook her head.

"Then do so, and cheer him up."

But Hetty had made a decision not to tell Hugo her news. Wait, she kept saying to herself. She wanted to be cautious. It would be so dreadful to disappoint him if something went wrong. She said as much to his mother.

Lady Flora said in a gentler voice than usual, "Hetty, you do realise that Hugo could be killed? Wouldn't you like him to have the pleasure of knowing about his child?"

"I just hoped to be able to tell him in person."

"You can't be too sentimental in wartime, my dear."

Julia, who had listened to this conversation, said only, "Did you ask the doctor about riding?"

"He said a reasonable amount of exercise was fine. We didn't specifically mention horses."

Julia's eyes were curiously still. If the coming baby aroused bitter jealousy in her, she was not going to show it.

"You must be careful," said Lady Flora. "Personally, I think you should leave horses alone in the meantime."

"We country women don't take too much account of these things," Julia said. "Didn't you ride when you were expecting your children, Lady Flora?"

"I did. For one thing my husband expected it of me. But not after the fourth month. One doesn't need to be foolhardy."

"I would do the same," said Julia. She spoke dreamily, as if she were visualising herself in such a condition. "However," her voice became brisker and harder, "since I'm not, Hugo and I can go on having our early morning gallops. Until you're available, Hetty, of course."

Hetty was stung.

"I'm available now. I thought that was what we were agreeing on."

"Then we really will have to work at your seat, won't we?"

Lady Flora looked at the two girls questioningly.

"But you're not expecting Hugo home, are you? Either of you?"

"No," said Hetty. She gave Julia a steady look. "And I think I would be the one to know."

Julia gave a small tight smile. "No one knows in wartime. Hugo's a pretty good fixer. If he can wangle leave, he will. Just to see that filly I bought at Newmarket. If nothing else."

Bitch, thought Hetty. Cool secretive bitch. Why couldn't Lady Flora see the potential danger of a jealous woman and get her out of the house? Was there a chance, when the baby was born and she had totally to accept Hugo's marriage, that she would be realistic and dispatch Miss Julia Pemberton for good? Perhaps Hetty would have to go to the lengths of showing her that letter, "*I will never give you up . . . Never, never, never.*"

In the meantime Hetty was not only unable to master the situation, she was also stubbornly determined not to be thought a coward by these supremely confident English women. She would continue riding, but with care. She was so longing to be able to meet Hugo in the sparkling early morning and show him how well she looked in riding clothes. Horses were the strongest link between him and Julia. If that could be weakened she would have won her first victory.

Was she lonely? Kitty was friendly, but abstracted, always busy with her hospital work or her gardening. Lady Flora's façade was impeccable, but beneath it, Hetty was sure, was a deep-seated antagonism and a resentment for the daughter-in-law whom she had had to accept because of a convenient bank balance. As for Julia, even without personal rivalry, she was not the kind of person whom Hetty would have wanted as a friend. They had nothing at all in common.

But this mattered little, for the good reason that she was not accustomed to having friends. She was getting on splendidly with the servants who, although at first surprised by her lack of formality, eventually decided that they liked it, especially the younger maids. Cook was still suspicious but beginning to unbend. Mrs Evans, the housekeeper, would never have unbent if she had been there to see how Hetty so capably took over her duties, going about the house and into the kitchen, the servants' sacred domain, freely and without apology.

Even Lady Flora was forced to admit that the house was running smoothly. She said more than once that she would like to have met Hetty's mother, who must have been a remarkable woman to have trained her daughter so well. Only practical, Hetty had answered. Most American women were.

But getting on with servants was a far cry from having

personal friends of one's own class. Lady Flora had murmured something about arranging a small "At Home", adding that it was too bad that circumstances had denied Hetty any of the brilliant social life she had expected.

Hetty, however, was reluctant to entertain a lot of stuffy county folk without Hugo at her side. She would go to church on Sundays and sit in the Hazzard pew to be stared at, but couldn't parties wait?

"Of course they can, my dear," Lady Flora said with a graciousness that indicated her relief. "Now if the boys were home for Christmas that would be wonderful. But I expect it's too much to hope for." In spite of the circumstances, Hetty didn't entirely lack companionship. The odd little boy Freddie, as solitary as she was, had taken to following her about. He wanted to talk about Achilles and Apollo and Hector, he said. The people Daddy kept writing about. Were they soldiers? Wouldn't Hetty tell him about them?

So she searched in the library for a copy of the *Iliad*. She had never read it herself, and doubted if even the well-stocked library in New York had had a copy of this book. But after Lionel's reference to the shining eyes of Zeus in his letter to her she had become as curious as Freddie.

Freddie curled up beside her in the big leather chair and she read aloud, "*Thus all night long they sat across the corridors of battle, thinking great thoughts and keeping their many fires alight . . .*"

How could a little boy understand this complicated and diverse collection of characters? By his complete attention he seemed to. He was like a little elderly scholar. Perhaps he just enjoyed the companionship and being read to.

"You'll make him into a Cambridge don," Kitty grumbled. "Are you going to do the same with your own child?"

"I intend that he'll be more than just a Master of the Hunt." Hetty said.

Kitty was amused. "What a thing to say in this house!"

"Then don't tell Hugo. Anyway, of course, he may be a girl."

"Then you'll have to go on trying until you get a boy. It will certainly be expected of you."

The haunting anxiety came back.

"If only there's time. Oh, Kitty, there's got to be time for both of us."

"Cheer up, the war will end one day. Or else –"

"Else what?"

"We'll get back wounded heroes." Kitty's eyes momentarily went dark. "I see too many of those. But better than dead ones," she finished briskly, although adding thoughtfully, "At least, some of them."

Then there was the day of the tea party. In the summer drawing room, not in the garden, because autumn, though balmy and golden, could be changeable and one didn't want the ladies to have to scurry indoors out of a sudden cold breeze. Fallen leaves lay like doubloons and tresses of dark golden hair on the smoky water of the lake. The lawns prickled with chestnut husks. There were not enough people available to tidy up, so the charming disarray would linger into winter.

The war in France seemed to be intensifying, rather than nearing an end. But Lady Flora had decided to have a modest female tea party, since so few men were available nowadays, and anyway only women enjoyed tea parties.

Hetty would have chosen to be anywhere, up in the roof rafters with Tom Grubb, in the library with Freddie, even down at the stables with Julia, rather than in the summer drawing room among all those formal women. She was three months pregnant, and therefore presumably safe from miscarriage. Now there could be no alternative to telling Hugo because eight or nine curious females would soon guess her condition. She had so treasured her secret, reluctant to share the coming baby even with its father – almost as though it could be something entirely her own.

124

But she must guard against a tendency to become too secretive. Surely the time for extreme wariness and suspicion was past. Even Uncle Jonas had written:

I am making a further transfer of money to your bank, as you requested, since you seem to have set your mind on rebuilding that tumbledown old house. But don't let these people bleed you dry. You're young and romantic now. You may feel very different about your famous Loburn in a few years. Personally I prefer fine solid modern architecture such as ours. Don't take offence at this advice. I am, as you know, a cautious business man.

There had been no trouble in that direction, thank goodness. She was accepted as the legitimate heiress to a large estate.

But the baby was private and personal, a delicate presence that was still entirely hers. It made this strange life, through which she was treading so carefully, real. In comparison with what she had already accomplished, she should be able to take a handful of inquisitive women in her stride.

They sat in their silks and laces and wide-brimmed hats, sipping tea out of Lady Flora's fine bone china, and being waited on by a slightly flustered Effie who had been trained to dress, not to feed, her superiors.

Hetty had been bidden to sit in their midst so that they could all talk to her. They had previously only seen her in church. Even with a war on she was living too secluded a life, they said. They could scarcely believe it was by her own choice. She was so charming, too. Were her eyes grey or green? Like the sea, weren't they? – though perhaps she didn't want to be reminded of that. And didn't Hugo love her dimples? And wasn't she longing for him to be home on leave? Not to mention how desperately, poor fellow, he must want to return to his bride.

Somewhere a cup clattered. It was Julia's. She had put it down too carelessly.

"Julia, my dear, ring the bell for some more hot water."

"Of course, Lady Flora." Submissive, slim and patrician, in her simple blue dress, furious behind her wide beautiful eyes. Did no one else sense that mounting rage in her?

It was the first time in public that she had had to stand back and watch Hetty, the foreigner, usurping what she had dreamed about being her position. She was finding it almost impossible to preserve the well-mannered obedience Lady Flora expected of her. Surely Lady Flora, who was a highly-intelligent woman, must be aware of this, and should have found Julia a safer, less emotional position. Was she then enjoying an explosive situation in the way of bored old ladies longing for drama? Or was it Julia who had privately begged to stay at Loburn?

No one else in the room appeared to be conscious of undercurrents. Unless it was old Mrs Entwhistle, the lady in black lace and diamonds, who said vaguely, "We had always thought it was Julia Hugo was devoted to, Flora. Didn't we, Margaret?"

Margaret, her elderly sister, concurred with a vague nod of the head, and Lady Flora outdid the determined vagueness of the two ladies with her murmur, "He was, of course. He still is, indeed. Dear Julia. We have made her one of the family. My boys are like brothers to her. Well, cousins, anyway."

And then a beak-nosed lady with sharp eyes said directly to Hetty, "I met a survivor from the *Lusitania* only last week. The Eversleigh girl, Flora. She had been visiting an aunt in Boston and was coming home to join the Red Cross. Katharine Eversleigh, Hetty. I may call you Hetty, may I not?"

"Of course," said Hetty, her throat dry.

"Did you happen to run into Katharine? She had a stateroom on the promenade deck."

"Wasn't that where you and your mother were, Hetty?" said Lady Flora with interest. "I seem to remember you saying that the lifeboats were launched from near your stateroom."

Hetty swallowed. She was afraid her voice would come out in a croak. Instead it was a whisper.

"Yes, we were lucky to be so near the lifeboats. But that still didn't save dear Mamma."

"Poor child. Adelaide, you shouldn't have brought up such a painful subject." That was a kinder voice.

"I can't hear what she's saying. You didn't run into Kate Eversleigh, Hetty?"

Hetty made another effort.

"There were so many passengers. We didn't know their names."

"Well, perhaps you'll recognise her when you meet her again."

"Again?"

"She's bound to be at balls and parties. Unless she's got herself sent to France with the Red Cross, which is quite probable. Brave gel."

Hetty pressed her hands to her cheeks in her habitual defensive gesture.

"I'm a coward, I confess it. I still can't bear to be reminded of that awful time."

She meant to look up pleadingly at her innocent persecutor, but found herself staring right into Julia's eyes, those enigmatic eyes with their held-back anger. She thought she detected a flicker of something else — awareness, excitement, determination?

Oh, bother this sunny drawing room full of chattering bejewelled parrots. She was going to make the winter drawing room hers, she suddenly decided, since she couldn't have the music room, and this lovely garden-facing room was so much a family retreat. It was where somebody like her belonged. And it had the advantage of facing the sweep of drive down which Hugo would come home. She would move the pictures she liked best from the gallery, and arrange brighter furnishings.

Yes, she would sit in there this evening before dinner and write to Hugo about their child. She made the letter up in her head.

Your mother had some of her friends to tea today and they all stared at me, and I'm afraid they guessed my secret. Hugo darling, I have been hugging it to my breast for three months until I was absolutely sure. Now I can safely tell you that we are going to have a child before next spring. I hope it will be a boy, not only for your sake but because I would dearly like a son. However, if it is not a boy we will try again. Does this make you happier in your miserable horrible trenches? I do so hope it does . . .

"Hetty! Hetty! Can you come here? Kitty's not home from the hospital yet and we can't find Freddie. Nanny has been searching the house and garden."

Julia was in the hall, and changed from her tea party dress into pullover and riding breeches.

Hetty sprang up. "I haven't seen him since lunch-time."

"Oh, dear, where is he? Pimm said he saw him on the edge of the woods earlier and he said something about finding Mount Olympus. Have you been putting these ideas in his head?"

Freddie had been so completely fascinated by Zeus, the Cloud Gatherer, the Queen of Heaven, Achilles of the fleet foot, Hector, Tamer of Horses, and the other immortals. What were immortals? "People who live for ever," Hetty said. "Not like us."

"I'd dearly like to see them."

"You see them in your mind, the way Daddy does."

"And the Black Ships," said Freddie. "Can I see them in my mind?"

128

"He's a very imaginative little boy," Hetty said to Julia. Of course one put ideas in a child's head, stocked his brain for future use. Julia didn't need to sound so accusing. "I'll come and look for him. He can't be far away."

"I'm going to saddle Monarch," Julia said. "We think Freddie may have headed for the Four Hills. His version of Mount Olympus. Do you think you could ride? Then we could take different directions."

Hetty didn't wait to change. She could scramble on to Bessie in her skirts. She had a horrible premonition of disaster. Freddie was small for his age, and not at all athletic. He could have tumbled into a ditch or, worse, into a stream. Water, dark and menacing, always came into Hetty's nightmares. She thought of the black lake beyond the yew trees. How terrible if that had to be drained. And if Kitty, and later Lionel, should come home to find their only son had drowned, while looking for the Black Ships of Troy.

Regret for stirring Freddie's too fertile imagination with the *Iliad*, and her permanent suppressed guilt, made Hetty feel sick. She hurried behind Julia's slim striding figure.

"Damn, the groom isn't here," Julia exclaimed. "I believe he said he was going to help harvest the last of the wheat. We'll have to do this ourselves, Hetty. Do you feel capable?"

"Of course I feel capable," Hetty lied. She was never going to be a bold rider. Truth to tell, she was still alarmed by horses, a fact Hugo would be bound to discover.

"Then you skirt the woods, and I'll go through them," Julia ordered. "Don't gallop. For God's sake, be careful. We don't want an accident. You're less likely to see a small boy if you're galloping madly, anyway."

The sky was still clear and bright over the hills, but in the valley the long shadows stroked the autumn grass. A cool wind was stirring. Bessie was fresh and wanted to gallop. Hetty tried to rein her in. She was so used to Julia at her side, watchful and careful, that she felt terribly alone and afraid. As she had been alone, clinging to a lifebelt in the endless sea. At first she couldn't search in the dips and hollows for Freddie's tow-coloured head. She was too intent on staying in the saddle. At last, however, Bessie settled down to a sedate trot, and she guided her nearer to the edge of the woods.

"Freddie! Freddie!" Her voice, or the horse's intrusive presence, stirred a tawny owl from its perch. It glided soundlessly, a small feathered galleon, across her path, making Bessie dart sideways in fright. She soon settled down again, however, but one prayed that no foxes or other woodland creatures would dart out of the undergrowth.

Where was Freddie? Surely he couldn't have reached the last of the Four Hills, his personal Mount Olympus. That was more than two miles away.

Were they right in assuming he was out in this evening landscape at all? Had Julia jumped too impulsively to conclusions? But what would Kitty say if he were lost? And Lionel, so dangerously scaling his own war-torn Mount Olympus?

One must – Hetty's thought was never completed. For there was suddenly an abrupt explosion in the woodland, something towering and huge dashed out, and Bessie, startled beyond measure, flung herself sideways and then into a gallop. Hetty hadn't a hope of staying in the saddle. Her foot caught for a wrenching moment in the stirrup. The last thing she was aware of was sliding rapidly and terrifyingly head first to the ground.

10

"Hetty!"

A small anxious voice came out of the mist, the memory of agonising pain, the weakness. She tried to move, pushing away the horrid debris floating on the waves, struggling to cling more firmly to the lifebelt.

"Hetty, you're not going to die, are you?"

"No, no, I'm a survivor," she shouted, and with reviving consciousness knew that her voice was inaudible to the bewildered little face at the side of her bed.

"Freddie!" Memory surged back. Her relief was so great that she was almost able to move her stiff lips in a smile. "You're safe!"

"I wasn't lost, Hetty. I was only up in the roof with Tom. He helped me up the ladder. Nanny needn't have got into such a taking."

"Now, young man, you must go!" Someone in nurse's uniform was pushing Freddie to the door. A nurse. Good heavens, was she ill?

Yes, she was ill. She felt pain in her head, and a nasty sinister ache in her womb. She had a sensation of nausea and deep apprehension.

"Are you a nurse?"

"I'm Sister Best, Lady Hazzard."

"Then where am I?"

Not in her lovely shadowy bedroom at Loburn, in the wide bed, with Hugo's side kept immaculately for his return. This was a small dreary room, the bed narrow and iron-framed.

131

"You're in the Cirencester hospital, my dear. You had a riding accident. You don't remember?"

She tried to shake her head, but it hurt. Beneath the sheet her hands lay on her flattened womb.

"My baby?"

"You've lost that, I'm afraid. Couldn't expect much else, could you?" Sister Best wasn't kind after all. Her face was humourless and disapproving. "Don't they teach expectant mothers in America to be careful?"

"Freddie – he was lost – we had to look – Nanny was in a taking. So was Julia." She was babbling.

"Should have left that to someone else. Now you must rest. Doctor will be in later."

Tears began to flow down her cheeks.

"Why are you so unkind to me?"

"I'm not unkind. I'm practical. Doctors and nurses spend their lives mending things foolish people bring on themselves. We have a military wing here full of seriously wounded soldiers. We haven't really time for silly young women."

"Then go away, go away!" Hetty whispered.

Nevertheless she drifted into sleep, not because the sister had told her to, but because she seemed to be so weak. Her next visitor, when she awoke, was much kinder than the stern sister. Kitty in her V.A.D. uniform, harassed as usual, but smiling, although her eyes were full of tears.

"Hetty, Hetty, what a terrible pity. Doctor Bailey tried so hard to save the baby, but it was no use."

"What's today?" Hetty asked, looking at sunlight outside the dusty window.

"Thursday. It all happened in the night, Head aching?"

"Yes, it is."

"You had some concussion, too. That's why you don't remember much. Freddie was devastated."

"Julia said he was lost in the woods, that he'd gone off

because of me reading him the *Iliad* and filling his head with myths.''

Did Kitty's face tighten? At least there was no doubt about the disapproval in her voice.

"Oh, Julia! I never would have thought she had it in her to panic. Cool as a cucumber always. And especially not to panic about Freddie. She scarcely notices his existence. Of course, Lady Flora isn't saying anything, but we're pretty angry that Julia allowed you on a horse under those conditions."

"She did tell me not to gallop. And I didn't until something scared Bessie. I don't know what it was, some great beast crashing out of the wood. Is there a bull at Loburn?"

"Or a horse," said Kitty drily.

Hetty stared at her.

"You can't mean – Julia?"

"Yes, I do. Accidentally, of course, but it was damned careless of her. She admits it."

Hetty lay very still, letting her suspicions take possession of her. Julia had planned this so that Hugo's baby would be lost. It had been no accident; it had been deliberate. Julia had been smouldering with jealousy for weeks. The tea party with the twittering old women admiring Hetty's looks and manners must have set it alight.

That must be true. After all, why should Julia be so upset about a missing child whom she didn't even care for? She had simply guessed what Hetty's reaction would be when told Freddie was lost, and had seized the opportunity to stage the riding accident that she must have been planning for some time.

Julia, the enemy!

The quiet cold voice in her head was speaking.

But perhaps you deserve this, Hetty, for all your own lies and deceits. You weren't meant to be the mother of the heir to Loburn.

"Was it a boy, Kitty? Could they tell?"

Kitty nodded. "Afraid so. But the doctor says there's no permanent damage. You can have a dozen children. Different from me. I have to make do with my little frog."

"Oh, Kitty. I would be happy to make do with your little frog. But supposing," Hetty added fearfully, "Hugo doesn't come home?"

"Oh, he'll come home. He'll be one of the lucky ones. He always got out of his troubles. Like finding an amenable heiress to pay his crushing debts? I've got to go now, love. My boys will be waiting for me. We've got two young airmen who crashed at the airfield and got badly burned, poor devils."

Burned, thought Hetty in pity, remembering Donald Newman with his youthful eagerness. Burning would be worse than drowning. Perhaps Donald had been lucky, after all.

"If your concussion is all right they're letting you go home tomorrow. But you'll have to rest."

And live again with her enemies? Julia, Lady Flora? But you never thought it would be a bed of roses, living someone else's life. So be quiet, be clever. Wait for Hugo to come home.

"That's the girl," said Kitty. "You're looking better already."

The servants, Effie and Elsie, had given the winter drawing room a great turning out.

"Mrs Lionel said you were going to have this room for your own, my lady." Effie was pink-cheeked with pleasure at having her mistress home and at having worked to please her. "Mrs Lionel put the flowers in and got Mr Bates to bring the pictures down from the gallery. The ones she thought you would like, but you can change them of course, she said. Shall I light the fire, my lady? Will you be sitting in here?"

The windows caught the dying afternoon light and the room looked alive. One of the pictures from the gallery was the lady in the faded yellow dress. How had Kitty known she liked that one? The tilted eyes seemed to follow her. For the first time she had the feeling of having come home.

"You've done wonders, Effie. Yes, light the fire. I'll have tea in here. I can rest just as well on the couch as on my bed. I guess plenty of Hazzard ladies have spent a long time resting on that couch."

"You won't be doing much of that, my lady, you're too energetic." Effie paused. Her face was full of honest affection. "We was all ever so sorry about the accident."

"Thank you, Effie. It was lucky I hadn't told my husband about the baby, so at least he won't be disappointed."

"I'd keep away from them horses, my lady. Nasty beasts."

Hetty found she could smile. "That's sacrilege in this house, Effie."

"Not with Mr Lionel and Mrs Lionel, my lady. They're not horse people, either. I wouldn't think Master Freddie is, neither."

"Well, thank you for your advice, Effie."

She wanted to lie quietly, enjoying the luxury of being home, in her own sitting room which, as time went by, would be a small world she had created for herself, filled with her best-loved treasures. The yellow lady with her provocative eyes was only the first of these. One wondered if she too had laid here from time to time, recuperating from little understood fevers, or too many pregnancies. Had she grown to be old and fat and ugly? Or was she like Clemency, doomed to remain for ever young and fair. Perhaps she had hated the winter drawing room and always sought sunlight. Perhaps she had had no secret to hide and no kinship with shadows.

Everyone must be made to ask permission to come in here, Hetty decided. Even Hugo.

But this order had not yet been made known, and presently, without knocking, someone opened the door. Lady Flora was a tall, slender figure in the gloom, insubstantial yet exuding too much authority to be excluded.

"You're not asleep, are you, Hetty?"

"No, I'm awake."

"Then I shall just come and have a little chat. How nice the firelight is. But why have you chosen this gloomy room? Kitty tells me you want it for your private sitting room."

"I like it. It has so much atmosphere. Besides, I can look out of the window and see Hugo coming home, can't I?"

Lady Flora sat on the edge of a chair, poker-backed as always.

"Yes, poor child. I hope that will be soon."

"He didn't know about the baby. Isn't that a good thing?"

"But you'll tell him eventually." That was a statement, not a question. The pale immobile face seemed to be saying, "Don't ever tell him." And indeed, before Hetty could answer, Lady Flora went on, "I do hope you're not blaming Julia too much. She's desperately upset. She says she'll never forgive herself, even though it was a pure accident."

"Did her horse run away with her?" Hetty asked innocently. "I thought she was too good a rider to let that happen."

"It can happen to any rider," Lady Flora said sharply. "You were both worried about Freddie, and perhaps neither of you were as careful as you should have been. I must speak to Kitty about Nanny. I don't think she watches Freddie closely enough. Climbing ladders, indeed! Who was to guess he was up in the roof."

"Or in the woods," Hetty murmured.

"There was good reason for thinking that. Pimm had found his hobby horse discarded on the path leading to the woods."

His winged Olympian steed, Hetty thought tenderly.

"It might have been there for days."

136

"I hardly think so. Anyway, that's irrelevant now. Except that Julia blames herself dreadfully, and is quite alarmed about facing you."

Julia alarmed? Never. She had probably organised the evidence of the wooden hobby horse herself.

"And you probably don't know, my dear, that had she not got help so quickly you might well have died. She was quite frantic."

"I'm far from dying, Lady Flora. The doctor just says I must be quiet for a few days."

"Of course. We know that. But when you're stronger you and Julia must be friends again. Remember, you have so much and she has so little."

"She won't have so little all her life."

"Why do you say that?"

Because she is strong, Hetty thought silently. We are really two of a kind, Julia and I. We try very hard to get what we want. Who will be the stronger? It simply has to be me. There's no alternative.

"She's very attractive. She must be admired a lot."

Lady Flora nodded and sighed.

"We're too many women in this house, that's the trouble. I wonder when the war will end. Oh, I see you've had Jacobina's portrait brought down. Do you like it particularly?"

The name, discovered at last, gave her pleasure.

"Yes. I wonder about her. What an unusual name."

"There's not much known about her. I believe she died in childbirth. The baby, too. So there's nothing left of her in this family. Except perhaps a ghost."

"I'll be luckier than that," said Hetty.

"Of course you will. By the way, my friends thought you were charming. Much too charming to be shut away here all the time, as if you were in a monastery. We decided you really ought to have a visit to London. Even in wartime there are a lot of things going on. Parties for officers home from the front. That sort of thing. They want bright young women. I can arrange introductions. I'd be happy to take you myself, if it weren't for my stupid heart. But you'll probably meet friends of your own from America. You'll call at the Embassy, of course."

"No, thank you, Lady Flora," Hetty said quietly and definitely, "I don't want to go to London until I can go with Hugo. Besides, as soon as I'm well enough I intend to do hospital work like Kitty does. They can't treat me as an alien now that I have a British husband."

"No," said Lady Flora thoughtfully. "I don't suppose they can." She might have been honest and added that she still did so, herself.

It was two weeks before Hetty could bring herself to leave the sanctuary of the winter drawing room in the daytime and her bedroom at night. By that time she had begun to feel stronger, and less plagued by the too familiar nightmares, the icy sea, so heavy on her limbs and the cries of the drowning, the more eerie one of the strange stirrings like old stiffened clothes in the wardrobe, and once, horrifyingly, when she thought she was awake, a misty face at the window. Jacobina's? Clemency's? Not Clemency's. She had never belonged here.

Doctor Bailey said, "Your mind still playing tricks on you? That will stop when you get your husband home. You're a healthy young woman. All you need is a normal marital life, then all these bad things will slip into the past. But in the meantime you're alone too much. Who do you see?"

"Kitty. Freddie. The servants."

"Then I'm going to give you an order. Lady Flora says you have been refusing to eat downstairs. You're perfectly strong enough now to eat with the family, for both luncheon and dinner."

The nervous thoughts came into her head. I'll have to see Julia. I haven't spoken to her since the accident. I've let it be known that I didn't want to see her. Although I've seen her through the window, striding across the lawn as if she owns the place. And I have to admit that she looks as if she ought to own it.

"And then," Doctor Bailey went on, "why don't you go into the hospital occasionally? There are some blinded young men there. They need letters written for them, and someone bright to talk to. They'll love your American accent. I'll speak to Matron. Will you do it. Lady Hazzard? Sitting alone brooding can be self-indulgent, you know."

Hetty was shamed out of her dream world.

"Of course I will. I had intended to, anyway. I didn't know about the blind soldiers."

"Good girl. So back to normal life, eh? I'll report to Lady Flora. She's been anxious."

Hetty obeyed the doctor and went down to dinner that night, telling no one but the servants of her intention. She took the three women by surprise. Kitty, in her usual exuberant fashion, exclaimed, "Thank heaven for another face! We're all boring each other to death." And Lady Flora unbent enough to say, "It is time you took up normal life again, Hetty. I understand how you have felt. I always turn to my piano in times of stress. I know you have your books and your needlework. But one has to live more energetically than that, especially you, a young woman."

Hetty looked past Lady Flora to her faithful shadow, Julia.

"I won't be riding any more, Julia," she said. "I don't care for horses, anyway. I'm writing to tell Hugo."

Julia flushed. Her eyes were fiercely bright, but whether from shame or pleasure Hetty couldn't guess. But when she spoke her voice sounded sincere enough.

"You can't blame me as much as I blame myself for that accident. Can she, Lady Flora? It was such an unnecessary thing to have happened. Hugo will never believe I could have been so careless."

So that was what disturbed her, not Hetty's miscarriage but Hugo's suspicions. He might not fret too much about his bride taking a tumble, but he would be furious

139

at losing his heir. Julia could not bear him to blame her. On the other hand it would be highly satisfactory to have this silly inept American girl out of the stables and no threat to those intimate early morning rides of which she was so jealous.

"Certainly you shouldn't ride when you're pregnant," Kitty said in her practical manner. "That's crazy."

"I won't ride at all," Hetty repeated. "I don't suppose I'll be ostracised for that. People will only think I'm a quaint American. Anyway, there won't be time for riding, there'll be too many other things Hugo and I want to do. For instance, Tom Grubb said there must be some of the original plans of Loburn around, and I intend searching for them. It's so exciting, like a treasure hunt. When we find them we can start planning restorations as they should be done. Uncle Jonas says I can have all the money I need. He can't refuse me because it's my money. Hugo will be terribly pleased, won't he?" She was playing her trump card. She looked defiantly at Julia. Answer that, she challenged.

Julia's eyebrows lifted delicately. "Is Hugo interested in architecture? I had never noticed. Had you, Lady Flora?"

"So many things come down to money," Lady Flora sighed, under her breath. She added more audibly, "Of my two sons I would have said Lionel was the one to enlist in support of such ambitious plans. Don't you agree, Kitty?"

"Goodness me, yes." Kitty flung herself into the discussion, unaware that she was taking sides. "He's been longing to take down the ceiling in the hall and expose the old beams. That's the oldest part of the house, Hetty. That and the winter drawing room. They go back to Tudor times. I should think those old plans are somewhere in the library behind those acres of books. Oh yes, Lionel will be off his head with excitement if he's allowed to scratch away at panelling and brickwork. But not

140

Hugo. I don't think you can convert him from being an outdoor man, Hetty."

So the winter drawing room had housed ladies in fur-trimmed velvet gowns and close-fitting caps trimmed with pearls. Ladies who sat stitching at fine tapestries and had small pug dogs nestling at their feet. Hetty's trump card had been out-trumped, but just now she didn't mind. Her instincts about that room had been right. A frisson of pleasure ran over her. Now, whenever this complex situation she had involved herself in became too nerve-racking, she could retire to the winter drawing room and deliberately re-create the past, in whatever colourful and peaceful terms she chose.

More practically, since she had to live in the same house as Julia, a semblance of manners would have to be observed. This did not make Julia any less of any enemy, but her misconception of Hetty as someone rich and pampered and naïve would eventually be her downfall. Little did she know that she was tangling with a tough slum child accustomed to being bullied, cheated and deprived, and with a strongly-developed instinct for survival.

However, Hetty didn't underestimate these stiff-backed English women either. After all, she had already had experience of Julia's methods. From now on it was not to be just antagonism but war. A ladylike war? Hetty doubted it. And suddenly felt brilliantly alive again.

Her new-found equanimity was all too short lived, however. The next week in the hospital ward, inhabited by long rows of young men, some lying flat and heavily bandaged, some sitting up and grinning perkily at the new arrival, some staring with a hollow unreachable gaze, she was nearly undone.

Kitty had arranged with the sister in charge for Hetty's visit, and had told her to go to the farther end of the ward where the partially or wholly blinded were.

It was bad enough that the high-ceilinged gloomy room with its iron beds and recumbent forms reminded her vividly of the room in Kinsale where she had recovered from her near-drowning. The awareness of human misery pressed on her with a deadly familiarity, and she had a choking feeling of being unable to breathe, of wanting to close her eyes and slip into unconsciousness.

But a cocky voice called after her, "Hey, miss, you going to waste yourself on chaps who can't see you? Come and talk to me." And to her relief she found that she could smile.

"Later I will. But I must talk to these men."

There were four of them, three with bandaged eyes and relatively unmarked faces, the fourth so muffled in bandages that there were only small holes for his nose and mouth. It was this pathetic form, this travesty of a human being, that drew her. She stood near his bed and said brightly, "Hi, boys. I've come to write letters for you, or do anything you want. Just talk, if you like. Were you all wounded in France?"

One answered quite cheerfully, "Me and Bert and Ken were. Donnie's an airman. Hadn't even got to France, had you, Donnie? Came down in flames at the flying field near here."

Donnie! Donald?

"How terrible. How –" Hetty's voice trembled. This wouldn't do. Stiff upper lip, Kitty had said. She bent over the mummified mask. "Can I do anything for you, Donnie? Do you want to send a message to anyone? I can write it for you."

There was the slightest stir in the bed. A faint hoarse voice issued through the hole in the bandages.

"You're . . . a Yankee . . . That voice . . I'm sure I know it . . . Who . . . are you?" Then there was a grotesque sound of triumph. "I've . . . got it. You're Hetty . . Hetty Brown!"

A nurse came bustling to the bedside, speaking in a low voice.

"This won't do, Lady Hazzard. You mustn't excite my patient."

142

Hetty had backed away, her hands pressed to her cheeks in the old panic-stricken way.

"He thinks I'm someone he knows. He must be wandering."

The nurse's expression remained calm and unsuspicious. "Not surprising, poor lad. He's a Canadian. What's more he nearly drowned on the *Lusitania* before collecting this."

Hetty could hear the muffled longing whisper. "Hetty, is it you? Can't be ... They said she drowned ..."

The nurse was pushing screens into place round the bed. She glanced at Hetty. "You're no use here if you're the fainting kind."

"I'm all right," said Hetty stiffly. "What will happen to – Donnie?"

The nurse's calm broke; her whisper was angry.

"I'm not God. Now go and be cheerful with the others. If you can't be, you'd better come back another day."

In the end she didn't disgrace herself. She managed to chat to the other three men and listen to their hardy jokes. No more sounds came from behind the screen. Donald Newman! How could it be that he had survived the shipwreck without her knowing? She wanted to go behind the screen and hold his hand. She despised herself for not daring to. She could have said it was only her American voice that had made him think she was this person called Hetty Brown.

But then she would have had to say that Hetty Brown must be dead, and the very thought of that made her throat dry up. How could she have anticipated what terrible pitfalls existed in a life of deception? If she had known Donald Newman had survived, would that have prevented her from embarking on her deception? How well did she know herself? How strong were her ambitions?

There was no use in imagining a different set of circumstances. But if Donald had survived, unknown to her, couldn't Clemency have done so, too? She could be suffering from amnesia and sheltered by someone. It wasn't likely, but in this nightmare moment anything seemed possible.

Could she go back to the hospital tomorrow? Yes, she told herself, she could. It was the least she could do. She would sit beside that travesty of a young man and talk to him about America, about Canada, about anything. And if he could answer her, she would listen. He wouldn't be able to see her tears.

However, the next day the bed at the end of the ward was empty. The same nurse saw her staring at the smooth white sheets.

"Moved to London," she said cheerily in a voice intended for the listening ears in the neighbouring beds. "To a hospital where they specialise in burns."

"Oh, I thought –"

The blue eyes glittered, daring her to speak her fears.

"The boys will be glad you've come again. They took to your voice. Cute, they called it."

And Hetty knew that Donald was dead.

Or was he?

Was she going to encounter him again at the some unexpected time?

Nothing was safe. Nothing. But at this point there was no turning back. Besides, she admitted honestly to herself, she didn't want to. Loburn beckoned, the return of Hugo beckoned, the prospect of having another child beckoned most of all. If she could achieve that last desire, she surely would have made amends for all her guilt.

II

Hugo was home. In the middle of the morning Hetty saw
him walking down the circular drive, his kitbag slung over
his shoulder. She couldn't believe her eyes. She had to
rush across the hall and out of the front door to see if he
were real. She was so glad to be the first to welcome him,
even ahead of Bates who hadn't known the master was
about to ring the doorbell, and therefore was not
stationed in the right position.

"Hugo!" She threw her arms round him. "It really is
you?"

He gave a smile that was uncomfortably not a smile.
His face was gaunt and yellowish.

"You sound doubtful."

"I've been inclined to see ghosts. Who doesn't nowadays?" She was babbling. "Why didn't you let us know
you were coming?"

"It was short notice. The C.O. said I could have four
days while the company is in rest billets, before the next
push."

"Four days! Is that all?" Hetty saw his tightened face.
"But that's magnificent," she said quickly. "How did you
get here?"

"I got a lift with some airmen on their way to the airfield. In an old Ford that threatened to expire at any
moment. Hadn't we better go in?"

"I don't want to share you with anyone," Hetty said,
clinging to his arm. The frown flickered between his
brows. She saw that he would have to be humoured. "But

I won't be that selfish. Shall we go in and ring the gong triumphantly? No, better not. It will scare your mother. Oh darling, you do look as if you're in need of rest and sustenance."

"I'm perfectly fit." The stiffness was in his voice again. "How's Mother? Julia? The horses?"

And me, your wife? Ask me how I am. And smile at me properly, Hugo, Please.

"Everyone's well." She sighed. "Only four days. We must count every hour, every minute."

Freddie said, "Why does Uncle Hugo look so angry, Hetty?"

"Angry?"

"You must have noticed," Freddie said in his elderly way.

"I don't think he's angry. Just tired and trying to forget bad things. Bad things happen in wars, even in Hector's on the plains of Sparta."

"His eyes stick out," said Freddie. "Is that from all the banging of the guns?"

Hetty had noticed that distressing feature, too. Hugo's bright blue eyes, so startlingly attractive when she had first seen them, had grown paler and somehow more bulbous. It must just be that his face was thinner, and stiffened into the mask of composure that he thought necessary to wear in all situations.

Four days were not going to be anything like time enough to ease the massive strain from which Hetty knew he was suffering. If she had sufficient time she would break down the barriers. What he needed was communication, loving, forgetfulness. But would she ever have time?

As it was the four women dined that night with a polite stranger. Kitty prattled, Lady Flora made vague irrelevant remarks, and Julia had a hectic flush in her cheeks and looked distressingly beautiful. Hetty remained almost as silent as her husband but not discontentedly so. After all, once again she held the trump card. She would presently be sharing his bed.

Though that turned out to be a farce, for, obviously in a state of extreme exhaustion, Hugo simply fell back on the pillows and slept.

She didn't sleep herself until the early hours, and then when she woke, it was daylight and he had gone.

Riding with Julia, of course.

He hadn't even asked how her own riding was progressing, nor whether she would care to be his companion this morning. It was Julia he met in the frosty dawn, and when they returned there was a distinct change in Hugo's attitude. He looked more relaxed, his eyes brighter, and with a glimmering of pleasure. He even looked at Hetty as if he actually saw her.

"Morning, darling. Hope I didn't disturb you when I got up. Julia's been showing me the new filly. Nice creature. We'll have her mated in the spring. Sorry. I'll be boring you. Julia tells me you've decided you don't like horses."

It was good to see Hugo looking so rejuvenated. Nevertheless . . .

"Not as much as children," Hetty said deliberately.

He put his arm round her waist, giving her a powerful squeeze.

"Julia told me. My poor darling. And you never said a word to me."

"I expect Julia told you how it happened, too."

"Yes. Wretched bad luck. She was crying, poor girl. She said she didn't know how to live with her guilty conscience."

"I expect she'll manage. We all do."

"It was an accident."

"Of course."

"And what have you got to be guilty about? It wasn't your fault, either. A bit foolhardy, perhaps. Our next

147

child will be born safely. It had better be, or I might start talking about carelessness."

She didn't mind his reprimand. Warmth flowed through her. Tonight was going to be different. He was rested, refreshed, they would make love, a child would be conceived. Which came first, his desire for her or for the eleventh baron, the new young lord to inherit Loburn?

Indeed, which came first with her?

"Hugo, I make you a solemn promise that the next time I will look after myself like a rare orchid, or spun glass."

"Just sensibly, dear girl. That's all I expect. And now tell me what Tom Grubb is doing up in the roof? Are we rebuilding Loburn?"

"We're beginning to."

"Absolutely splendid. You're a capable woman, aren't you?"

"And healthy as well," said Hetty. "I expect we'll end up with ten children. We'll help to repopulate the world."

It was the wrong thing to say. The shadow flickered in his eyes.

"Then let's get mortality out of our minds. We've both had enough of that."

That oblique remark was the only one he made about what had been happening on the battlefield in Flanders, the long terrible battle of Ypres, the uncountable dead.

They went upstairs early that night. There was a bottle of champagne on ice in the bedroom, just as there had been on their wedding night. Julia had disappeared earlier, almost tactfully, damn her. So had Lady Flora, but not to go to her room. She was playing the piano in the music room. Hetty thought that the pure muted sound would make a delicate romantic accompaniment to their love-making. She was wrong. A Brahms nocturne was not suitable to the violence of Hugo's attack on her.

Attack? Surely not. Just a frenzied physical release,

lacking tenderness or thoughtfulness. It was behaviour that was surely uncontrollable, for she was sure he would not willingly have hurt her or ignored her pleasure.

Or would he? Did she know this man, his mind over-full of the dark memories of war?

Of course she didn't know him, war or no war. She might discover that he had a brutal streak which he no longer intended to conceal. Or his mind could be full of Julia, her hair streaming in the wind, galloping ahead of him over the Four Hills. His supreme ideal of beauty, Hetty suspected bitterly.

The sound of the piano was far away, slightly melancholy, totally unsuitable. She remembered suddenly how Effie had said that Lady Flora always played the piano when she was upset. Why was she upset tonight when her eldest son was home and in good health? Because he was in bed with the wrong woman?

"Give me some more champagne, darling?"

"I'm sorry, was I a bit sudden for you?"

She smiled into his thin face, the bones pressing against the sallow flesh, the slightly prominent eyes lacking any semblance of tenderness.

"A bit. But we have all night."

And the next time it was better. If anything it was she who, through tension, tiredness and perplexity, lacked genuine response. However, one could simulate. She was discovering more than she had bargained for. Women were versatile, in many different ways.

The precious four days did not result in a regained love and tenderness. That had been too much to hope for. But Hugo wanted her every night and held her as if he would like to crush and consume her. It seemed as if he were driven by some monstrous futile anger against the whole clouded and stormy universe. It was only after this physical assault – for that was virtually what it was – that he could sleep.

And only after he had been out riding with Julia, or alone, that some of the rigidity went out of his face.

Kitty said that he was beginning to look like half a dozen pompous irascible old colonels and brigadiers she had known. Surely he was too young for that. Hetty would have to soften him after the war. She could do so if she tried.

"Do you think so?" Hetty said wistfully. "He seems to be permanently angry."

"How can the way he behaves in four days be permanent? You just haven't got time now, that's all. And I don't believe you have ever really got to know him, have you?"

"I thought – in New York –"

"He was a debutante's dream?" Kitty was blunt, as usual. "Well, he was never that, in my opinion. He hasn't got half of Lionel's brains. But he's usually a good-natured fellow. He's suffering from a bit of shell shock, I think. We're beginning to see more of it among the men just back from the front. It takes time for them to recover. But they do, with help."

"Oh, I'll help," Hetty said fervently. "If only I can guess how."

"I suspect you've done that partly already." The slight bruise on Hetty's throat hadn't escaped Kitty's notice. "I hope you've got a baby out of it, at least."

Hetty looked doubtful. "I wonder if this is the right time, the right conditions."

"You think you'll have a squalling angry tortured little brat? Don't be silly. He'll be yours. You'll be the mother."

Hetty's eyes filled with tears.

"You're always so kind to me."

"I think you deserve a bit of kindness. I really do." Kitty shrugged in her casual way. "Freddie thinks the same. Confer with him."

Then Hugo was gone, and it was late November and

they read that snow covered no-man's-land, and the men in the front line trenches slept in their great-coats, and balaclavas and mittens, and almost never took their boots off, yet still got frostbite and a host of other ills. The ground became too frozen to dig new trenches, and when a thaw set in they nearly drowned in mud. The wounded did actually drown.

The icy waters of the Atlantic would be preferable to that horror of suffocation.

It was terrible reading about it, or hearing it from the lips of survivors, men with amputated fingers or toes, one of whom said cynically, "They say there'll be cowslips and larks and poppies and other nice things in the spring, but I don't believe it. There'll just be bones, you know. Just bones sprouting up out of the earth."

By Christmas it was rumoured that the Gallipoli campaign had been a failure and might have to be abandoned. All that heroism and tragedy, the blue Aegean running with the blood of the most splendid young men on earth, and for a lost cause. But Kitty was jubilant; she only cared that Lionel might soon be home.

Hetty was not jubilant about anything, for there was not to be a baby. She had a feeling of time racing by, of too many uncertainties, too many dangers.

And Julia was up to something.

She and Lady Flora had been visiting old friends in Bath, staying overnight and returning the following afternoon. Like mother-in-law and daughter-in-law, Hetty thought, watching them descending from the Rolls, clutching hats and scarves which threatened to be snatched away in the sharp November wind, clutching each other, too, and laughing.

They had enjoyed their brief stay away, particularly Julia who looked more animated than Hetty had ever seen her. That surely couldn't have been the result of enjoying something as mildly stimulating as a musical soirée and a sedate dinner party, where, as far as Hetty could discover, the youngest male was on the wrong side of fifty.

The secret came out eventually.

"We met a friend of yours, Hetty," Julia said airily.

"You couldn't have!"

"Oh, but we could. Couldn't we, Lady Flora?"

"Don't tease the child," Lady Flora said quite kindly. "It was only the Eversleigh girl, Hetty. She says she did meet you on the *Lusitania* although you did tell us you didn't remember her."

"No, I don't. Everything's so blurred. I don't seem to have Miss Eversleigh's memory."

"Perhaps you were a bit too occupied with a certain young man," Julia said slyly.

"Don't be a bitch, Julia," Kitty interrupted. "Everyone has shipboard flirtations. Except Kate Eversleigh, probably. Didn't there always used to be a flap about getting her a partner for the Hunt ball?"

"Girls, you're behaving like schoolchildren," Lady Flora chided. "Anyway, Hetty will be able to see whether or not her memory is reliable when Kate comes tomorrow."

"She's coming here!" Hetty couldn't keep the alarm out of her voice.

"Just to tea, my dear. On her way to London. She's catching a troop train on her way to France with the Red Cross. You may think her a dull person, but I must say she has plenty of courage."

"And you never told us what a gay little creature you were, Hetty," Julia was determined to persist with her petty persecution. "Who was the irresistible young man you spent so much time leaning over the rail with?"

"Nobody, nobody!" Hetty cried in a high strained voice. "At least he's nobody now because he was drowned. They all were. Except Katharine Eversleigh, and me. That's why my memory is so bad. It wants to shut out things." She added more steadily, "I would

152

rather not see her, if you don't mind. It sounds hateful, like forming a survivors' club. How long were you in the water, Clemency? Who fished you out?"

They were all staring at her in surprise. Afterwards Kitty said it was because she had called herself Clemency for the first time. They had hardly known whom she was speaking of.

She did see Katharine Eversleigh, of course. By the next day she had collected herself and knew that she was capable of being in command of the situation. After all, she had had plenty of practise at being quick-witted in tricky situations. Something the dull Miss Eversleigh with her secure upbringing in an English county family would know little about.

And indeed this was how it turned out to be. Katharine Eversleigh was a well-built plain-faced friendly young woman who wanted only to congratulate another survivor.

"Of course I don't expect you to remember me, Lady Hazzard. You were always so popular, weren't you? Always the centre of attention. And such lovely clothes. I could have snatched that green silk dress off you, if you can imagine a carthorse like me in moiré silk."

Hetty knew the dress she referred to. Clemency had liked it, too. She had been inordinately fussy about how it was ironed. It had taken exactly an hour, and after one wearing it had all to be done again. There was no way Hetty could have forgotten it.

"It was an adorable dress," Katharine was going on. "Young Mr – I don't think I ever heard his name – admired it too, didn't he?"

Had this large, seemingly good-natured, young woman been primed by Julia?

"You must mean Mr Merrit. His family was in sugar. Terribly rich. Actually he got to be rather a bore. Adulation gets to be so artificial. Mother and I were planning ways of ditching the tiresome young man. But eventually it wasn't necessary. The Germans –" the high affected note went out of Hetty's voice. She had gone very pale. "Well, they did it for us, didn't they? Were you –?"

"Yes, I was lucky. Our lifeboat got launched safely. We had no idea until afterwards how many were upset into the water, how many people never got ashore, at least not alive. But now here I am –" Miss Eversleigh sensed the uncomfortable atmosphere and gave an awkward laugh, "sticking my neck out again, going to France, though I don't suppose I'll get too near the German guns."

"You astonish me, Hetty, being such a wicked little flirt," Julia murmured. "Isn't she a marvellous actress, Lady Flora?"

Lady Flora was giving Hetty a long thoughtful gaze, obviously trying to conjure up the vivacious young woman in the green silk ball gown. She was frowning a little, and it was left for Kitty to say, "Can you blame Hetty if such an awful experience washed some of the frivolity out of her? And what was wrong with a bit of frivolity, anyway? Hugo obviously admired it."

"I'm married now," Hetty said, with stiff dignity. Then, "Yes, I was frivolous once. Not that long ago either, althought it seems an awful long time now. I led that kind of life. Hugo knew and he enjoyed it, too. But he's changed, as well." She looked challengingly at the listening women. "How can one not, after what we've been through?"

It was left for Julia to say, rather ineffectually, "It is a pity about that lost trousseau. I wonder how you can be contented with provincial clothes. Yes, Cirencester is distinctly provincial, Kitty, and you can't deny it. But Hetty doesn't seem to want to go to London to shop."

Hetty's chin lifted sharply.

"I'll do that when my husband comes home permanently. Just now it would be pointless to get oneself up like a gadfly. I have no intention of doing it."

There was a brief awkward silence, Katharine Eversleigh looking bewildered and uneasy. She put her cup and saucer down with a clatter, and Julia, who had not given up the private game she was playing, said. "Did you suffer a sea change, too, Kate? I mean one as complete as Hetty's?"

"I wasn't in the water so long. I wasn't in danger of drowning. And I didn't lose my mother."

"Or your maid?" Julia suggested.

A look of distaste came into Katharine's mild brown eyes.

"I don't think we should hash over those old things, Julia. It does no good. It's only very distressing." She added briskly and cheerfully, "I have a feeling that after tomorrow there are going to be worse catastrophes in my life. But I do wish you luck, Hetty. May I call you Hetty? Don't have nightmares about that time. We've survived. We ought to be congratulating ourselves, and making the most of our lives. I mean to, anyway."

"Oh, so do I," Hetty agreed firmly. Julia suspected something, but could prove nothing since she didn't know what she suspected. She would never know. How could she? There was no need to be afraid.

12

It seemed that Christmas was spent to the background of the piano being played in the music room, though there was nothing so seasonal and ordinary for Lady Flora as Christmas carols.

She was fretting in her unspoken way for her absent sons, so the delicate nocturnes were interspersed with requiems.

The day before Christmas Lady Flora, accompanied by Julia, distributed Christmas gifts to convalescent soldiers and Julia was mistaken for the new young Lady Hazzard. It seemed to be a great joke to everyone but Hetty. Other modest entertainments took place.

The vicar and his wife, Mr Edmonds the manager from the bank in Cirencester, Doctor Bailey and one or two neighbouring farmers were invited to Loburn for hot punch or whisky, as they preferred. There was a Christmas tree for Freddie, and a small and rather subdued party for the much diminished staff. It was all, in Julia's words, unutterably morbid. There were no carol singers, and there wasn't even any snow.

Hetty caught Julia's morbidity, for a letter had come from Uncle Jonas suggesting that it would be a sensible idea if she were to go and see that her mother's grave was being cared for.

I understand ferry boats are still running to Ireland, and it's your duty, my dear. Don't want thistles or shamrocks, or whatever, growing all over it. And I trust you to have made all enquiries possible about the fate of your maid. This is not only humanity, but an employer's duty. I'm not so fit myself; doctor gives me gloomy warnings to which I pay no heed. I shall go down drinking my brandy if I feel like it. Judging by the casualty lists, your husband seems to be on the lucky side. Though the new offensive they're talking of on the Somme may tell a different story. We don't know too much about it over here. I hope we have the sense to keep out of it . . .

And Hetty was going to have the sense to keep away from that windy Irish headland where she could do no good whatever. Mrs Jervis had had far too much attention all her life. Now she would have to do with only the odd prayer from a nun or a passing priest.

At last the Gallipoli campaign was over, the men slipping out silently night after night, not daring even to whisper. Not only because of the alert ears of the enemy, but because of the dead buried on the tortured hillsides, their own comrades who might feel deserted. The withdrawal was the most successful operation of that doomed campaign.

Some weeks after the end of the Gallipoli fiasco a letter came from Lionel in hospital in Alexandria. He had got another bout of fever but was recovering and would surely then get leave. All the fit men were being sent to France where the Somme offensive was gathering strength. The sunburnt young Australians and New Zealanders, casual, heroic, and splendid in stature, were gratefully received and sucked into another form of trench warfare. Not unscalable heights this time, but the flat desolate stretch of no-man's-land, glimmering evilly with mud and stagnant pools and unspeakable debris.

Hugo's letters had become shorter, less frequent, and completely unemotional. He was in good shape, he hadn't had a scratch, he hoped the roof at Loburn was finished and watertight, that Hetty wasn't overdoing the hospital work, that everyone was well. He had no word of any leave at present.

Then there was a knock on Hetty's bedroom door early one morning. She thought it was Effie with her tea tray. She looked at the bedside clock. Six-thirty. Hugo?

Her heart beginning to thump, she called eagerly, "Come in!" However, her visitor was already in, unable to wait for permission. The small head just showed above her bedside.

"Hetty! Hetty! Daddy's home. He came in the middle of the night, at five o'clock. Mummy laughed like anything and then cried, and then he went to bed because he was tired."

Hetty's first reaction was sharp disappointment that the unexpected arrival in the early morning had not been Hugo. She chided herself for her selfishness and kissed Freddie, and said, "How lovely! Tell Mummy to come and see me the minute she can."

Kitty came half an hour later, still in her dressing gown, her expression a mixture of joy and anxiety.

"Hetty, he's so thin! And utterly exhausted. He came back on a hospital ship to Southampton, and then escaped from a troop train – so he says – and got someone to drive him here. He's not medically discharged yet, and I'm insisting on him reporting to the hospital as soon as he's had a rest. I'm really praying that he won't be fit for active service again, though I don't suppose I want an invalid husband either. It's malaria, and they ran short of quinine on board ship, so he'll soon improve when he's properly treated. Lady Flora's buzzing about like a queen bee, but even she's not going to get to see Lionel until he's rested."

"Kitty darling! What wonderful news, Lionel home and not shot to pieces. That's what I dread so much for Hugo, some sort of mutilation."

"Yes, I know. But malaria's no joke, either. I have to keep going in to look at Lionel and make sure I haven't been dreaming. Hugo won't get badly shot, Hetty. I just know. He could always look after himself. And when he gets home they'll be the Hazzard brothers again. That's how they've always been known. And we'll be the Hazzard wives."

The shape in the high-backed wing chair beside a fire that needed replenishing was scarcely more than a shadow. Hetty had been sitting at her embroidery frame for half an hour before she noticed that it was there. It was only when she switched on the lamp beside her that she saw the two dark eyes looking at her. For a second, fantasy possessed her. Here was Jacobina's lover – for she must surely have had one – and he would have been a slim quiet cavalier like this, wrapped in a bottle-green velvet robe, his dark head tilted against the wing of the chair.

"You must be my sister-in-law," said a weary voice. "I've been watching you. You make a picture of grace. Who told me Hugo was going to marry a chatter-box American? Or did I just think of a type for Hugo – like happy families, horsey husband, neighing wife."

Hetty hardly dared to open her mouth. She had an instant and overpowering desire that he should like her voice, the words she said, her looks. "A picture of grace." He must have thought he had been looking at the Tudor lady, busy with her long-ago needlework.

"You thought I was Jacobina. That lady." She pointed at the yellow portrait. "I thought you were a ghost, too. You're Lionel, of course. It did surprise me to see someone sitting there."

"And I woke up and saw you," he said. "But why were you so surprised to see someone here?"

"Because you didn't make a sound, and because this is my room, and I selfishly made a rule that no one was to come in without my permission. The winter room. I suddenly fell in love with it. And no one else wanted it. Lady Flora and Julia have the music room and the summer drawing room, and Kitty has her own suite. I wanted somewhere of my own. I'm still rather an alien here."

"Still?"

"So I sit in this room, kind of wrapping it round me like a soft old cloak. No, Kitty doesn't let me be an alien, nor Freddie. But – your mother – she's distant. And Julia –"

"What is Julia?"

Hetty couldn't resist her answer. "I think of her as a high-stepping chestnut mare, rather mean at times. Oh –" she put her hand to her mouth, "Whatever is making me talk like this? Are you one of those men who make women say indiscreet things? Let me put on some lights so I can see you properly. And I'll ring for Effie to bring some tea. Will you have tea with me?"

"If I'm permitted to stay. This room used to be a favourite retreat of mine, too."

"Oh, did it? Then I must give it back to you."

"I'll refuse it. Or can't we share occasionally? Hetty, do stand still a minute, will you? I've been looking at scruffy unwashed males for so long I'd almost forgotten there was another sex."

Hetty stood in the firelight, not knowing what opinion he was forming of her. She wished vaguely that Hugo had sometimes looked at her with this deep totally absorbed interest. Then she forgot Hugo and was aware only of the thin face, the sunken fever-bright eyes. Satirical brows, narrow curving lips, an emphatic chin. A clever face that could be full of intolerance, or alternatively of sweetness. Or so she guessed.

Why had she not asked to see photographs of him, why hadn't she been prepared for this? Freddie's father who wrote funny letters about mermaids, and the gods of Olympus. Kitty's husband.

He stared at her for some moments. Then all he said

was, "Lucky Hugo. Let's have that tea, shall we? I suddenly feel hungry."

Hetty went to ring the bell. She switched on more lights and felt her cheeks hot.

"You've decided that I am a chatterbox?"

"I've never heard a chatterbox with a charming voice like yours. So if you are, another of my theories will have been proved wrong."

Now that the lights were on the room was ordinary again, or as ordinary as it could ever be, with its old panelling and its deep-set windows. The dream they had both walked into for that brief few minutes, for she knew that he, watching her at her needlework, had been in the same dream as hers, had gone. He was a very tired sick soldier, perhaps hallucinating a little, and she was still bedevilled by her private ghosts.

She had the instinct to know the situation was a little dangerous. But she could control it, she was growing harder all the time.

"And the other theory?" she said lightly.

"The reason you married Hugo. Have I the right to ask for any explanations?"

"I expect so. You're Hugo's brother. Well, then, Hugo married me for my money and I married him to get a title and to live in an English manor house and to curtsey to royalty, and all that. That's what they've told you, isn't it?"

"More or less."

"It's only a fraction of the truth. I want to love Hugo and have him love me, if only we ever get enough time together. That's the real situation. And it would have all been a success if I hadn't arrived in such bad shape, and he hadn't had to leave almost immediately for the front. There's really nothing more to say. Here's Effie. Bring tea for us here, Effie. Is Mrs Lionel home?"

"Not yet, my lady, but she said she'd be back by five. She couldn't not go to the hospital because there was a dying man she'd promised. And excusing me, sir, she said you was asleep and not to be disturbed."

"Then when she arrives tell her we're waiting for her in here," Hetty said. "And ask Bates to build up the fire. It's still chilly in the evenings. You'll feel it, Lionel, after Egypt. You're terribly thin, aren't you?"

"There's a great deal more to say," Lionel said.

"About what?"

"Your marriage. It intrigues me. Vastly. You're not in the least a hostessy fashionable ambitious lady. You look as if you think too much, for one thing."

"I suffered a sea change," Hetty murmured. "That's what Julia says."

"Perhaps you did. You had a particularly horrible time, Kitty told me."

"But I never was a hostessy lady," Hetty said, and experienced the greatest relief to be speaking, for once, complete truth. "Hugo fascinated me. He still does. And I'm already besotted by Loburn, which pleases him. We've got all our lives ahead of us and we're going to be very happy, and have children, and repair and rebuild Loburn in the way it should be done. I'm going to start looking for the original plans which I'm told should be somewhere in the house."

"Of course. What a marvellous idea. Will you let me help?"

"Oh, yes. I'd be so happy if you would."

Looking at his face which was full of lively enthusiasm, she couldn't resist adding, "I only wish Hugo was more interested, but architecture doesn't appeal to him, Julia says. The way you're looking now is the sort of look he'll have when he has a newly-born colt or filly in his stables."

Lionel laughed and began to cough. Hetty exclaimed in remorse, "We're talking too much. I think you should be quiet now."

He did become quiet, but not before he said, "For a

162

minute you had a tiny little viper's tongue in that delicious mouth. How intriguing."

Kitty found them half an hour later. Lionel had fallen asleep again, as suddenly as a child. For the first time Hetty saw Kitty looking cross and put out.

"How could you have let him come downstairs? You can see the shape he's in," she whispered angrily.

"Don't blame me, Kitty. I just looked up and saw him sitting there. So I rang for tea and we talked a little and then he fell asleep."

Hetty was so overcome emotionally that tears began running down her cheeks. "Oh, Kitty, you're so lucky, you have your husband home. If only I had mine."

Kitty's anger vanished and she came and clung to Hetty, weeping herself.

'Oh, goodness! Lionel might wake up. Don't let him find two wailing women."

"Did that soldier die?"

"Private Albert Mays? Yes, he died. But I was there to hold his hand." A great sob came up out of Kitty's throat. "He saw I had kept my promise, and he put his hand in mine and just went to sleep. Poor kids. That's all a lot of them are, wanting their mums' hands to hold."

Hetty looked at Lionel's sleeping face. She felt overcome with an aching sorrow.

"And this one, Kitty?"

"We'll get him up to bed. Doctor Bailey is looking in later. He says it sounds like a week or ten days in bed and no visitors. Not even Freddie except for a few minutes at a time. Lady Flora isn't going to like that. And the rule applies to you, too, Hetty, and to Julia."

"But won't he be lonely?"

"I'll be with him," Kitty said simply.

The ache in Hetty's throat grew sharper. She was afraid that she was never again going to like sitting alone in the winter drawing room.

The next time she saw Lionel was ten days later. Then, dressed in army uniform, he was being helped into the Rolls, with Pimm on one side of him and Kitty on the other. He was off to a medical board. Kitty was hoping he would be invalided out of the army, but more likely the verdict would be extended sick leave. At least, after today's interview, he would be allowed more freedom. Hetty guessed that he would take it, with or without permission. Freddie had said that lately Daddy had been getting pretty irritable. Plain cantankerous, Nanny said.

That morning Hetty found the house, in spite of its size, stifling and claustrophobic. She set out on a long walk through the woods, across the bottom meadow, and on to the narrow winding road leading to the village. She encountered only sheep grazing, a startled cock pheasant erupting with a clatter from the long grass, a dappled troup of cows like a patchwork quilt, and two of Hugo's horses kicking up their heels in delighted freedom.

Far off, like a gnat buzzing, one of the aeroplanes from the training field hung in the sky, before plunging in what looked like a perilous dive. It was a beautiful morning, both exhilarating and poignant. Too many young men, like the unlucky flier, Donald Newman, were dicing with death, being killed or irreversibly damaged. Maimed in a way that, if they were animals, they would be humanely killed. Instead, they were kept alive to extract their price from those who had to care for them. Supposing Hugo came home scarred beyond recognition, or physically helpless? Supposing Lionel was returned, like repaired goods, to France and the terrors of the big Somme offensive?

Not Lionel, with his acutely sensitive face, his fascinating mind.

But you mustn't think of him, you must think of your husband. Lionel is Kitty's.

In the village the few people about looked surprised to see the young Lady Hazzard, the foreign lady, trudging along like one of them. She had been regarded as something of a recluse. They bobbed and said, "Good morning, my lady," in a friendly way. Hetty wondered what purchase she could make to show her goodwill. Should she have coffee in Mrs Bryce's little dark teashop? But a sudden stronger impulse had seized her. She turned down the lane leading to the church, crossed the small green graveyard, and went into the beeswax and hymn-book-smelling gloom.

She wanted to sit quietly, perhaps to pray. She had never been trained to prayer, for her mother had grown too cynical to believe in a God who had allowed her and her child to suffer so much hardship. One fought for oneself, that was the only certain way of achieving anything. But even if it were impossible to be aware of a benevolent deity, Hetty liked the mysticism and the poetry of the old incantations. She could forget, or find forgivable, her misdeeds, her deceit, her guilt. She could sense beauty touching her.

Lord, now lettest thou thy servant depart in peace, she murmured under her breath as she knelt on the worn hassock and buried her head in her hands. She was just an innocent young woman praying for the welfare of two men, husband and brother-in-law.

But even that she could not do wholeheartedly, for she was suddenly overcome by a feeling that someone was watching her. Turning her head sharply she saw a young woman in the opposite pew. She must have been there when Hetty went in, for her prayer, or meditation, had ended. She had been staring at Hetty, surely, for as soon as she caught Hetty's look she sprang up and slipped quietly out. She was wearing a fine black veil over her head and face, but even so Hetty knew with shocked certainty that she was Clemency. The dark head, the neat profile, the slim waist, the dancing step.

For a moment Hetty thought she would faint, her skin cold, her heart thumping like a beaten drum.

165

Then, galvanised into action, she rushed out of the dim church into the sunlight. There was nobody in sight. She dashed across the graveyard, recklessly treading on graves. In the distance, too far off to be identifiable, there was a woman with a shopping basket. That couldn't be Clemency. She would never come back to haunt with a shopping basket! Indeed, she had never carried a shopping basket in her life. Anyway, the woman was turning into Mrs Bryce's teashop, probably for something as mundane as a cup of tea and a bun.

Hetty sighed bewilderedly, knowing she must have suffered another hallucination, another trick played by her stretched nerves.

She could hear voices from beyond the yew walk, the vicar's and the clear low tones of a woman. They were emerging from the shadow and coming towards her. The woman, bare-headed, was Julia who immediately affected great surprise.

"Hetty! I didn't expect to see you here. The vicar and I were discussing the garden fête for the Belgian refugees. Lady Flora is to open it."

"We hope you will be able to attend, Lady Hazzard," the vicar said unctuously.

"Why, of course –"

"You're looking strange, Hetty. Are you ill?"

"No, I'm quite well." In desperation Hetty added, "Did you see anyone come out of the church just now?"

"No. No one. Did you, vicar?"

"I saw you, Lady Hazzard."

"There was a woman praying. She –" Hetty bit her tongue. She had been going to say, "She looked like me."

"People do come in to pray," the vicar said, smiling gently. "I imagine you have been doing the same thing. For your husband, of course."

Across the short expanse of sunlit turf Hetty met Julia's gaze, so bland and calm, yet completely cold, completely unsympathetic, and again with that underlying look of puzzled suspicion. Had it been Julia in the church? She could have snatched off a black veil and put it in her pocket. She would never say so. She would enjoy bewildering Hetty further.

But if Clemency were really wandering through the village, Julia's enmity, in comparison to this threat, was insignificant.

"I'm going home," she said wearily. "It's past lunchtime. Kitty and Lionel should be back."

"Wait a moment. I'll walk with you. Good morning, vicar, and thank you. I have all the information Lady Flora needs."

"Wait." Now the vicar was detaining them, his elderly face suddenly enlightened. "I think, Lady Hazzard, the woman you saw would be Jane Smith. She slips in and out of the church since her fiancé was killed on the Marne."

"She did wear a black veil," Hetty said in relief.

A lock of the vicar's sparse grey hair lifted in the wind. Something autumnal came into the late spring morning. "So sad. So many young women looking like elderly widows."

"But where did she disappear to?" Julia murmured as they walked away. "Into thin air? Anyway, what I don't understand, Hetty, is why you should have been in a state about seeing another woman in the church."

"I wasn't in a state."

"You were. White as a ghost."

"Oh, shut up," said Hetty rudely. Leave me, she added silently. Stop watching me. Get out of my sight. I would be so happy never never to see you again.

But she's part of your destiny, said a voice, very coolly and soberly and so distinctly that it was amazing Julia didn't seem to hear it. And then it added: she never will leave you until that's resolved.

It was the second time that someone had uncannily spoken to her out of mid-air.

Lionel and Kitty were home, and what was more Lionel had come down to luncheon. No more solitary confinement for him, he said. He was to have nourishing food and stimulating companionship until his next medical board in two months. His lungs were affected, Kitty explained, as if such a calamity were a benediction. With rest they would improve, but it was unlikely he would be fit for active service again.

"We'll get you well, darling, but not that well," Kitty said cheerfully. "Isn't it bliss to have a man in the house again? But you can't sit around idly, Lionel. What will you do? Work on your book?"

Lionel's dark eyes sought Hetty's across the table.

"Not yet. First, Hetty and I are going to begin a search for those plans we were talking of. We'll start rebuilding Loburn this summer."

"Loburn, Lionel dear, is your brother's," Lady Flora pointed out.

"And Hetty, as his wife, has authority, Mother dear. Didn't Hugo give you *carte blanche*, Hetty?"

"Yes, he did." She was suddenly so shiningly happy that the uncanny events of the morning might never have happened.

The woman in the church had been that sad young woman, Jane Smith. Not Clemency come to warn her that, having succeeded in marrying Hugo, she must not now fall in love with his brother.

Soon it was full summer and Lionel was much stronger. It wasn't that Hetty intentionally sought his company, nor that he sought hers. It was simply that they were thrown together by similar interests, and the absence of other people. Kitty's hospital work absorbed so much of her time, and she was a compulsive gardener. Lionel no longer needed nursing so she must get on with these important occupations. Besides, she said, pushing up her tumbling hair in her familiar gesture, she wasn't a clinging wife. Lionel would hate it if she were. So how fortunate it was that he had Hetty to share his passion for the reconstruction of the house. Surprising, too, that little rich New Yorker being so involved in an old house. It had turned out to be her natural gift. But she would be less involved when Hugo came home. If Hugo came home . . .

Lady Flora's health was deteriorating, and she spent most of each day in her room, or playing the piano. The marvellously pure notes sounded through the summer dusk, and would be for ever bound up in Hetty's memories of Loburn that summer. Only Julia, if anyone, knew what was going on in Lady Flora's head. But Julia's time was spent more and more with the horses, obsessively grooming them and exercising them, in case Hugo suddenly arrived. Hetty didn't mind this any more. Indeed, she scarcely thought about it. Everyone in this house seemed to have an obsession, and she not the least. Being with Lionel in the library, reading old documents in faded handwriting, discovering fascinating pieces of family history, sometimes not speaking for hours but always knowing he was there, as absorbed as she was, gave her complete contentment.

Lionel said that he had never had time to do these things before. In an unexpected way the war had its advantages. And Freddie, at the precocious age of five, had got to know the *Iliad*, as had Hetty. Hetty had a bent for literature. Had she known? He had supposed the life of a rich young socialite in New York wouldn't have given her either the time or the inclination to be academic.

"My mother would have fainted with horror," Hetty said, thinking of Millicent Jervis, strong-minded, bossy, ambitious. "I think perhaps not my father. But he died when I was very young. Oh, I did learn to read and write," she added, straightfaced. "And I have a very good imagination."

She remembered the young woman in the church, the voice issuing from the bandaged head in the hospital, the vague rustlings and sighings coming from the wardrobe at night. "Too good," she said wryly. "Better even than Freddie's."

"I have nightmares, too," said Lionel, guessing her thoughts.

But yours aren't from guilt, Hetty wanted to say. Those nightmares are the worst kind. They sit on your shoulders for hours afterwards, like black hard-eyed birds.

However, since Lionel's return the bad nights had been less frequent, and she had moments of such pure happiness that she felt it shining out of her. Happiness that permitted no thought of past or future, and which was completely impossible to conceal, were anyone watching her.

Lionel was watching one day. He said, "I think we ought to have a party. How long is it since there was a party at Loburn? Not since the war began."

"Without Hugo?" Hetty said uncertainly.

"It would be splendid if he could get leave, but I doubt if a party would be considered sufficient grounds. No harm in writing and mentioning it, though. He must be due for leave. He might be able to wangle something. He's a good manipulator, old Hugo. Gets what he wants. Let's plan a party, Hetty."

"You plan it. You and Kitty. I don't know people. But yes –" she knew her eyes were showing her pleasure – "it would be fun."

"But you always refused to go to London, Hetty," Kitty said. "That's where you'd meet people. Here, we'll be down to the war rejects and the walking wounded, such as my own dear husband. Why are you suddenly so keen on it?"

"I don't know. It's mid-summer. The long evenings are so beautiful. And who knows, Hugo might get some leave. Loburn *en fête* might just pull him home."

"Now you're fantasising. Things like that don't happen. Well, I suppose we could have some of the doctors and nurses from the hospital, and anyone who's home on leave. Lady Flora will have a list of old pals, and Julia could ask her hunting friends. One or two retired colonels *et cetera*. I still can't understand why Lionel's going along with this idea, though. He never liked parties much, and especially not the hunt ball variety."

"He's got things to forget, too," Hetty murmured. "Music and dancing – it's one way, isn't it?"

"Like taking an anaesthetic," said Kitty. "Well, all right. Lady Flora will enjoy it. And Julia who dances like a dream. I suppose I can doll myself up. But I shan't get a new dress. Shall you?"

"Maybe," said Hetty dreamily. She had never been to a party in her life. Kitty wouldn't believe her if she told her that.

"Yes, I will get a new dress," she said decisively. "Something rather crazy and wonderful. I just feel in the mood."

Kitty gave her a long look.

"Then you'd better pray that Hugo gets home."

"Hetty! Hetty!" Julia called a few days later. "The postman's just been and your dress has arrived. Can I come in?" But she was already in the library where Lionel and Hetty were attempting to decipher a particularly fragile old document, the faded writing like the veining of an autumn leaf. She had a long box in her hands.

"Isn't it exciting? Lord and Taylor, Fifth Avenue. You never told us you'd sent to New York for something. Is it particularly special?"

"How odd," said Hetty. The all too familiar dryness was in her mouth again. "I didn't send for anything."

"Then your family must have sent it to you."

"I haven't got a family, except Uncle Jonas, and the day he bends his stuffy financial brain to choosing women's clothes –" she was chattering, and Lionel was watching with a questioning lift of his brows – "will be a surprising one," she finished lamely.

"Why don't you open it?" Lionel said. "Let us see the famous Wall Street brain's choice."

"Yes, open it," begged Julia. "Do let us see."

What did she expect to be in the long dressmaker's box? A doll? A dead doll? They all helped to demolish the wrapping paper until the white cardboard box tied with blue satin ribbon was exposed. A letter was attached. Ridiculously, Hetty's hands were shaking as she tore it open. It was typed neatly on Lord and Taylor notepaper, and read:

Dear Madam,

In response to your request we have had made a replica of the green moiré silk gown you lost at the time of the sinking of the *Lusitania*, and which you said had been an especial favourite. Miss Natalia, who always made your garments and has retained the pattern and your size, assures us it is an exact copy. We now have pleasure in despatching it to you, hoping that it arrives safely and gives you much pleasure. As you requested, we have sent the bill to your uncle, Mr Jonas Middleton.

We beg to remain,
Your obedient servants,
Lord and Taylor

Hetty tentatively lifted the tissue paper.

"It's – my green silk," she whispered. She made an enormous effort to speak naturally. "The dress I wore for the last ball on board ship." She couldn't control a deep shudder. "It's kind of uncanny."

"Do take it out of the box and let us see it," begged Julia. "Shall I?" Her inquisitive fingers couldn't keep away from the dress. "It's a little crushed, I'm afraid, but Effie can attend to that. She irons and goffers terribly well."

So do I, Hetty thought, irony taking over from her black sense of nightmare. I know every gather, every fold of this dress. If it is the same one. And it is, she thought dazedly, as Julia shook out the shimmering silk. Miss Natalia wouldn't make a mistake. She was a very clever dressmaker. If she hadn't been, Clemency would never have continued going to her.

"Oh, it's gorgeous!" Julia breathed. "Isn't it, Kitty?"

"I thought Hetty had stopped being interested in clothes," Kitty said. She was looking at Hetty in a puzzled way."Does a man in the house have anything to do with this rejuvenation?"

Hetty flushed angrily. How could she explain that the dress arriving had nothing to do with her? Who had ordered it? That was the terrifying question. She shuddered again, overcome with morbidity. The dress spread out over a chair was like Clemency rising triumphantly from the waves.

"Oh, Kitty, you know me better than that," she protested. "Yes, I did intend to get something a little crazy for the party, but I haven't done that yet. I truly know nothing about this." She fingered the silk distastefully. "It must have been the idea of one of my friends, Adele, or Betty or Lucy or –" She pressed her hands to her cheeks. "They had all seen my trousseau and knew this was my favourite dress."

That must be how the garment had come to arrive. Must be. Ordered by someone who knew Uncle Jonas's address. And hers, too. Lady Hazzard, Loburn near Cirencester, Gloucestershire, England. The label was correctly addressed.

Lionel said easily, "If this was meant to ravish Hugo, Hetty, you'll still allow the rest of us a preview, I hope."

"For our modest party!" It was the first time Hetty had heard Kitty speak snappishly to her husband. "It will be much too dressed up."

"It will be a sight for tired eyes. Do us all good," Lionel's voice was equable, but final. The conversation, as far as he was concerned, was finished.

Lady Flora sent for Hetty later that day. She said she would like Hetty to have tea upstairs with her.

Hetty frankly didn't relish a tête-à-tête. She had never been at ease with the stiff, elegant old lady, and wondered what had provoked Lady Flora's sudden attention. The arrival of that wretched dress? The puzzle of it was weighing her down and making her have impossible fantasies. Who could have ordered it? Surely a letter would arrive with an explanation. If not, she would have to write to Lord and Taylor for information. But that would take so long and in the meantime Effie, with cries of admiration, had hung the dress in the wardrobe to rustle like small sea waves in the night.

"Come in, my dear." Lady Flora was sitting at the window in her usual high-backed chair. The tea table had been drawn up to her and her hands were hovering over the delicate china. "I think you prefer lemon, don't you? Isn't it ridiculous that after a year there are still so many things I don't know about you? Or is it my bad memory?"

"What is it you want to know about me, Lady Flora? Don't I run the house properly?"

"Oh, excellently. Surprisingly well. And you look so charming, too. What a tragedy that you and Hugo have had to miss the first year of your marriage. There's so much this war has to answer for. But you are as happy as possible, under the circumstances, aren't you?"

Hetty answered carefully, "Yes. As you say, as much as one can be in these times."

"Sometimes I think you have a haunted look."

"I do feel haunted at times. Lionel does, too, and Hugo."

"My dear child, I do understand. That's why I'm glad there's going to be a party at Loburn. It will do us all good. And I hear you have a wonderful new dress sent especially from New York. How clever of you to think of

174

doing that. You must have been desolated about losing all your lovely trousseau."

"On the contrary, Lady Flora, I don't want to be reminded of it. It seems frivolous, after such a tragedy. That's why I can't understand that dress arriving or who asked for it to be sent. But I intend to find out."

"What an intriguing puzzle." Lady Flora's large dim blue eyes had the ghost of a sparkle, as if she were diverted and amused. "Someone who meant well by you, of course."

"Of course," Hetty agreed, not believing her words for an instant.

"Someone who didn't think of the painful memories the dress would evoke," Lady Flora observed.

Uncle Jonas? The housekeeper, Mrs Crampton, who had once written asking for information about her. Miss Natalia herself? After all, she, a little wasp-waisted woman with pinched lips, had visited the house dozens of times for fittings, and had become deeply interested in Clemency's romantic future.

No, it must have been someone closer than that.

Not Clemency! How *could* it possibly be Clemency, attempting a macabre revenge?

"I expect," said Lady Flora in her clear precise voice, "it could bring back that awful sensation of drowning. But you must overcome that. People have only seen you about the village and in church on Sundays, looking just a little mousey, if you will forgive me for saying so. You have been much too retiring. Why not look like an heiress for once?"

"No, I would only look like a peacock and that isn't suitable in these times," Hetty said stubbornly.

"You're wrong. What you will look like is the girl Hugo came back from New York talking so much about. You've scarcely given us a glimpse of her, you know."

"You make me feel like an impostor!" Hetty burst out unthinkingly.

"Nonsense! How could you get that impression? When I meant is that you're only a shadow of that girl. But how can you be otherwise, with Hugo away so long, and you losing your baby, and always waiting and waiting for news. My poor child, these times are very sad. Will you have some more tea?"

The beautiful limpid eyes could surely not look so completely innocent without being innocent.

Hugo wrote:

> Wish I could be home for the party, but leave doesn't look possible at present for various reasons that I can't mention. Though, my God, I am overdue for it. I hear you have a sensational new dress from New York. Time the Yanks sent us something towards the war effort, but I don't much like you wasting it on patched-up officers home on sick leave. Such as my brother, Lionel. I hear that you and he have found a lot in common. But the new dress was meant for me, I hope.

Yes, it was meant for you, Hetty said aloud in the quiet bedroom. More than you'll ever know. But I hate it, hate it, and I have the craziest suspicions which must be unfounded. Do come home, Hugo. I really need you rather badly . . .

She was getting into the habit of talking aloud to herself. It was a dangerous habit. One day someone might be listening.

Then Uncle Jonas's letter arrived, and she tore it open in the greatest haste. Now there would be an answer to the mystery.

There was not, however. Uncle Jonas merely said:

> I have had a rather large account from Lord and Taylor for a garment you asked them to send you. I have paid it, of course, but it has left me astonished at

the price of ladies' clothes. However, this is your own money, so I won't do anything but caution you about too great extravagance. No one knows what state the world's economy will be in after this European war is over. Disasters on the stock exchange can happen overnight. So don't let your husband and his family think there is a bottomless well.

And that, exasperatingly, was all he had to say.

13

Lionel silently passed the scrap of paper, faded brown, with curling edges, to Hetty.

With difficulty she read the pale handwriting.

My dear husband,

I never meant to deceive you but you had been away so long and your mother had got up the masked ball to amuse us all and cheer our spirits. It was mid-summer eve and balmy, the moon shining. I had a momentary madness. Oh, my dearest husband I had been lonely for so long. Now I am with child . . .

"Jacobina!" Hetty exclaimed.

Lionel nodded. "Dated 1720 if I can decipher the figures correctly. The year George I came to the throne. Exit Queen Anne, and exit Jacobina. Yes, it must have been she."

"And no one knows what happened after her husband got that letter?"

"Only that her baby didn't live, and soon afterwards she died in mysterious circumstances. Perhaps from the result of harsh treatment. Naturally the family hushed up the scandal."

"But they kept her portrait."

"It wasn't destroyed but I should think it was relegated to the attics for a century or so. Until some romantic like you unearthed it and tried to believe poor Jacobina wasn't a wanton, but just high-spirited and reckless."

"And warm-hearted and loving and lonely and neglected by her husband. Surely one lapse should have been forgivable."

"I expect the same rule applied then as it does today. So long as the guilty parties aren't found out. Is that description you just gave me one of yourself, by any chance?"

"In some ways."

"Warm hearted and loving?"

"I hope so."

"I would think so. And other things that you have been too modest to say. Charming and witty and amusing, when not pressed down by secret worries."

"Secret worries?"

"You jumped when I said that. What are you guilty about, Hetty?"

"Not because I'm pregnant like Jacobina," Hetty answered sharply.

"Then what?"

She had to invent an answer. "Perhaps because I'm mistress of this lovely house and I've hardly had a chance to know my husband. It seems a cheat, somehow."

"And perhaps because you haven't been treated very well," Lionel said. "Not by my mother, anyway. She still makes you feel an outsider, doesn't she?"

"A little. But I'm fighting back."

"You have to understand English people like her. They're cool and reserved and disciplined, but quite passionate underneath. When Mother decides to accept you it will be whole-heartedly. So keep on fighting."

"Lionel, how nice you are. If it hadn't been for Kitty and darling Freddie, and now you —"

"Yes? What would you have done?"

He expected her to say she would have gone right back home. Little did he realise she could never do that.

"Oh, I'd have kept on. My mother taught me to face challenges."

Lionel began to smile.

"I'm beginning to admire the Americans more all the time. I'm very glad to have you here, Hetty." He touched her hand. It was the briefest of gestures but the contact sent the warm blood spinning to her head in a way that no touch of Hugo's had ever done.

She said, "I think I'd better read that letter of Jacobina's again. It might be salutory."

Something flashed in his eyes. "These are reckless and uncertain times. Life could be very short. It's only common sense to live as happily as we can."

Not common sense. Not sense at all. Falling in love would be a new and dazzling experience, but she simply couldn't allow it to happen. What a mess it would all be. She must begin a difficult exercise in self-control by spending less time in Lionel's company and reminding herself that she was a rich and important lady, mistress of this wonderful old manor house, and eventually to be mother of its heir. Those things were sufficient. They must not be put in jeopardy by an illicit love affair.

But she didn't think she could have faced her next ordeal without Lionel's help.

A letter had arrived from the American Embassy in London. The mystery of the dress from Lord and Taylor's, still unexplained, had been bad enough, but this was infinitely worse.

Someone from the Embassy had written asking her if she would attempt to identify a young woman, almost certainly a passenger from the *Lusitania*. She had been sheltered by an elderly Irish couple, turf cutters, who lived in an isolated cottage some miles from Kinsale, and who had picked up the young lady half dead from drowning, and suffering from loss of memory some months ago!

They were illiterate peasants. They hadn't known of the sinking of the *Lusitania*. They had been waiting for the young lady to regain her memory and tell them who she was. The wife had cared for her and grown fond of her. They were a lonely couple. Now, the young woman did simple tasks in the small dark cabin, still apparently unaware of who she was or where she had come from.

Recently a nephew of the old people had come from Dublin to visit, and had said they must notify the authorities at once. Someone might be searching for this luckless young woman, and already so much time had gone by. So, reluctantly, the old man had made the long journey by donkey cart to Kinsale, and told his story.

We still have a short list of survivors to be identified, [the letter from the Embassy said]. We think there is a possibility that this young woman could be your missing maid, who appears on the passenger list as Miss Harriet Brown, aged twenty-two years. The young lady has now been brought to London and the wife of one of our staff, Mrs Pamela Brough, is very kindly looking after her. Would it be asking too much of you, Lady Hazzard, to travel to London and see this young person? It would surely be of great comfort to her family to know she was still alive, even in this distressing state, and I am sure comforting to you, too, if by any chance she is your lost maid.

Hetty was shuddering uncontrollably. Now her fancies that she had seen Clemency sitting in the church, or looking in her bedroom window seemed trivial, harmless. This was the real confrontation. Clemency alive, albeit without memory.

What memory might Hetty's face set alight in her dull shocked mind?

Was this the end of all the things she had begun to cherish so deeply? She couldn't bear it. She would rather jump in the dark lake beyond the yew avenue. To die by drowning would surely be ironic justice. She could join that other luckless lady, Jacobina, who had perhaps ended her life there. She, too could come back as a shadow on the garden wall, a rustle of silk skirts on a summer evening.

"Hetty, have you had bad news?" came Julia's voice. The ever watchful Julia. "You look as white as a sheet." The voice went on speaking at large to the people round the table. "Poor Hetty doesn't get many letters, but they all seem to give her a shock."

Sudden sharp anger at Julia's inquisitiveness and maliciousness partially dispersed Hetty's nightmare. The blood flowed back into her face and she was able to say, in a tone of despair,

"It's not finished yet."

"What's not finished yet?" Lady Flora asked quite gently. "Please forgive our curiosity, Hetty. We know that letter isn't from the front because it was in a very rich-looking envelope. Not the kind they issue to the troops."

"It was from the third secretary at the American Embassy in London, Lady Flora. And when I said it's not finished yet, I meant the sinking of the *Lusitania*. This letter says there's a survivor who could be my maid Brown. They want me to go and try to identify her."

"A dead body!" exclaimed Kitty.

"No, no, she's alive, but she's lost her memory. She's been looked after in an Irish cabin in the hills somewhere, and only just discovered."

"You'll have to make a journey to Ireland?" asked Lady Flora.

"Oh, no, it's not as complicated as that. She's been brought to London and I suppose will be sent back to America – I mean if she can't be identified."

"And if she can?" queried Lionel interestedly.

"Why, then –" for a second Hetty held her breath as if she were about to jump into freezing water – "I'll bring her back here. She can live somewhere in this big house and not bother anybody, can't she? What about the grey room? You all said that was so beautifully quiet for someone in my shocked state when I arrived."

There was a brief uncomfortable silence among the women, until Julia asked the inevitable question, "And if she recovers her memory?"

Then I'll have to strangle her, or drown her ... The terrible words jumped into Hetty's mind. However, she was able to answer quite coolly, "In that case, she can be given a position, but I must assure Effie that there's no danger of her being superseded."

"How very unexpected this is." Lady Flora's usually passive face had taken on an alertness, as if life had suddenly become more interesting. "It will be rather an ordeal, but of course you must go and see this poor girl, Hetty. When will you go?"

"Tomorrow. I'll call the Embassy today."

"I'll come with you," said Lionel.

Kitty started up. "Don't be absurd, Lionel. You're in the middle of your convalescence."

'Hetty can't go alone."

"Why ever not? She isn't going into a morgue."

Lionel looked courteously at his wife. "Ah, come, darling, we Hazzards are more hospitable than that. Aren't we, Mother?"

"Perhaps. But I think you should respect Kitty's wishes, Lionel. She's concerned for your health."

"Oh, goodness me!" Julia cried. "Are we to be landed with a semi-idiot girl, as well as Lionel having a relapse?"

Something exploded in Hetty. She pushed back her chair noisily.

"Shut up, all of you! I shall attend to this as I think best, and I don't need my hand held. I'll catch the first train in the morning. Pimm can take me to the station, and I'm old enough to know how to hire cabs, and even to make myself understood in my quaint American language."

She was flushed and belligerent, taking refuge in anger to conceal her churning fear, whipping up a storm over her hurt that Kitty had thought it necessary to play the possessive wife.

"Bravo!" muttered Lionel, and Lady Flora said soothingly, "There's no need to get hysterical, Hetty dear. We do all know how that shipwreck haunts you. You should be more like Katharine Eversleigh, who has such a sensible practical temperament. But won't it be wonderful if that strange woman *is* your faithful maid?"

The train slowly puffed its way out of the small railway station. Pimm, on the platform, gave a respectful salute and turned away. Hetty sank into a seat and allowed herself, for the first time in the last hideous twenty-four hours, to shiver and cry a little. But this was not a situation to be relieved by tears. It was one of overwhelming, nerve-stretching dread.

She was going to look into Clemency's eyes and Clemency into hers. Clemency's may well be vacant, but something would stir, some appeal, some accusation.

One thing was certain, she could never never bring a half-witted Clemency back to Loburn, to live there even in the isolated grey room like an unexploded bomb. She would have to plan something else, something kind and humane, but definitely final.

The door of the compartment opened. It was Lionel. "I came after all," he said simply. "I couldn't risk you getting lost in London. It's a big city. Besides, I wanted to come. I thought after you have settled this interview we could go and look at the historical places all visiting Americans like to see. Or, alternatively, since I'm a selfish fellow, I could show you my favourite places."

Hetty's tears had dried like magic.

"Lionel! What ever will Kitty say?"

"Do you know something, my dear sister-in-law? I'm getting a little tired of being an invalid. It's very boring. And Kitty really has let this nursing thing go to her head, really she has."

184

"She wants to keep you home and safe."

"Is that a thing to do to a man?"

That all too rare radiant delight was coursing through Hetty again. It would be gone in a moment. Especially when she began to think of the difficulty of deciding Clemency's fate, with Lionel watchfully at her side.

So she said nothing but relaxed, leaning back in the seat. Presently he moved across to sit beside her. A little later he took her hand and held it in his. She knew she should take it away, but didn't.

"You're scared," he said. "Your hand's cold. Give me the other one and I'll warm them both."

Inevitably, at the American Embassy, Lionel was mistaken for her husband. After a feeble attempt to get matters straight, Hetty decided that this game of impostors was becoming dangerously addictive. More satisfyingly, she saw that Lionel was enjoying it. He caught her eye, gave a small warning shake of his head, and made no protest when he was addressed as Lord Hazzard.

It was a different matter when they arrived at the terraced house in Chelsea, a neat dwelling with bay trees on either side of the front door and a shining bronze door knocker.

The shattering cold had possessed Hetty again. She was gripping her hands to hide their trembling.

"Lionel, it would be best if I were taken alone to see this girl. In case she's very nervous. I mean, a man, a complete stranger –"

"Might frighten her to death," said Lionel gravely.

"Don't you dare laugh at me."

"Hetty! Hetty! Hold my hand. Stop shaking."

The door opened and a neatly-dressed parlour maid stood there.

"You'll be Lord and Lady Hazzard? Will you step inside. The mistress is expecting you."

A blonde woman, uncomfortably like Clemency's New

York friends, chic, well-groomed and vivacious, came hurrying to take Hetty's hand.

"Do come in, Lady Hazzard, Lord Hazzard." She showed them into a small charming drawing room. "Will you have coffee or hot chocolate, or something stronger, before going upstairs?"

Hetty said in a dry hoarse voice completely unlike her own, "I'd rather go at once, if you don't mind. After all, poor girl, she's been waiting more than a year."

"I don't think she knows much about that, Lady Hazzard. But seeing you might spark something in her memory. That's what we all thought. I'll lead the way, shall I? Lord Hazzard –"

"He'll wait downstairs. He never knew – my maid."

The girl sat at the window in a small bedroom overlooking a neat garden. She seemed absorbed in whatever it was she saw, roses in bloom, a robin, grey London pigeons on the next door roof. She was slim-waisted, dark-haired, graceful. She only turned her head when the American woman spoke quite loudly.

"Harriet! Harriet, here's someone to see you."

The dark head turned slowly, slowly. Hetty groped for something to hold on to, the back of a chair. The room was swimming round her.

The sunburnt freckled face, the turned-up nose, the smallish blue eyes, were not Clemency's. Pert and merry it must once have been, this poor little bewildered countenance. But never Clemency's.

Hetty could shake her head, breathing deeply in blessed reprieve.

"Not remotely like her. I'm sorry. All your trouble for nothing."

"All your trouble, Lady Hazzard. You've had a wasted journey. But we felt we must try every avenue."

"Should I talk to her?"

"She won't understand."

"I thought she had only lost her memory."

"No, worse than that. She's like a child. Perhaps she always was, who knows? Well, I guess we'll get her sent back to the States and cared for. Perhaps some day someone who knows her will turn up. Isn't this war just terrible?"

The vivaciously pretty woman, as sparkling and fresh as a spring morning – already Hetty had forgotten her name because this episode must be completely erased from her memory – led the way downstairs.

Lionel looked up in sharp enquiry. Hetty shook her head.

"A complete stranger. Poor creature. There's nothing we can do."

"You've had a wasted journey, Lord Hazzard."

"Not wasted, Mrs Brough." There, he remembered the woman's name. He was much more trained in courtesy than Hetty. "We have other things to do in London. So shall we get on, darling?"

Hetty murmured, "I'm so sorry for that poor child. It makes one realise how lucky one is oneself."

She tucked her hand in Lionel's arm. She wanted to hurry away before the American woman saw the glow of relief in her face.

Out in the street, the relief came bursting out of her. She gave a little skip, exclaiming in a heartfelt voice,

"Thank goodness that's over. What a lovely day it is. How shall we enjoy it? Suggest something, Lionel. Could we go on the river? Are there still boat excursions in the middle of a war? There must be something for soldiers and their girl friends to do." She blushed in embarrassment. "I didn't mean it that way for us."

"Pity," said Lionel. "Of course we can go on the river. We can walk to one of the landing stages from here." He was looking at her curiously. "But what a funny girl you are. Half an hour ago you were shivering with terror, and now you're skipping like a child. Did you escape from some nightmare in that room upstairs?"

Hetty lowered her head. She began counting the paving stones, an old trick to induce calm.

"I suppose I did. Anything to do with the *Lusitania* makes me go cold. I guess it's always going to."

"I can understand that, but I don't understand why you seemed relieved that that poor waif wasn't who they thought she was."

"Brown. Harriet Brown. No, I wasn't relieved about that, Lionel, only that the ordeal was over. Oh God, I don't want ever to have to think of that horrible time again." For a moment she was sombre. "But I'll have to, of course. All my life, I expect."

The sun was shining warmly on her face, and the horror fading. Euphoria seized her again.

"Lionel, let's have a lovely day."

"If you go on looking like that we'll have an idyllic one. What a strange little creature you are, jumping from light to dark, dark to light."

"Don't we all?"

"No one as passionately as you."

They caught a boat just about to leave on its cruise through Putney, Richmond and Teddington. It was only half full, women with children, some very young soldiers with their girls. Lionel guided Hetty to the bow where there were empty seats. He said that he had never gone down the Thames on a river boat before, and marvelled at the pleasures tourists had.

"Wait until I take you round New York harbour," Hetty said, and then wondered whatever had possessed her to say such a thing, as if she and Lionel would eventually make much longer journeys than the one today.

"Did you do that with Hugo?"

"No, I didn't. I don't think he would have been interested. We didn't have much time together in New York."

"I know that. You married a stranger. You've told me."

"No, that isn't fair. He wasn't a stranger. And he was

188

so handsome. I can tell you, all my girl friends envied me madly."

"Hetty, you're chattering again."

"You keep asking questions."

"Why do you think Hugo wouldn't have been interested in going round New York harbour? And that I would?"

"Well – Hugo would have preferred a horse to a harbour ferry. And you would choose the boat."

"You're laughing at me."

"I have to if I'm not to get angry with you. The way you keep nagging me about why I married Hugo. Do I ask you why you married Kitty?"

"Do you want to know?"

His glance was suddenly so direct and challenging that she flushed and looked away, abruptly nervous.

"I'm sorry, Lionel. It's none of my business."

His fingers stroked her wrist lightly.

"No, it isn't your business. And I have no business asking questions about you and Hugo." He slid his arm round her waist. "Lean against me. Be my girl properly for today at least."

She did as she was told, leaning her cheek against his tunic, half-closing her eyes. If she was to be his girl for today the day must be made to last for a long time. Hugo, Loburn, the possible heir, were yesterday's and tomorrow's problems. Today she was going to be in love with the sun and the glassy green water and the floating swans. And Lionel of the gentle thoughtful face, who would look so well in a portrait at Loburn. If Hugo were killed in France, as he could so easily be, Lionel would become the eleventh baron, inheriting Loburn. What then? The thought slid in and out of Hetty's mind. Would she be the loser after all? Or could she persuade Lionel to leave Kitty and Freddie? She was so deeply committed now by her deceit that even this did not seem too big an obstacle. At all costs, Loburn must remain hers, like salvage from a shipwreck, which, as far as she was concerned, was exactly what it was. She hadn't sunk herself so far in perjury to end with nothing.

Immersed in her thoughts, her nerves contracted and she gave a great shudder.

"What's the matter? You can't be cold."

"A little. Only a little."

"Then I'll hold you closer."

The problems faded, peace came back.

When they got home, however, just before the summer dusk had turned to dark, it was Lionel who was shaking, not with cold but with fever. Kitty was furious.

"How could you do such a stupid thing, Hetty? How could you allow him to go to London and have such a long day?"

"She — d-didn't. I s-stole a march on her." Lionel's teeth were chattering and he was about to collapse. It had been a dreadful train journey, the illness had come on him so suddenly.

"Well, you were mad. You're still convalescent. Am I to spend all my time getting you well only to have you behave in this crazy way? Now you're going straight to bed. I'll help you upstairs."

"S-sorry," said Lionel to no one in particular, and then he was whisked away on Kitty's capable arm.

Hetty was almost as tired as Lionel. The emotions of the day had exhausted her. She was in no mood for Julia's interrogation which was about to come.

"Well, tell us, Hetty. What about the girl? Did you recognise her?"

"No."

"She might have changed a little?"

"She was no one I knew, certainly not my maid."

"How sad," said Lady Flora. "Did she talk to you?"

"No. She was like a child. Or half-witted if you prefer that description."

"There's no need to sound so hard, Hetty dear."

"I'm sorry. It was very distressing. But I can't cry about it."

"But what made you so late home?" Julia asked. "Surely it didn't take you this long to see the girl?"

"No. We went on the river. It seemed a nice way to spend the rest of the day." Hetty looked steadily at Julia. "You've all been telling me I should go to London and see things. I didn't invite Lionel to come but he did anyway, and I enjoyed it. He did, too, until he got a bit overdone. Now if you'll excuse me, I'd like to go to bed."

She woke to daylight and Freddie's face at her pillow.

"Hetty, Mother's pretty angry with you."

"I know."

"For making Daddy sick again."

"How is Daddy?"

"He's had his medicine and he's asleep. I'm not to disturb him."

"So you're disturbing me instead."

"I thought we might play Hector and Achilles and Helen."

"Helen?"

"Helen of Troy. Daddy was telling me about her. He said you would make a good Helen."

"I think sometimes we might play another game," Hetty said uneasily. "Your mother's perfectly right, the *Iliad* is much too advanced for a five-year-old. We'll all be living in a fantasy world."

"What's that?"

"A world of dreams that is sometimes rather nicer than the real world."

She thought of Kitty beside Lionel's sickbed. Beneath her rumpled and careless appearance, Kitty was a strong-minded woman who would fight for what was hers.

"Life isn't all romance and heroes," she said to the earnest little face beside her. "It's much more often simply doing what you're told and obeying rules. Not so much fun, really. But safer."

"How dull," said Freddie precociously.

She sat in Jacobina's garden every afternoon while the summer deepened and the colours in her needlework were the colours about her, the fresh green of the grass, the coral and cream of the roses, the rich blue sky. She knew that she was trying to perpetuate the scene in every way possible, supposing it should not last for her.

At last Lionel was permitted outdoors again and he found her there. He looked skeletally thin and pale, but the quick delight was in his eyes.

"Hetty, why didn't you come and visit the invalid? Relieve his tedium?"

"I don't think Kitty would have approved. I'm still in her bad books."

"Nonsense. She doesn't hold grudges. And I apologised for my thoughtlessness. Not abjectly, but just humbly enough. And one thing that has pleased her is that this relapse makes it less likely I'll pass my next medical board. It looks as if my soldiering days may be over. Are you pleased, too, Hetty? What's the matter? You look so serious."

Hetty took a letter from her pocket and handed it to him.

"Hugo," she said. "This arrived today."

"What does he say?"

"He's got some leave at last. He'll be home for our party. Isn't that good luck? He must have pulled a string or two. I begged him to if he could."

"Hetty, you sound just like a hostess."

"How does that sound?"

"Brittle. Efficient. Not my companion on the river at all."

"That was another day," she said. Her voice was even. She must never let him or anyone know that she was quaking inside with nervousness. She expected to find Hugo changed. That was inevitable after his long ordeal in a nightmare world. But how changed would he find her? And did her determination to make their marriage a success remain as total as it had been? Was she thinking of the way out, the simple admission that the records in the parish register were a forgery?

Never.

Never, never.

The thing was to avoid Lionel's company as much as possible. That perceptive face that made her heart turn over with delight could be her undoing.

14

Bands of sunlight stretching across the lawn had the yellowness of sunset. The day had been exceptionally hot, the garden floating in a heat haze that made it seem like a mirage. Was everything a mirage, and had it been so all the time? Tiredness and anxiety were making Hetty's mind woolly and confused. She rose from her vigil at the window. She must go upstairs and get ready for the party. People would soon be arriving, and although no one now felt in the mood for a party, it was too late to cancel it.

All yesterday and again today had been a time of impossible tension. Hugo hadn't specified the time of his arrival but from his letter Hetty had assumed it would be some time on Friday, later perhaps rather than earlier. She had stayed up until after midnight, waiting. Now it was Saturday evening and he still had not arrived, neither had there been any news of any kind.

Julia had spent most of the twenty-four hours lurking compulsively near the telephone and Hetty had sat at the window of her drawing room, watching the long shady curve of the drive. Lady Flora had played the piano a great deal, the house echoing with the dreamy melancholy music. At meals, the only time when they were all together, everyone was taut and listening.

"Trust Hugo never to be definite with his plans," Julia said in a sudden outburst. "You know that, Lady Flora. He's always liable to change his mind."

"You can't change your mind about specific leave," Kitty said. "Can you, Lionel?"

"I shouldn't think so, unless there's suddenly been a reason to cancel it."

"What reason would that be?" Hetty asked tensely.

"Oh, an unexpected enemy attack, a shortage of officers, orders from headquarters. But I don't suppose it's any of those things. Hugo's probably just had trouble getting transport down from the lines. The railway may have been shelled. He may have to wait until tomorrow."

"If I know Hugo, he'd have taken a motor cycle. Or a horse," Julia said, with a short unhappy laugh.

"It's not much use conjecturing, is it?" said Lionel. "We'll just have to wait."

Lady Flora, who was looking alarmingly fragile, her eyes set in smoky blue hollows, said calmly, "I know he'll arrive. I'm his mother. I sense these things."

"Then look into a crystal ball and put us out of our suspense," said Kitty flippantly. Hetty realised uneasily that Kitty had particularly wanted Hugo here for the party, if only to restore a little balance. It was altogether too much to expect Lionel to look after four women. Especially when one of them was Hetty, who was surely going to knock everyone's eyes out with that gorgeous green silk dress that no one in this war-deprived country could match.

Hetty had thought she could never bring herself to wear the dress since it reminded her so sharply of Clemency and of the mystery of its arrival. She had thrust it out of sight in her wardrobe and tried to forget it.

However, she had realised that not to wear it on this first suitable occasion would arouse suspicions. Another subtle reason was that she could carry off her welcome to Hugo more convincingly if she felt like Clemency. Clemency was Hugo's. Hetty was no longer sure whose she was, except that behind her eyelids, inside her skull, it was always Lionel's face that appeared.

Effie, escaping from duties downstairs, had come to help her to dress. As she tugged at the tiny buttons down the back of the dress, Hetty heard Clemency's scolding voice so clearly – "Brown, you're clumsy, you're pinching me" – that she drew in her breath in an audible gasp.

"Sorry, my lady, am I pulling too tight? The waist is just a fraction small. You must have put on a little weight."

No, she hadn't. She had always been an inch bigger round the waist than Clemency. But that was a fact that Miss Natalia at Lord and Taylor's would not have had in her records.

"It does catch me a little, Effie. It's so hot, I feel swollen with heat."

"It's thundery weather. There'll probably be a storm later."

"Not before midnight, I hope. We want to be in the garden."

"Can't tell, can you, my lady?"

"I wonder if we should go on with this party now that my husband hasn't arrived."

"You have to, don't you, my lady?" Effie said sensibly. "People expect it of you to go on as usual in spite of the war. Sets an example, they say, though I don't know who to." Effie had a nice turn in irony. "Could it be the Germans? Anyway, his lordship's bound to arrive before the night's over. You cheer up. You look ever so lovely."

"What's Miss Julia wearing?"

"I don't know, my lady. It won't be anything new, I don't expect. Do you think just a mite of rouge on your cheeks? You look a bit pale."

"I'm scared."

"About the master?"

"About everything." She was clenching her hands. It was this damned dress filling her with apprehension. Would the nightmare that Clemency was watching her never grow less?

"I guess I'm just in a nervous mood," she said.

"It's the thundery weather, my lady. And the waiting."

After Effie had gone she felt too nervous and restless to stay alone. She made her way downstairs, intending to look over the preparations as she had seen Mrs Jervis do a hundred times in New York.

She didn't expect to come on Lionel and Kitty, and indeed backed out of the drawing room when she saw them. She sensed that they were having a private conversation, but as she turned to go she distinctly heard Kitty say, "You're in love with her, aren't you, Lionel?" and she stopped compulsively to listen.

"Yes, a little, I think," he said, and a shiver of dismay and delight went through her. Of course it must be she to whom Kitty was referring.

There followed a long silence. Go away, Hetty admonished herself. You'll hear too much and regret it. But she stood rooted in her elegant green gown. A Clemency figure. Clemency would have listened and gleefully turned her gained knowledge to her advantage.

Then Kitty said in a rush, in a hopeful eager voice,

"You've been so ill, darling, you're having hallucinations. I see this happening all the time with the men in the wards. We call their fantasies waking nightmares."

"This is far from being a nightmare."

"Whatever it is, you'll wake up from it. You must. It would be all so impossible. So intolerable. That little cheat from New York."

"Why is she a cheat?"

"Because she's both bold and terror-stricken. Every now and then something scares her. We've all noticed. I didn't at first, but now I do. Your mother and Julia always have."

"Oh, come, Kitty. You have far too much common sense for this kind of nonsense. All that scares Hetty is whether she's going to get her husband home safely or not. Poor girl, let's be kind to her."

"Don't you spend too much time with her tonight," said Kitty ominously. "You and her with your heads together in the library all day. I won't stand for it, Lionel. It's not fair."

"Silly girl," said his voice at its most tender. Hetty slipped away, determined to listen no more. The overheard conversation had done nothing to calm her agitation. Did Lady Flora and Kitty truly think she was a cheat? She had always known Julia's feelings, but they had been induced by jealousy. Lady Flora perhaps had been prejudiced. She wouldn't have wanted an American daughter-in-law. But Kitty had been open and friendly and kind. If she were to go over to the enemy there was no one here whom Hetty could trust. Anymore than they can trust you, said her inner voice. Except Lionel, of course.

And thinking of him sent the spontaneous delight coursing through her veins. Supposing, Hetty found herself thinking, Hugo didn't come home tonight, supposing he never came home because he had been killed in France. Lionel would be the new owner of Loburn, and their collaboration over its restoration could grow closer and closer. Life could become intensely exciting.

She remembered Kitty saying once that they would be known as the Hazzard wives. But – sharing one husband? Never! Things would have to be better arranged than that.

The shock, when she came face to face with Clemency at the end of the dimly-lit hall, was appalling.

Her eyes flinched away, and so, surprisingly, did Clemency's.

"Isn't that dress a little tight for you, Hetty?"

Hetty spun round, pale and breathless, to face Julia who must have followed her across the hall. But hadn't Julia seen Clemency?

Stupid, stupid, it was her own reflection in the long smoky mirror which had always been in that corner. She must have looked in it dozens of times. But never before when she had been wearing an arresting green silk dress that roused the sharpest memories of her late mistress.

"Just round the waist," she admitted reluctantly. "I must have put on a little weight."

"We hadn't noticed it. Your other clothes aren't too tight?"

"Then Miss Natalia has made a mistake in cutting."

"I thought she was such a paragon."

"Everyone can make a mistake some time."

"Indeed," Julia agreed. "Indeed."

Hetty hated being caught by Julia in a vulnerable moment. The way that woman watched her was intolerable. Now even Kitty had begun to watch her and call her a cheat.

"This dress is uncomfortable, you're perfectly right. I don't think I will wear it after all."

"Oh, do keep it on. After all your trouble in getting it sent from New York. All the same, Lady Flora and I were both a bit surprised when we saw it. We thought it rather flamboyant for someone as quiet as you. You are quiet, aren't you? Or are you just pretending?"

"I didn't send for the dress," Hetty said angrily. "You know I didn't."

"Even so it was your taste. Once. Or was it? A pity the size isn't quite right."

Hetty turned away from the probing gaze. But that was a mistake, too, for she was confronted by the mirror and the startling image of Clemency again.

"Lucky you," said Julia. "I haven't had a new dress for over a year. My old white satin has to appear again."

The white satin, whatever its age, made her look regal. She had piled her hair on top of her head so that she seemed inches taller. Her flat body was as straight and slender as a taper. It only needed her eyes to glow, as they undoubtedly would when Hugo arrived, for her to be astonishingly beautiful. But just at present the anxiety showed beneath the make-up. She was even more tense than Hetty, which no doubt accounted for her pin-pricking behaviour.

How were they to get through the evening?

As it happened, there was no time for Hetty to change her dress, or even to worry about the evening, for the first guests were arriving, a group of officers from a nearby convalescent home.

The men hesitated between Hetty and Julia, and finally formed a circle round Hetty.

They introduced themselves, apologising for their assorted infirmities, a stiff leg, an arm in a sling, an empty sleeve . . .

"We've still got the insides of our heads intact. We hope. Is that tall good-looking lady our hostess? Should we have spoken to her first?"

There were more people arriving and greeting Julia with uninhibited cries of pleasure.

"Hunting types," muttered one young lieutenant to the other, and turned back to Hetty with relief. "May we stay with you? You look friendlier than her."

"I am, too." Hetty laughed, enjoying their admiration.

"You're an American! Say, that's interesting."

"My name's Hetty. Actually I'm Lady Hazzard," she smiled mischievously. "And your hostess. But do call me Hetty."

She beckoned to Bates to bring drinks for the embarrassed men, and looked frankly at their infirmities, the empty sleeve, the leg that would probably remain permanently stiff. "Aren't you all lucky, you won't have to go back to the front again. My brother-in-law may be invalided out of the army, too. My husband is another matter. We're expecting him home on leave this weekend, but he hasn't turned up. I'm sure he will before the party's over. We mustn't let that spoil the fun."

She didn't miss the quick significant look that passed

from one to the other. In their experience, anyone who didn't turn up was dead.

As she had anticipated, this was going to be a long and difficult evening, and how hot it still was. The green silk, too tight for comfort, was sticking to her. What did she do next? Lady Flora would not approve of her allowing herself to be monopolised by three young army officers, but she had never been to a party before, something no one realised.

"Don't go away, Hetty. You're the prettiest girl here," one of the young officers was saying.

"I'm not going away. But you must meet other people. Sit down if you want to, or wander in the garden. It smells delicious in the dark. Oh, here's my sister-in-law. Kitty, these boys are from the convalescent home. Maybe you nursed them in hospital?" She lowered her voice. "Do I have to talk to those hunting people?"

"Of course. You should talk to everybody. Surely you know that?"

The scolding whisper made Hetty's cheeks flush. Now the room was full and very noisy. Words reached her from Julia's friends. "Nice filly he's got, ha ha ' Did that mean a horse or herself? "The one in the stables is better," Julia answered, and there was a burst of laughter. Hetty sought for innocuous people, the nice bank manager, the vicar and his wife. Clemency, she knew, would not have behaved like this. She would have made herself the centre of attention all the time. But no one here knew that, except Hugo, and still there was no sign of him. As time went on she had an overwhelming urge to be near the door, not only so that she would be the first to welcome him when he came, but to breathe some fresh air.

A hand closed gently round her bare arm.

"I was right from the beginning. You *are* a mermaid." She had jumped at his touch.

"Oh, Lionel, I'm so edgy, waiting for Hugo."

In contrast to the pallor of his face, his eyes looked deeply black.

"Jacobina waited longer than you have. Don't you remember what she wrote? *You had been away so long and I was lonely* ... It's appallingly hot in here. Do you think we could stroll outside for a while? We won't be missed now Julia has her gaggle of elderly colonels. Do people like that ever lower their voices, you were going to say. No, never."

"Those young officers –"

"Nurse Kitty has taken command there. And Mother's got all her old admirers round her. The Hazzards at play. We haven't exposed you to this kind of nonsense before, have we? Do you want to run away from it?"

"I can't, can I?"

"You can do anything in the world you like." She wondered if he were a little drunk, but already he was guiding her towards the door, and she was longing for the cooler air, and the darkness.

"Are you very upset that Hugo hasn't turned up?"

"Of course I am. I'm desperately worried."

The gravel crunched beneath their feet. They walked towards the yew walk and the black glass glimmer of the lake. It was very dark, with no stars. Surely that massing blackness over their heads was thunder clouds. Kitty had said to Lionel, "*That little cheat from New York.*"

With some subtle questioning, was that description what he was setting out to establish now?

"If Hugo never came home again –"

"Don't say that!"

"There would be me and you still." He drew her closer to him, in the darkness, and then she was in his arms. The radiant excitement was blotting out all discretion, all sense. She had so longed for this kiss.

And now I am with child ... Jacobina's forlorn words slid in and out of her mind. Lionel, this is wrong ...

202

Kitty, Freddie, Hugo, they're all watching. Everyone watches me all the time.

But what was wrong about such a natural melting together? It had been inevitable from the day of their first meeting when he had stirred in the chair by the fire and gazed at her.

"Hetty!" He drew away. "Let's sit by the lake. We have to talk."

Before they could move however, there was a brilliant flash of lightning and the flowers in the garden sprang out at them, roses, night stock, rosy petunias, in an arabesque of colour that almost instantly vanished. A portentous roll of thunder shook the warm air.

"Damn!" said Lionel. "Do you mind getting wet?"

The merest quiver of dread touched her.

"Not on this hot night. Lionel, I should tell you, I overheard something you and Kitty were saying this evening. She accused you of being in love with me, and then she called me 'that little cheat from New York'. Why did she say that?"

"They're all jealous of you."

"Do you think I'm a cheat?"

"Only when I'm not allowed to kiss you."

There was a rustling in the bushes and trees, as raindrops began to fall. Hetty felt her bare arms splashed, and her face.

"Lionel, how can we be in love? There are too many complications."

He was quiet and persuasive. "Let's just enjoy ourselves at this minute. Later –"

The thunder crashed again, and in mid-sentence Lionel's words were drowned as a cloudburst descended on them. Water ran down Hetty's neck and into her eyes, blinding her, and trickled into her mouth chokingly. Cold drenching streams of water that brought back powerful memories of drowning, of being weighted down by heavy skirts, unable to move, to see, to breathe. The nightmare was so vivid that she momentarily lost consciousness.

She recovered, to feel the rain still falling on her face, and Lionel holding her, and a dim memory in her head of screams.

"Clemency! Clemency!" The distraught voice floating over the sea.

Had that been her voice? Oh, dear God!

"We ought to get out of this," said Lionel. Was there just the least stiffness in his voice? "It's easing off a little. We'll slip in the back way. Don't worry, we won't be the only ones to get a drenching. Feel better now?"

Hetty stirred. She felt achingly tired.

"Yes. Sorry. What happened?"

"I think you fainted. Scared of thunderstorms?"

"No. Only of water."

"Of course. I understand. Afraid your dress is ruined."

"I'll have to change. So will you. Oh dear, you won't catch a chill, will you? This time Kitty will never forgive me."

Kitty, the wife.

"Lionel, we haven't talked."

"No. We were rudely interrupted. By God, I imagine."

"I thought I heard some screaming." Her voice was tentative. "Was it me?"

"Yes."

The thunder crashed again, farther off, a retreating menace.

"Words?"

"Not very intelligible."

But she knew he had heard her crying for Clemency who was drowning. What was he to make of that?

Trembling, her cold wet fingers clinging to his they made their way back to the house and were able to slip up the garden stairs unobserved. They did have a little luck.

Not much, however, as the next day proved. The

yellow telegram with its stark message, that Major Lord Hazzard was seriously wounded in France, arrived just after breakfast.

This time it was Julia, not Hetty, who fainted.

15

"Do you want to talk, Hetty?" asked Lionel in his gentle courteous voice, catching up with her as she walked up and down, up and down, the gravel drive.

"What would I say?"

He shook his head slowly. "There isn't anything to say, I suppose. You'll have to stay with Hugo. I'm sure you've already made that decision."

"Yes, I have. Of course."

Of course I have, she added silently and furiously. Because I am not so heartless as to leave a sick husband, and besides that would mean leaving Loburn. Which is one thing I will not do, now or at any time. It was the only thing in this rocking world which represented stability. Clemency would have agreed, had she been faced with this situation. They were both granddaughters of a highly successful American property man, after all.

"Kitty tells me I fantasise." Lionel looked hollow-cheeked, and very tired. "Perhaps I do."

Was he telling her he didn't love her, he had only been playing a game? Her chin went up.

"We've encouraged you," said Hetty. "Freddie and I. We loved your *Iliad* stories. I expect it's dull, being a convalescent. Hugo will find that, too."

"But he'll have you," Lionel said briefly.

No, he'll have Julia. And you'll have Kitty and Freddie, and their life won't be messed up and there won't be any more of those irridescent dreams. Besides, you don't entirely trust me after last night, do you, Lionel? I can see

t in your eyes . . . Why, why? Why is it always me who is
he outsider?

This thought came back to her frequently in the days
hat followed. She thought of Julia's regal beauty in her
vhite satin dress. No wonder she had been mistaken for
he lady of the house on the night of the party. She would
ave been much more suitable in that role than this vola-
ile American who, even after a year, remained a stranger.
As if there were some insurmountable barrier between
er and an English family.

Of course there was – but this was not as they thought,
er nationality. It was her guilt.

After two anxious weeks of trying to get news of Hugo
and the extent of his wounds, they heard at last that he
vas in hospital in France, and would be sent back to
England when he was fit to travel. He had suffered severe
njuries, losing a leg, and an eye.

The last, no doubt, explained the letter from his batman
o Hetty.

Dear Lady Hazzard,

I been to see the Major in hospital and he has asked me
to write to you and tell you he don't want anyone to try
to come and see him. Specially you. You'll have to be
patient, my lady. Nasty wounds upset a man's mind. I
know this as well as anyone, having been 1 year and 6
weeks at the front. You better respect his wishes. I'm
ever so sorry to lose him, he was kind and considerate,
a real gentleman.

Yours respectfully,
Andy Wright (Cpl)

Lady Flora was unexpectedly kind.

"Come, my dear. Sensitive men don't like their wives
o see them in extremity."

But Hetty had never thought Hugo a particularly sensitive man. If he had been, how could he have allowed his

mistress to stay on in the house after his marriage?

"Why am I always being punished?" she burst out.

"Punished? I don't know what you mean. You are only one of thousands of young wives whose husbands have suffered dreadful injuries. You simply must be brave and accept things as they are. Wait patiently until Hugo comes home. That is what we all have to do." She added thoughtfully, "Unless there is some special reason why you think you ought to be punished."

"Why ever should I think that?" Hetty said aggressively.

The big limpid eyes surveyed her. After a long pause, Lady Flora said, "Perhaps because you're an American and aren't buoyed up by patriotic feelings, since this isn't your country's war. Though I would have thought by now that you would have felt completely on our side."

At last she escaped from Lady Flora's subtly barbed tongue. The gloom of the winter drawing room on a summer afternoon was exactly suited to her mood.

Serve you right, serve you right. This is your punishment for your wicked deceit, being tied to a disabled bad-tempered difficult husband for the rest of your life.

But she was still Lady Hazzard, she told herself over and over. She was still entitled to be mistress of this lovely old house, even if she had an impotent husband. Impotent? No one had suggested that, except perhaps by innuendo. As Lady Flora had wisely counselled, one must wait and see. But her chances for love had gone. Lionel, with his beautiful face, his charming fantasies, had taken that away.

If she sometimes thought she heard Clemency laughing at her in those haunted days, she told herself it was pure fancy. Clemency couldn't go on tormenting her all her life, could she?

People forgot. One day no one would remember how she had been a shivering naked waif dragged out of the sea. With only the badge of gold round her wrist to establish her identity. The bride from the sea.

Freddie, at least, remained her friend. His shining owlish eyes were fixed on her in awe and sympathy.

"Daddy says Uncle Hugo will have a black patch over his eye. He'll look like a pirate. Will you like that, Hetty?"

"Oh, I expect I won't mind it too much for myself. Only for Uncle Hugo."

"You won't be frightened?"

"Of my husband? Goodness me, no."

"Mummy says he'll be a bad patient. Does that mean he's going to die?"

"No, no, it means he may be a bit difficult. Angry. That will be a good sign. It will mean he's getting better."

"Why don't you cry, Hetty? Julia cries."

"Julia's a silly emotional woman," Hetty said sharply.

Freddie stared at her, his gaze far too contemplative for a five-year-old.

"Well, I love you, Hetty, no matter what they say."

Hetty smiled steadily at the staunch little face. "What do they say, Freddie?"

"They say it was a mistake you and Uncle Hugo getting married."

"Who says it?"

"Oh – they do. Nanny, too, once, but Mummy told her to mind her own business."

Hetty said, "It wasn't a mistake."

"Oh, that's good, Hetty." Freddie jumped up and down with relief. "I didn't want you to go away."

"I have no intention of going away, little frog. But I'll need you as a friend."

"Against the Trojans?"

"Exactly."

If she was not allowed to go to France to see Hugo in hospital, she at least insisted on being entirely responsible

209

for the preparations for his return.

He was not to go to a military hospital in England, he was to be brought straight home to Loburn. She had managed to find a male nurse, a grey-haired ex-ambulance man, Patrick Mahoney, who had been wounded and invalided out of the Ambulance Corps. He was physically strong and imperturbable, used to coping with angry frustrated young men who hated infirmity and their permanently broken bodies. The officers were often the worst, he said; other ranks were more phlegmatic. Perhaps they had been used to expecting less, he said philosophically. Hetty liked him. His stoical manner would not irritate Hugo. He could sleep in Hugo's dressing room, while Hugo occupied, as was his right, the big double bed, the Loburn marriage bed.

Julia said agitatedly, "You're not expecting to share that bed with him, are you, Hetty? It would be quite impossible. I mean, an amputated leg. Oh, poor darling Hugo."

"But he'll recover," said Hetty quietly. "There are such things as artificial limbs. We'll get him fitted as soon as it's possible. In the meantime I plan to move back to the grey room. My first haven, remember?"

"Haven?" Julia had flushed.

"After the cold sea, that's what it seemed."

The summer moved slowly and serenely on, darkened only by the news from France, the mounting casualties and the all too familiar stalemate of the Somme battles. And by the waiting. Hugo's arrival was delayed and then delayed again. What was happening? Something about his wounds not healing. News was indirect. Nobody had had a letter from Hugo himself. Perhaps he was unable to write.

Then suddenly, with no warning at all, he arrived home.

Hetty had been at the military hospital, doing her usual

task of writing and reading letters to the badly incapacitated men. Kitty was there, too, and when they returned home together, Bates came out, his usual aplomb vanished. He looked an old man, shaken and distressed.

"The master's home, my lady."

Hetty held her breath.

"Oh, Bates, how is he?"

"Didn't look that good, my lady," Bates seemed strangely evasive. "But it was a long drive for him."

"Where is he?" asked Kitty.

"He went upstairs, madam. Said he didn't want to see anyone at present."

"He could walk?"

"On crutches, madam. With some difficulty, I observed, but he refused help." The reason for Bates' evasiveness became clear. "It's no use your going up, my lady. He's locked his door."

Oh God, it was going to be worse than she had anticipated.

"But of course I'm going up, Bates. He won't refuse to see his wife. Has someone telephoned for Patrick Mahoney?"

"That's no use either, my lady. His lordship made it clear he didn't want anyone."

"But he must have someone. He has to eat and undress and wash and all that."

"Those were his lordship's orders, my lady," Bates said. He was plainly upset. "Perhaps he'll listen to you."

"He'd better. He hasn't come home to starve himself to death!"

"Go easy, Hetty," Kitty said quietly. "You've seen how a lot of these boys come home."

Shaken and crying and half-demented, or utterly silent, sitting huddled on their beds, refusing to respond to anybody.

But Hugo wouldn't be like that. He was older, an officer, brave, self-disciplined.

"Has anyone tried to persuade him to open his door, Bates?"

"Yes, my lady. Lady Flora, and then Miss Julia."

Did he refuse to speak to Julia, too?

"Did he say anything?"

"Not as far as I learned, my lady. Lady Flora decided he must have fallen asleep. Which is very likely because he did look done in."

"I'll go and see," Hetty said.

"Oh, my lady –"

"Yes, Bates?"

"Be prepared for a shock, my lady."

"Of course. We know he had bad injuries. He can't be anything but greatly changed."

She tapped gently at the door.

"Hugo!" No answer.

"Hugo, it's me, Hetty."

"Hugo, it's your wife."

The silence continued.

"Hugo!"

She was afraid he might have fallen and be lying helpless. Or that, as his mother had surmised, he had collapsed on the bed and fallen so deeply asleep that no polite knocking was going to rouse him.

Kitty had come up the stairs to stand beside her.

"Would he be likely to be sleeping so soundly?" Hetty whispered.

The two women looked at each other. In Kitty's experience, and less completely in Hetty's, few of the men back from the front slept soundly unless drugged. They twitched and turned and cried out in half sleep, and came sharply awake in terror when disturbed.

"He's being bloody minded," Kitty said. "He can be. That's a side of him you haven't encountered, perhaps."

"I hardly know him at all," Hetty admitted. "I've never

had time, and the circumstances have always been unpropitious."

"No peaceful cruises on the river," Kitty said, but without malice. "Poor Hetty. But you're not the only wife who's had a rough time. At least you have your husband home, whatever shape he's in." She rapped loudly on the door, and spoke in her authoritative nurse's voice. "Hugo, are you listening? You've got to let us in. Otherwise we'll have to get someone to come and take the lock off the door."

The silence continued for a moment, then there was a shuffling sound, and something gave a loud crack. Hetty jumped, startled, but Kitty grinned and said, "My guess is he's just given something a violent whack with one of his crutches. Good sign. The more angry he is, the more alive he is."

"Come on, Hugo," she cajoled. "You've got to let us see you some time."

At last his voice, loud and furious, answered. "Can't I have any privacy even in my own home?"

"As much as you like," Hetty called. "But just unlock the door. We're worried about you."

"You don't need to be. I'm only half dead so far. I'll see you when I decide to, not before. And don't listen to old Bates's horror stories."

Hetty couldn't keep the nervousness out of her voice. "What do you mean?"

Kitty nudged her to be silent.

"Come on, Hugo. I've been nursing badly wounded men for over a year. You can't shock me."

"Go to hell," came the uncompromising response.

"Very well," said Kitty cheerfully. "You take a rest. Come downstairs when you're ready."

"Or ring the bell," Hetty called. "It's right beside the bed."

"My God, are you making me an invalid?"

The outraged voice made Hetty shrivel. She was nearly in tears.

"Kitty, what have I done wrong?"

"Nothing, nothing." Kitty had taken her arm and was leading her away.

"He's locked me out of my own bedroom!"

"That's the least of it, I would think," Kitty said shrewdly. "You'll have to be patient. He's a bit immature, Hugo. Lionel would have faced this in an entirely different way. He would have been philosophical and rather saintly. Old Hugo is going to roar like a bull. Both methods are a bit trying. Which do you prefer?" she said slyly.

"I don't know. I just want to run away."

"Not you. You're not the running kind. Are you?"

Not after getting this far, Hetty wanted to say. She was glad Kitty was friendly again.

When the family assembled for dinner everyone was subdued. Julia had been crying and made no secret of it. Her patrician nose had a red tip, her eyelids were swollen. Lady Flora was determinedly cheerful, asking why they were all so glum when Hugo was home and in no danger of dying.

"That's what I say," Kitty agreed. "He's a bit shell-shocked but he'll recover from that in time. Bates says he's wearing a bandage over one eye and walking on crutches. It's not the worst, is it? Bad enough, of course." Kitty's common sense was sometimes extremely irritating.

"What about that male nurse you had arranged for, Hetty?" asked Lady Flora. "Shouldn't he be sent for?"

Hetty shook her head. "No. That was a mistake."

"But how do you know if you haven't seen Hugo?"

"That man upstairs doesn't want a nurse. He would think it an insult. Didn't you hear him shouting?"

"He was always aggressive," Lady Flora said helplessly, and Julia began to weep again.

"Oh, do shut up, Julia," Kitty said impatiently. "I've got a great dislike of women weeping over their wounded.

Self-indulgence, I call it "

"It's Hugo's leg. He won't be able to ride. It's just too tragic."

Lionel was watching Hetty. When she met his eyes he came across and squeezed her hand.

"Chin up," he whispered.

Tears springing to her eyes blurred his profile. She felt as if she were losing him for ever. The beautiful summer was over.

"Well, come along," said Lady Flora briskly. "Let's go into dinner. By the way, Hetty, cook was asking about a meal for Hugo. I suggested a tray be left outside his door and he could collect it when he felt near starvation. Don't think I'm callous, but I never could tolerate tantrums from my sons."

"Tantrums?" Hetty queried.

"That's all this is. Hugo wants a lot of attention. He always did."

Indeed her words were borne out in the next minute, for Elsie, who had been carrying a laden tray into the dining room, suddenly screamed and there was a shattering crash as the tray was dropped.

"Good God, girl, how can you be so clumsy?" came Hugo's unmistakable voice.

Hetty was first into the room. She stopped short. No wonder Elsie, now down on her knees gathering up the broken plates, had screamed. For the electric light had been turned off, and the long white tapers in the silver candelabra had been lit. At the head of the table, a little indistinct in the wavering candlelight which no doubt had been his intention, sat Hugo. Upright in his chair, dressed in uniform, shoulders square, head high, one protuberant blue eye blazing angrily, the other hidden by a black patch, a horrific red puckered scar that drew up the corner of his mouth, down his right cheek.

In the smoky yellow light he looked macabre, sinister. He was smiling. His crooked mouth made his smile malevolent.

"Come on in, everyone. I'm not a monster. What was that damned silly maid scared of? Dropping all the food. Doesn't she know there's a war on, and good food shouldn't be wasted?"

Hetty tried to speak and failed. He *was* a monster, she was thinking frantically. War had made him mad, as well as disfiguring him so cruelly. The handsome husband she had boasted about in New York. No, it was Clemency who had done the boasting.

Everyone was stricken into silence. Hugo, sitting there surveying them with his one good eye must have thought them a group of frightened sheep. But not entirely, for someone suddenly switched on the lights, and the room was brightly illuminated.

"Who did that?" he roared.

"I did, dear boy," said Lady Flora calmly. "It's so stupid, but I really can't see to eat by candlelight any more. I tend to choke on fish bones. We're all perfectly delighted that you feel able to join us, Hugo. It's been such a long time. Hasn't it, Hetty? Aren't you glad to have your husband home?"

Lady Flora's cleverly inane words made Hetty able to approach that horribly distorted face, and put dry lips against the undamaged cheek. If one looked at him from this side, she reassured herself, he was as handsome as he had always been. She was very careful not to wince at contact with his flesh. But inevitably her eyes slid to his trouser leg, folded back above the knee, and the tremor that passed through her communicated itself to him.

"You've got half a man back, wife. Have a good look at him." Hugo deliberately thrust the disfigured side of his face at her. "Make you feel sick?"

"Hugo, for God's sake shut up," Lionel exclaimed in a tense voice. "Your histrionics may help you, but the rest of us don't find them amusing."

"That scar will improve," said Kitty bluntly. "Is that what you're worrying about?"

"And this?" Hugo said, tapping the black patch over his eye. "Would you like to see the empty socket?"

Julia gave a sharp cry and ran to kneel beside him, pressing her head against his thigh. "Hugo, we all love you."

"Don't do that, for God's sake," he said irritably. "Get up. Aren't we ever going to eat? I've had nothing since leaving France early this morning. And where's Bates? Ring for Bates, Mother. Let's have a bottle or two of some decent claret. Unless you've drunk it all while I've been away. What about you, Lionel? You managed to avoid the shells? Damn whizz-bang got me. I was just coming on leave."

His strange tortured gaze moved round the table.

"Well, Hetty, have they anglicised you yet? What's the news from New York? Uncle Jonas still holding the purse strings?"

"Hugo, what a thing to say," his mother exclaimed in a shocked voice.

"It's true enough, Mother. Hetty-Clemency, or Clemency-Hetty, whichever she prefers, has to insist on her rights. No one dislikes parting with money more than a Wall Street financier, especially to a giddy young woman with a profligate husband."

"Hugo, you're talking too much," Hetty said mildly. She reached out to touch his hand. She was trembling inwardly from his mocking use of her name coupled with Clemency's. He thought them one person. As in fact they now were.

He moved away from her touch, as if gentle human contact unnerved him. She noticed, with dismay, how his hand shook as he lifted his soup spoon to his mouth. He let it clatter down, and shouted again for Bates who had, unwittingly, come to stand at his blind side.

"Yes, my lord."

"Dammit, Bates, stand where I can see you. I'm not blind. Fetch a couple of bottles of the 1897 claret. After dinner I want some port in the library. Perhaps you'll join me, Lionel." He made an impatient movement. "I wish all of you wouldn't stare at me like that. And if you're anxious, I can assure you I can drink a half bottle of port without needing to be carried upstairs. When I come to that, you can put me in the ground. But I plan to sleep in my own bed tonight."

His remaining eye, red-rimmed and tormented, sought Hetty's. "I might warn you I won't be wanting company. Will you mind? You mustn't be in too much of a hurry to beget the heir."

"Hugo, you're doing nothing but showing off," Lady Flora said crossly, as if the nightmare monologue were nothing out of the ordinary. "Tomorrow I hope you'll have the grace to apologise."

"Like hell," muttered Hugo, the puckered scar aslant his cheek quivering pinkly against the dark flush of his skin. "Home sweet home." He suddenly looked exhausted. "We used to sing about it in the trenches. Home sweet home!"

The nightmare meal was at last over, and Hugo made his way, teetering dangerously on his crutches, to the library, followed by Lionel. Julia inevitably began to weep.

"But he didn't once mention the horses," she wailed. "That shows how dreadfully he has changed."

Had Jacobina got back a husband like this from his wars? Angry, unreconciled, completely self-absorbed, loathing himself and everybody else? If this were so she must have been glad of her lover's baby in her womb.

Hetty wondered how she could make herself go to bed with that furious travesty of a man. But she would have to if she too wanted a baby in her womb. And she did. It was the only sweetness left to her. That and Loburn.

What would you have done, Clemency?

16

After that first day Hugo didn't lock his door. That, however, was his only concession to normality. He began a pattern of behaviour that was frightening. He refused to leave his room until dark, obviously reluctant to be seen, then he came downstairs to dinner, following the ritual of the candles burning in a dim room, a too liberal quantity of wine to drink, and two hours later an unsteady return upstairs.

After the first night Lady Flora made no objection to the candles. Hugo's temper was too uncertain. She recognised that it was not, after all, the exhibitionism of a spoiled and arrogant young man, but something darker and more sinister.

Hetty too made earnest efforts to avoid arousing Hugo's temper. Going into the big master bedroom, as she did on one pretext or another, she would see him sitting in the armchair at the window, his back to the door, only the back of his blond head visible, the hair curling crisply and attractively, giving no hint of the ruined face.

Hearing her entrance, sometimes he remained silent, sometimes he grunted, "What do you want?" She invented the need for articles of clothing. "Have I driven you out of your room?"

"You know very well you have, but not for ever, I hope."

He seized on the last part of her answer.

'Don't be such a liar. Julia always said you were a liar."

"And do you think I am?"

"Well, you don't have to pretend you don't mind my gargoyle face."

"I'm not pretending, Hugo. And I do mind it, but mostly for your sake. I'm just trying to find you again. Don't you get awfully bored sitting here doing nothing all day? Couldn't I talk to you, or read to you?"

The dark flush had risen in his face.

"No, I don't want to talk, and I was never one for books. You should have married Lionel if you wanted a literary man."

Yes, Hetty thought painfully. Hugo was more right than he knew.

"Well, I didn't. I married you. And I hate to see you so unhappy."

"Unhappy, Christ! Who could be happy? Just leave me, will you? Just get out."

"Give him a little time," Doctor Bailey had said to Hetty. "Be patient and try to coax him to be more communicative. He ought to talk about these dark things in his mind. We don't want to have to send him to a hospital, do we?"

"No, no. I'll keep him at home. That's my duty."

Doctor Bailey seemed a little surprised at her choice of words. But they were exactly true. This was Nemesis. She was paying for her wickedness.

But was she to go on paying in this way for the rest of her life, living with a husband with whom she could not communicate, and for whom she felt nothing but pity and revulsion? The prospect appalled her.

What are you going to do, Hetty? Give up and go back to New York? How could she do that with Uncle Jonas certain to discover her deceit? Besides, after being an heiress, it would be very little fun to be poor again. After being Lady Hazzard it would be no fun at all reverting to plain Hetty Brown.

No, she must gather up the remnants of her courage, and be a loyal wife to that poor bewildered angry man sitting alone hour after hour. It was only another challenge, perhaps the most severe of all. But hadn't she boasted that she was not one to be afraid of any challenge?

All the same, it came as a bitter blow when Lionel announced that he and Kitty and Freddie were looking for a house, and planning to leave Loburn. That had always been their intention when Hugo married, but the war had intervened. Now was the time.

He looked at Hetty with his gentle compassionate gaze, and said that this was the only thing to do. It was practical as well as honourable.

"I might really fall in love with you if I stay here," he said, with a touch of flippancy that did not disguise his underlying seriousness. "Be a good girl and stick it. You will, you know. And it might turn out better than you think."

"How?" Hetty cried miserably. And then, ashamed of herself, "Of course I intend to stick it. I had no intention of doing anything else."

Lady Hazzard of Loburn. She was still that, at least.

Nevertheless, she sobbed for hours after Lionel's talk with her, and in the dusk, pressing her tear-wet face to the window, saw a dripping drowned face, looking in.

"No!" she gasped, moving away. The face moved away, too, and melted into the night.

Surely it had only been her own, dimly-mirrored in the glass. She had suffered that trick of Clemency's once before, in the mirror downstairs. She wouldn't be caught like that again.

She remained pale and shaken, however, and almost decided she could not go down to dinner that night. The candlelit dining room and Hugo's unfriendly intimidating figure at the head of the table seemed too much of an ordeal. She thought of this situation going on after Kitty and Lionel and Freddie had gone, after Lady Flora had died and Julia departed. There would be just herself and Hugo left like figures in a never-ending play.

"What's the matter, my lady? You seen a ghost?" Effie had come in to turn down the bed.

"Yes, I think I have, Effie. My poor husband who is hardly anything more than a ghost."

"Oh, he'll perk up, my lady, don't you worry. Give him time. He can't ride his horses, that's half what he's fretting about, I'll be bound. He's trying to get used to the notion of no more hunting. That was his life, wasn't it?"

"Yes, I expect that's a good deal of the trouble. And then he's terribly sensitive about his damaged face. But he'll have to start seeing people some time."

"He will when he's good and tired of his own company," said Effie vigorously. "Begging your pardon, my lady, if I'm speaking too boldly, but with you beside him he'll recover."

It was tempting to make a confidante of Effie. After all, she was the kind of company Hetty had been used to most of her life. But this tendency to familiarity must be watched. Everything must be perpetually watched. It was very wearing. And lonely.

Lady Flora had become kinder, however. Her large eyes were concerned as she regarded Hetty.

"You're looking tired, my dear. You should get out more, before the summer is over. Couldn't you persuade Hugo to walk with you in the garden? He did seem better at dinner last night, don't you think? Less irritable. And that scar on his face is fading. Can you convince him of that?"

"Oh, dear, no. I don't dare mention it."

"So you both pretend it doesn't exist. And other things, like not sharing the same bed."

Hetty flushed. She had been afraid that Hugo had become impotent. It would be so dreadful if she forced him to prove this fact.

222

"What would really set him up, Lady Flora, is a good gallop with Julia. Since he can't have that, I just don't know what I can suggest that he will listen to."

"He has to realise that there are other things in life besides horses and hunting. That makes for a narrow outlook. So no sentimentality, Hetty. Be firm with him. Make him face the truth. Tell him you're beginning to be sorry you ever left New York," she added. "Make him stop thinking of himself."

As if Hugo had heard this conversation, or knew of it and guessed what had been said, he actually shook himself out of his apathy the next day. He sent for his estate manager, old Fred Ryman, and then for Julia.

Fred was one thing. He had been longing to talk to the master ever since his return, about practical things such as crops, harvests, livestock, repairs. Julia was another matter. Hetty watched her run eagerly up the stairs. She had either overcome her abhorrence of Hugo's disfigurement, or perhaps her tenacious love made it of little importance. She had longed to be needed, and perhaps this summons was to be her opportunity.

Hetty made herself keep well out of the way. If this cool blonde English girl, Hugo's first love, could do anything to improve his state of mind, then she must be allowed to try. This was not a time for jealousy. It would be wonderful to see Hugo more cheerful, she told herself sternly. Let it be unimportant who achieved such a miracle.

There was no miracle, however . . .

Julia came downstairs, looking angry, chagrined and disbelieving.

"I won't do it," she was saying. "I simply won't do it." She saw Hetty and said hysterically, "It's unthinkable. He's not in his right mind."

"What has he done?"

"He's ordered me to sell the horses. You can't have an estate like this without horses. You simply can't."

"Especially if you can't ride them," Hetty said drily. "That's what he means, Julia. Neither he nor I can ride them, and Lionel and Kitty are leaving. So there would be only you. It's hardly sense to keep a string of hunters for one person, and she only an employee who won't be here for ever." It was splendid getting even with Julia for once. The memory of her lost baby goaded her.

Julia had gone scarlet.

"That's not the reason. It's Fred Ryman's fault. He says with the war continuing there are going to be shortages of fodder, and it's a luxury keeping stables."

"Isn't that true?"

"I don't regard good hunters as a luxury."

"Maybe you don't, but a man with one leg may have a different way of looking at such things. You'll have to do as Hugo asks, Julia."

Julia's anger had turned to a cold animosity.

"Who are you to give me orders? You act as if butter wouldn't melt in your mouth but what are you, really? Nothing but a good housekeeper. If you hadn't had all that money Hugo wouldn't have given you a glance."

"You make Hugo sound very mercenary," Hetty said stiffly.

"Well, of course he was where you were concerned. He had to be. We all understood that. But –"

"But what?"

Distress about the horses had made Julia indiscreet, perhaps, about what had passed privately between herself and Hugo upstairs.

"It wasn't intended to last, your marriage of convenience," she said cruelly.

"I don't believe you."

"Oh, yes, it's true. It's still true. We all know what you are."

"What am I?"

The alarm signals were sounding in Hetty's head. *The little cheat from New York* . . .

224

"Certainly not what you pretend to be," Julia retorted, and refused to enlarge on that cryptic remark.

It was all rather silly, like a schoolgirls' quarrel. Hetty refused to allow Julia's remarks, which surely constituted an empty threat, to upset her. Surely the important thing was that if Hugo could give orders to his manager, and make this momentous decision about his horses he was improving at last. Was the tyrannical unnatural behaviour of the past weeks coming to an end? Would he soon be wanting her in his bed and could she be sure she would not quiver with revulsion if he did?

She had never loved him, that was the trouble. A loving wife would have ignored the surface disfigurements. If this had been Lionel – but Lionel's beautiful face, marred and disfigured, would have broken her heart. She would have taken him in her arms and held him for ever.

Hugo was different.

But she was Hugo's wife.

He had begun another habit which was even more disturbing than his solitary confinement in his room, that of prowling about the house, opening doors silently and frightening the maids. In spite of his crutches, he moved with little sound. Effie said shamefacedly that his disfigured face with the black patch over one eye peering round the door made her think of robbers.

"Hugo, you must really stop startling the servants like that," Lady Flora said at dinner. "I believe you're enjoying it."

Hugo gave his lopsided grimace that was meant to be a smile, and a pleased one at that.

"Do they think I'm an ogre? Splendid. I might as well get what fun I can out of the way I look. That's due to me, don't you think? And I must say the servants seem damn lazy over their work. Dust all over the place."

"They manage very well," Hetty said defensively. "This is a big house for a small staff. Please don't criticise them, Hugo, or they may leave and how would we replace them? All the younger women are going into munitions."

"It's not only the servants I'm criticising. I find my wife and my brother closeted together in the library rather frequently. What do you two get up to?"

Now Hugo was grinning evilly. His undamaged blue eye challenged Hetty.

"We're going through old papers, Hugo. I want to find out everything I can about the house, because if we're to restore it as it should be done we ought to know its history."

"We've come across some amazingly interesting stuff," Lionel said in his courteous manner. "I should think some of the documents haven't been looked at for a couple of centuries. Hetty has quite a talent for this sort of thing."

"Why should an American be so interested in the history of an English family?" Hugo asked suspiciously.

"It's my family now, Hugo," Hetty replied. She looked at him steadily. "Whether I regret the fact or not."

"Of course you regret it," Hugo exclaimed loudly. "A pretty young thing like you stuck with this spectre who makes the servants scream in fright."

Lady Flora sighed. "You will persist in being melodramatic. It would be more to the point if you inspected the repairs Hetty has already had done. Have you ever expressed your gratitude?"

Now the tyrannical blue eye was fixed on Lady Flora.

"What for? She loves the house, she says, so isn't it a privilege that she has such a satisfying way of spending her dollars."

Kitty leaned forward indignantly. "Hugo, you really are the end. Boorish and intolerable. If no one else will tell you that, I will. You can't go on punishing everyone for your misfortune. We all have a limit to our patience. Lionel and I will soon be leaving here, thank goodness, but the others have to stay. Unless Hetty decides to go back to America, of course. I, for one, wouldn't blame her if she did."

Did Hugo look startled? He turned to look at Hetty, showing the undamaged side of his face, the clean handsome profile that was still profoundly exciting.

"But she won't go," murmured Julia, almost inaudibly. "Will you, Hetty?"

"No, I won't. I have no one but Uncle Jonas there. Here I have my husband and the house, and all the things we're planning to do."

Hugo swallowed the remainder of his wine and beckoned to Bates to refill his glass. The dark flush was in his cheeks again.

"Did you say your husband?"

"That's what I said."

It seemed to Hetty, suddenly, that the brightness in the blazing blue eye could have been from tears. Hugo crying! There was a constriction in her breast. She wondered if he sometimes shed tears sitting in his room alone. She had never before thought of that.

It was the morning after this dinner-table conversation that Hetty came on Julia in Hugo's and her bedroom, bending over her private desk. She knew that Hugo had gone downstairs, and she had slipped up to see that the room had been tidied for his return. She was thinking of the remark he had made about the servants leaving dust. An unfair remark, but the complaint ought to be checked.

And there was Julia caught redhanded.

"What are you doing?" Hetty asked sharply.

Julia had hastily closed the desk and stepped backwards.

"I was looking for the bill of sale for the filly we bought at Newmarket."

"In my desk? What would it be doing there?"

"Oh, goodness, I'm sorry. I thought this was Hugo's desk."

"Did you?"

"Yes, I did. I had just begun to look. I've scarcely touched anything."

"Don't you think the library would be a more appropriate place to search? That's where Hugo keeps his business papers, as you must know."

Julia raised alarmed eyes.

"Yes, I did know, but I couldn't find anything there. Since Hugo spends so much time in this room I thought he had probably moved his papers. I do apologise, Hetty. I'm not entirely rational since the horses have begun to leave here."

Then she was gone before Hetty could make any comment about her being irrational, or very shrewd and calculating. What had Julia really been looking for?

She checked her desk to see what papers or letters were immediately visible. Uncle Jonas's letters, some from the bank, the one from the American Embassy about the unidentified survivor from the *Lusitania*, and the one Mrs Crampton had written a long time ago enquiring for Hetty Brown. Also, of course, Hugo's brief and uninformative letters from France. Nothing incriminating, surely. But no one in her position should keep old letters. They might eventually provide the missing clue to a mystery.

Was Julia looking for the answer to what she imagined was a mystery?

The Lord and Taylor letter about the green dress? Did that say anything that could be regarded as suspicious? Or did Julia think there might be love letters from Lionel? Was she looking for some damning evidence to produce to Hugo? She was a mean devious woman and Hetty believed her capable of anything.

The day the last of the horses were led away Hugo got very drunk, and fell down the stairs, crashing like a felled tree. Astonishingly he was not seriously hurt, but he was shaken and his temper not improved. Bates and Hetty helped him upright and got him to a chair where he sat glowering, waiting for the glass of brandy he had ordered Bates to bring. He refused to have a doctor sent for.

"A pity I didn't break my neck," he said.

Hetty, badly shocked herself from fright, lost her patience and exclaimed, "Oh, for heavens sake, I'm sick of all this self-pity. If you won't have a doctor and only intend to sit here getting drunker, I'll leave you to it. The boys in the hospital need me more than you do. Perhaps Julia will be kind enough to come and hold your hand."

It seemed that this was exactly what did happen. When Hetty returned from the hospital, tired and depressed, but no longer angry, she was told that Julia had sat with Hugo for an hour, sometimes weeping, sometimes trying to hearten him. Later she had helped him upstairs.

All the things his wife should have done.

He didn't come down to dinner that night, and nobody had any new suggestions about what could be done to revive his old cheerful spirit.

"The war is terrible!" Kitty suddenly exclaimed. "If my son ever has to fight in a war like this I'd rather he didn't grow up. You're lucky after all, Hetty, not having a son."

"You really believe that?" Hetty said sadly. She knew now that she never would have a son or a daughter. She was just to be a figurehead, mouldering in company with the old house, for the rest of her life.

Clemency, Clemency, is this your revenge?

"You can share Freddie with us," Lionel said. But suddenly he seemed too mild, too bland. "When we move we won't be too far away. Freddie will have his own notions about seeing you."

"All this Hector and Achilles business," Kitty grumbled. "At his age he should be interested in Jack and the Beanstalk and things like that."

"No, I don't think fairy stories are for Freddie," Hetty

said. "He's too precocious. Actually, I had been thinking of trying him with Charles Dickens. Do you mind, Kitty?"

"Don't ask me, ask his father. He's the one with the literary tastes."

"Splendid idea," said Lionel. "We may get a budding young Oliver Twist in the house, of course. But it will liven the place up."

The experiment was a great success. Freddie listened with rapt attention to the adventures of David Copperfield, begging Hetty not to stop reading. Now that the afternoons were drawing in they made an assignation in the winter drawing room at five o'clock. It was quiet there and they were undisturbed. At least Hetty had thought they were undisturbed until the afternoon she heard a slight sound at the other end of the room, and turned to see the door softly closing behind a tall figure.

"Is that you, Lionel?"

"It isn't Daddy," said Freddie. "It's Uncle Hugo."

"Uncle Hugo!"

"He comes every afternoon to listen. He sits in that chair where you can't see him."

"But why doesn't he say he's there?"

"I expect he likes to be invisible," Freddie said sedately. "Go on with the story, Hetty. You're wasting time."

After a lot of thought Hetty decided to say nothing to Hugo about having discovered his presence at the reading sessions. All she did was raise her voice a little so that it would be clearly audible to the listener at the back of the room. The sessions took on significance. Freddie had always been a most rewarding audience, but now she read with an undercurrent of excitement. She found that she liked Hugo being there.

17

Autumn was making itself felt, with early storms and a
sharp drop in the temperature. Leaves began to fall. The
wind sighed and moaned round the old house, with
ghostly echoes of a thousand past years.

Hetty was finding the grey room chilly and sad. It
reminded her too much of the first days of her arrival at
Loburn in a state of shock, distress and disorientation.
The wind in the trees was like waves breaking. Sometimes
it rained with a sound of icy water being flung against the
windows. She would wake from a dream, cold and rigid,
and full of apprehension. It was then that she thought
Clemency stood at the foot of the bed watching her silently.
Clemency had never been silent in her lifetime, so how
could she stand so immobile now? She must deeply hate
Hetty for the warm blood in her veins, the ability to
laugh, talk, cry, love . . .

Half awake and in the lingering throes of nightmare,
Hetty wondered if she might be going a little mad.
The year had been such an enormous strain. She was so
weary of keeping her own counsel, and unbearably
lonely.

*But you can't turn back, can you, Hetty? There's no
turning back.* Clemency's voice was echoing from the
nightmare, and a moment later a nudging at her side made
her sit upright, screaming. Clemency was there. She was
getting into bed with her!

A cold hand on her shoulder pushed her back on to the
pillow.

"Stop that noise. I'm not a ghost." Hugo's voice. "I'm coming in with you. Do you mind?"

"N-no." She whimpered with suppressed sobs. "Hugo, you scared me. Put the light on."

"No. No light."

Of course, there was his distorted face, his maimed body, both more acceptable in the dark. Or so he must think. But feeling his heavy body forcing its way between the sheets beside her, and knowing by his breath on her cheek that the crooked mouth was inches from her own, she began to shake uncontrollably.

"Don't cringe! For God's sake, don't cringe from me!"

"I'm – not."

"Then kiss me."

The angry autocratic voice was turning her into a puppet. She moved towards him, making herself feel for his lips.

This is what you have to do, Hetty. Clemency again. *This is part of your debt to me . . .*

She thought she would shudder again when their flesh touched, but he lay so unexpectedly still, letting her lips nudge and caress his, that the sensation lost its eeriness and became rather pleasant. She kissed his unmarked cheek, and then, with temerity, let her lips touch the wrinkled and fading scar, finding to her own surprise that she felt no revulsion.

His arms tightened round her. In the darkness, she couldn't see whether his good eye, the one that blazed such anger and bitterness, was open or shut. She explored, and felt the bristling eyebrows, the thick soft eyelashes. Gently, a feeling of sensuousness spreading through her, she kissed the closed eyelid, and heard his breath go out in a long sigh.

She remembered fleetingly their frenzied, tense, almost impersonal, love-making so long ago, and realised that the slow stirring in her body, the quiet growing rapture, and his own trembling, naked against her, were utterly

232

different. He was being so disciplined. So unexpectedly thoughtful, waiting for her, waiting to be certain that she was not reluctant or disgusted. And she had thought him impotent. She gave a little gasp of laughter.

"All right?" he whispered.

"Oh, yes. Oh, yes."

"You didn't think it would be all right?"

"I want to feel your leg." Her fingers found and dwelt on the roughened skin of the stump. "There. Now I know all about you. You haven't any more secrets."

He pressed hard against her, crushing her in his grip.

"I've been wanting you for days."

"You never told me."

His voice was gruff. "I was afraid you wouldn't be able to bear me."

"Hugo, oh, you fool. All this time wasted." She spread her legs. Her voice came deep and sensuous. "And what on earth are we waiting for now?"

In the dawn, with the room lightening, Hugo stirred. Hetty had scarcely slept, although she had had half-dreams that Clemency, watching them from the end of the bed, wasn't a malevolent ghost after all.

But with the daylight some of Hugo's uncertainties had returned. He moved away from Hetty, saying that he didn't suppose she particularly enjoyed the sight of him.

"Actually," she said thoughtfully, raising herself on her elbow to trace the scar on his cheek with her fingertip, "I think you look rather distinguished. I've thought so for some time. But I didn't want to pander to your vanity by telling you. You used to be a very vain man."

"I know. An arrogant sod."

"I like you better the way you are now. With your honourable wounds. And this subject is now closed. It's never to be raised again."

"Remarkable girl," he murmured, drawing her down beside him.

"But I think you'd better go back to your room if you don't want the servants talking. Effie will be here with my morning tea tray shortly."

"Dammit, let them talk. You're my wife."

Hetty was suddenly uncertain herself.

"Hugo, I can't make up to you for your horses, not being able to hunt, all the things you're deprived of."

"Can't you?"

"Well, can I?"

"You might try. I always did admire you enormously, you know."

"Admire?"

"I'm not one for pretty speeches."

"But you loved Julia. Is that what you're telling me?"

"A long time ago. She had a marvellous seat on a horse. But now she's got a bit shrewish. And I look at you."

Hetty's voice roughened.

"Who told you that you couldn't make pretty speeches? Anyway, if we're being frank I ought to tell you I thought I was falling in love with Lionel."

"You wouldn't have for long. He's a nice chap but a featherweight." Hugo lifted his head off the pillow, so that she could see the strong thick column of his neck. "A woman like you needs a man to dominate her a bit. I knew that when I first met you in New York."

The warning finger touched her. Was she never going to be able to relax?

'I was pretty spoiled and impossible then, I guess. I think we both had our eye on the main chance."

"I expect we did."

"Hugo, we've never talked like this before. As friends."

He grinned and his mouth seemed only slightly crooked.

"We've both changed a good deal. That's something the war has done."

"Would you have fallen in love with that girl you knew in New York? I mean, as time went by."

"I doubt it. Nor she with me."

"We're talking of her as if she's someone else altogether," Hetty said compulsively.

"Isn't she?" His blue eye was actually twinkling. "Certainly I didn't bargain for too much of your mother's company."

Hetty moved back to their shared bedroom that day, and without a word being said the whole house knew what had happened.

Lionel went out for too long a walk, got chilled, and retired to bed. He had never shaken off his malarial fever.

Julia looked ashen-faced, the corners of her mouth pinched, her eyes blank. She couldn't be unaware of the new sparkle in Hetty's eyes or her quiet contentment. Nor, unless she was deaf, could she have failed to hear Hugo humming tunelessly as he walked about the house. He had become very agile on his crutches.

Would she give up now, Hetty wondered, and could afford to have pity for the girl who had written, "*I will never give you up, never, never, never . . .*"

Lady Flora sent for Hetty, and said briskly, "Well, Hetty, so the invalid has decided to recover."

"Yes, I think so. I'm taking him to London next week to have consultations about an artificial leg. Pimm will drive us up." Hetty couldn't prevent herself from smiling radiantly. "Yes, he really is recovering."

"Well done, my dear."

"Oh, it was nothing to do with me. It was just that he was – ready." She felt her blush, and looked up to see the kindness in Lady Flora's wide beautiful eyes.

"I wouldn't say it had nothing at all to do with you," she said. "You're a very attractive young woman. Especially now you're happy. It's the first time we have seen you happy, Hetty, do you realise that?"

"I hope we may have a baby," Hetty said in a rush.

"Why, of course you will. And this time you will take the greatest care. I will see to that myself."

"Yes, ma'am," Hetty said instinctively and realised that she had fallen into the old subservient way of speaking to a superior.

But Lady Flora didn't seem to notice, or perhaps she liked Hetty's humility, for she smiled and said, "I'm just going to have tea. Won't you join me?"

She might have known that none of this could last. Especially when she was sure that she was pregnant. She had reached her goal and the satisfaction of this achievement was too great and too underserved. It was not surprising that it was about to be snatched from her.

The letter was beside her place at the breakfast table. She had a distinct and unhappy feeling of *déjà vu*.

"I see you have a letter from America, Hetty," Kitty said pleasantly. "How nice for you. You haven't heard from New York for a long time, have you?"

"No," said Hetty. Her mouth was dry. She had recognised Uncle Jonas's handwriting. There was no reason why he shouldn't write to her, nor was there any specific reason for her apprehension. She only knew that if she weren't careful her hands would shake and Hugo would notice.

"Hetty always gets upset about letters from New York," Julia observed to no one in particular. "She seems to anticipate bad news."

Hugo was opening his own mail. He looked up to say, "I don't know why you're all staring at her so inquisitively. She might prefer to read her letter in private."

But that would be highly suspicious, Hetty decided, ripping open the envelope and taking out the thick notepaper covered with Uncle Jonas's distinctive writing.

My dear Clemency,

I can't think what this business of "extreme importance" is that you want to see me about. I wonder if you realise how difficult and hazardous it is to come to England at this time. However, since I am your Trustee, and for poor Millicent's sake, I have pulled all the strings I can, and have finally obtained a passage on a cargo ship, the *Erin*, which I am sure will be highly uncomfortable.

As you, of all people, must be aware of the danger of German U-boats in the Atlantic, I can only think your matter of extreme importance must be urgent. It would have been kinder to elucidate a little. Are you having trouble with your bank? Or your husband?

Well, I mustn't be a tetchy old man. I will enjoy seeing Loburn and you, my dear, of course. The *Erin* is scheduled to dock at Southampton on the 12 November. I have cabled for a car to meet me and drive me direct to Loburn. This will avoid trouble for you, and you can expect me when you see me.

Your affec. Uncle Jonas

P.S. I am too old for this sort of thing, so that business of yours had better be important.

"What is it, Hetty?" asked Hugo. "Bad news. You look upset."

Hetty had frequently wondered how the end would manifest itself when it did come. So this was how it was to be, with Uncle Jonas denouncing her. She sat dazed with shock, unable to speak. Uncle Jonas was arriving to see the young woman whom he supposed to be his niece, only to be confronted by a stranger. For he of all people must recognise that she was not Clemency whom he had known from birth. Even if she could deceive him with the story that her year in England had changed her greatly, what business of extreme importance could she invent? More significantly, someone, and it must be someone in this house, had treacherously written to him asking him to come.

Hetty's anguished eyes took in the breakfast table, with the shining silver and fine china, the warm comfortable room, the people round the table, her family now, surely. And at the opposite end Hugo, no longer flushed and violent and irascible but a rather slow and quiet man whom she had grown to love.

What would happen when he heard of her monstrous deception? Would he fall into one of his old rages and order her to leave the house for ever? Very likely. He was a proud man. He would never tolerate the mother of his child being a servant and illegitimate and a deceiver.

"Hetty!"

"Oh, sorry, Hugo." Somehow she pulled herself together. "I was lost in thought. This is surprising news. My Uncle Jonas is on his way to visit us. His ship docks on the twelfth. That's in three days. It's so soon."

"Whatever brings the old boy over here? He's a bit foolhardy crossing the Atlantic in the middle of a submarine war."

"Business of extreme importance," Hetty said numbly. Her gaze went round the table again, Kitty, Lionel, Hugo, Julia. Julia! The cold blue eyes had given the smallest flicker.

A small scene flashed into Hetty's mind of Julia bending over her desk, searching for something. A bill of sale for a horse, she had said. But was it not in reality Uncle Jonas's address? So that she could play this last treacherous trick on Hetty.

For hadn't there been other tricks — the dress from Lord and Taylor's, for instance, the dress that didn't quite fit. The insinuations, the watching, the slowly gathered evidence, the enmity inspired by bitter jealousy.

Oh yes, it all fitted. Hetty was tempted to accuse Julia now, at the breakfast table, in front of everybody.

But such an act would mean a confession by Julia of

238

her suspicions, and above all Hetty didn't want Hugo to hear that. There might be too much truth in them. She had no alternative but to wait, face Uncle Jonas, play her part until the end, and trust to luck staying with her. Perhaps it would.

Having made that decison, Hetty became calm. She decided what room Uncle Jonas should have and had it carefully prepared. She arranged menus which she thought he would like. She talked about him to Lady Flora.

"He's a little stuffy grey man, rather plump, only interested in finance, his own and other people's. At first he was very opposed to my coming to England to marry Hugo. He didn't like so much of my money being put into a venture not of his planning."

"So he's coming to look over the investment?" Lady Flora enquired shrewdly.

"He must be. I don't think you will particularly like him, Lady Flora."

"Oh, we have his kind in Threadneedle Street, too. And he is your family, my dear. Of course we will like him.'

Apart from the preparations for Uncle Jonas's arrival, Hetty did one other thing that made her wince with distaste. She began wearing Clemency's heavy gold bracelet. She had hidden it away ever since the shipwreck, unable to bear the sight of it. But now it must be brought out to give her the right identity, to prepare herself for being called Clemency.

Only one day later than expected, Uncle Jonas arrived, a little bundled-up figure climbing out of the hired Ford motor car and gazing up at the façade of the house.

Hetty didn't wait for Bates to let him in. She ran out eagerly (wouldn't Clemency have done that?) crying, "Uncle Jonas! How wonderful to see you."

He allowed himself to be embraced. He didn't look at her very hard. His small stone grey eyes were watering from the cold wind.

239

"Well, Clemency. A bit decrepit, this famous house, isn't it? Needs a bit of paint and refurbishing."

"I know, Uncle. That's what I want to talk to you about. But not yet. Come inside. You must be tired and frozen. How was the journey?"

"Hellish. A rolling old tub, permanent black-outs, and disgusting food. But we never caught a glimpse of a U-boat, and I'm here safely. I could do with a good tot of Bourbon, though."

"Scotch, Uncle Jonas. We don't have Bourbon. Bates, take in Mr Middleton's luggage and bring drinks into the library. Hugo's waiting for us there."

"Hugo?"

"My husband, Uncle Jonas."

"Of course, of course. I'm getting forgetful. Anno Domini, I'm afraid. An old gentleman like me shouldn't be travelling across the world. But I'm still quite capable of sorting out your affairs, Clemency. I'm not forgetful about money."

Hetty, although not daring to relax, noticed with relief that the old man was totally self-absorbed, fussing about his comforts, his small grey eyes looking inward. He had kissed her but scarcely looked at her. Now he was saying, "You look fine Clemency. Your husband's finished with the war? Badly wounded, wasn't he? I must say this war's no parlour game. We're trying to keep out of it. No business of ours. Ah, so this is the library. Fine room. I'd always heard English country houses had fine libraries. Ah – Lord Hazzard. By jove, old man, they've knocked you about a bit. Recovering?"

"Splendidly. With limitations."

"Ah! Damned cold journey I had here. Clemency said something about some whisky."

"Here it is, Uncle. Come and sit by the fire."

"Yes, I will. Now that's real cosy. I could sit here for an hour or two. I can't make a long stay, Clemency. A day or two to get your problems sorted out, a quick look at London, and then I'll be on the same old tub back to New York."

Hetty stiffened as she heard Hugo's question.

"How do you think Hetty – I mean Clemency – looks? We call her Hetty, you know."

"Do you? Can't think why. Didn't know it was a name in our family. Why, she looks just fine."

The sunken tired old eyes looked at her briefly, and Hetty made herself smile warmly.

"Hugo and I are expecting a child, Uncle. Does that please you?"

"That's nice, I guess. My, if Millicent were alive she'd be right over. Poor Millicent. Her grave all right, Clemency?"

The twinge of ice down her spine again.

"Yes. I send money to the Convent sister. They see it's looked after."

"Good. That Scotch isn't bad at all. May I have another? And now, both of you, tell me what this urgent business is which you brought me over about."

Hetty caught Hugo's questioning glance.

"It could wait, Uncle Jonas. You have the rest of the family to meet, Hugo's mother and brother and sister-in-law."

"Business comes first. Out with it, my girl. Have you got into some trouble?"

"No. No, indeed." Hetty plunged desperately. "It's only that I so love this house, and it needs an immense amount of money to be spent on it. Almost all my inheritance, I would say. Hugo and I have been planning it. We don't want to wait until the end of the war. And it is going to be our child's inheritance."

"If he's a boy, yes. But I'd remind you you won't be spending all your inheritance, Clemency. You still have the Fifth Avenue and Long Island houses, you know. Freehold. Like gold. And talking of gold, I've taken the opportunity to bring over your mother's jewellery, all that

241

didn't go down with her on the *Lusitania*. If it isn't to your taste there's no reason why you shouldn't sell it. Get some advice on an honest jeweller, though."

Hetty was blinking back tears. It couldn't be so easy, fooling this astute old man. It was too much to believe.

But she was realising rapidly that Uncle Jonas was only astute regarding property. People didn't count half as much. He scarcely saw people. Nor was he going to be particularly interested in doubts and mysteries. He would brush them aside as embarrassing complications in the straightforward administration of an estate. He would rather not know about them. Not that he did know about them. It was obvious that it had never occurred to him that this young woman they called Hetty, attractively anglicised, and running an important house capably, might not be his niece.

Three liberal measures of Scotch whisky later, and thoroughly warmed by the fire, the old man began to look relaxed and benevolent.

"Ah! Feel comfortable for the first time since I set foot on that old ship. Think I'll go to my room and have a rest. What time do you have dinner?"

"Seven-thirty. Uncle. We don't have many servants, it's hard to get them with the war on, and we don't like keeping them up late."

"Good. Suits me fine. That'll give us time to have a business discussion after dinner."

"Hetty, why have you been so secretive with me?" They were in their bedroom preparing to dress for dinner. Hugo was indignant enough to bring back her nervousness.

"What do you mean? Oh, the money for Loburn. Well, I thought I had been rather brilliant about that." She was improvising again. "I want all my inheritance brought over, not just dribs and drabs, and I couldn't have an endless cross-Atlantic correspondence with Uncle Jonas. There are ways to handle him, and they're not by

242

letters. He's too clever and cautious about the written word."

"But he's amenable after a few glasses of Scotch?"

Hetty grinned.

"And he's not averse to a good brandy, either."

"I'll remember that after dinner. You're too clever by half, you know. Come here and kiss me."

She liked his autocratic voice, and allowed herself to be folded in his arms, relaxing gratefully. She believed the worst was over.

Clemency, you won't spring any more horrid surprises on me, will you. That money is of no use to you any more, nor your mother's diamond brooches and necklaces.

"Are you talking to yourself, darling?"

"I'm only saying that I'm going to flout the Bible and build up treasures on earth. We're going to have the most beautiful house in England."

"You always did steer yourself against fate, didn't you?"

She was startled.

"What do you mean?"

"Well, thinking you can be happy with a one-eyed monster for a husband."

"But I am! I am happy, Hugo!"

"Don't be so intense. You're not trying to convince a jury."

A jury! Why did Hugo use such a terrible comparison?

Dinner was going to be a further test, when everyone was there, Lady Flora observing with her acute intelligence, Julia longing for Hetty to make a mistake and give herself away.

It began well enough. Uncle Jonas looked pompous, indeed, distinguished, in his dinner jacket, and was obviously charmed by Lady Flora. He addressed her frequently as "dear lady" and launched into monologues about life in New York, sometimes adding, "Clemency will remember that, of course," or "Clemency's mother could tell that story better than I can."

"It's strange hearing you called Clemency, Hetty," Lady Flora remarked. "But I do think Hetty suits you better. Or are we just familiar with it?"

"And that other girl," Julia interjected, sharply and clearly. She looked slightly drunk, her eyes too bright, her colour unusually high.

"What girl, miss?" Uncle Jonas asked. He fixed his small stony eyes on Julia with no particular interest. He wanted to continue his conversation with Lady Flora.

"Why, Hetty's maid. Didn't Hetty tell you she had to go to London recently to try to identify a girl, a survivor from the *Lusitania*. She was very upset about it."

"You didn't tell me this, Clemency."

"There was no point, Uncle Jonas. The girl turned out to be a complete stranger." Hetty paused, then said calmly, "They had thought she might be my missing maid. You remember Brown? Harriet Brown."

"Oh yes, that young woman. I can't say I remember what she looked like. Sad thing though. She never was heard of again, was she?"

"No," said Hetty.

"Well, fortunes of war. This is a splendid claret, Lord Hazzard. And you've an excellent cook, too." Uncle Jonas was getting comfortably fuddled. "I can thoroughly sympathise with my niece."

"How, Uncle Jonas?" Hetty asked tentatively.

"Why, in wanting to restore this fine historic mansion. Well worth while. Damned worth while. You're doing a service to the nation, and I have nothing but admiration for this country. I'll have your stocks converted into cash as soon as I get back, Clemency. Better still, I'll send a cable to my broker from here. In case the U-boats get me, eh? Eh?"

18

Hetty could scarcely believe that fortune favoured her again. Uncle Jonas's visit was an unqualified success. The day he left for London, and a brief stay in the Ritz Hotel, Hugo accompanied him, Pimm driving them in the Rolls. Hugo was going to have a last fitting of his artifical leg and, if all was well, he would come home wearing it. He was in good spirits at the prospect, so the goodbyes were jolly, and full of friendship and goodwill.

Lionel and Kitty, Freddie, Lady Flora and Hetty stood waving from the steps.

"Nice old boy," said Lionel. "I wouldn't have thought an American could have so much sympathy for the fate of an English house."

"I'm glad," said Kitty. "Because if Hetty has six daughters it will be Freddie's one day." She gave Hetty a friendly glance. "You ought to take your first baby to New York and show it to Uncle Jonas. He's rather lonely, you know."

"Yes, I ought to. When the war's over, of course." Hetty was utterly astonished that she was shedding tears at Uncle Jonas's departure. And not tears of relief, but of real sorrow.

"Everybody's packing bags today," Freddie remarked.

"Everybody?" Hetty asked.

"Well, Uncle Jonas and Julia. That's two people."

"Julia!"

Lady Flora moved.

"Yes. Julia has decided to leave us. She misses the

horses too much and I can't keep her fully occupied. She's bored."

"But where's she going?" Kitty asked. "You always said Loburn was to be her home."

"That was a long time ago. Now she's able to take care of herself. I've advised her to take a secretarial course. She's excellent at writing letters."

Hetty's eyes were drawn unwillingly to meet Lady Flora's enigmatic gaze.

"You know, Hetty, your Uncle Jonas was under the impression that you employed a secretary, but of course you don't, do you?"

"What are you getting at, Mother?" Lionel asked.

"Nothing of importance. Are you and Kitty rushing off house-hunting again? Then perhaps Hetty will come and take hot chocolate with me. I warn you, Hetty, I shall be needing more of your company now that Julia has gone."

"Of course, Lady Flora," Hetty said numbly. "Shall I come up now?"

"If you would." Lady Flora shivered. "It's chilly. Departures. They're sad, whatever their reason."

There was no alternative but to come out in the open at last. Hetty sat facing Lady Flora in her charming green and white sitting room, and said bluntly, "How did you know that Julia wrote that letter to Uncle Jonas? And the earlier one to Lord and Taylor for the dress? I guessed, because I knew her motive, but how could you guess?"

"There." Lady Flora sat by the fire warming her hands. "Now we're cosy. How did I guess? Well, I simply insisted that she confess. I admit it wasn't a pleasant experience. I had once hoped Julia would be my daughter-in-law. I was very fond of her. We shared our dislike of your coming to Loburn, Hetty. I apologise for that. You must have noticed."

"I noticed you were always suspicious of me. You asked a lot of questions."

"Exactly. I thought they needed asking. But where I gradually accepted your answers, Julia refused to. Oh dear, this is all very distressing. I can only tell you that she became more and more jealous of you until she was determined to destroy your marriage. At the beginning I had sympathy for her, but not since I've seen how clever you have been with Hugo in his worst moods, so quiet and compassionate and tenacious."

"I'm a tenacious person, Lady Flora."

"Indeed you are. You put up with Hugo's horrible behaviour where another woman, even Julia, would have given up. So I came round to your side, and when I discovered what Julia was doing I couldn't approve at all."

"What was she doing?"

"Look! I'll show you. She had made a list of the reasons she had for suspecting you were not Clemency Jervis. She meant to show it to Hugo when she had final proof."

"Uncle Jonas's visit was to provide that?"

"Precisely. Will you read this?"

"Must I?"

"Of course you must. Unless you're afraid."

"I'm not afraid," Hetty lied.

Distastefully she scanned the neatly written page of assumptions, accusations and supposed evidence, all insubstantial, but all undoubtedly adding up to a disturbing picture.

(a) This young woman arrived in a nervous jumpy state, said her engagement ring had come off in the sea but not her old bracelet initialled with the letters C.M.V. Hugo didn't seem to think this unlikely, but Lady Flora and I did.

(b) She was always in a panic over any letters that arrived for her, as if she was afraid of what they might contain.

(c) She refused to be called Clemency, as if the name held horrors for her.

(d) She had unexplained frights, such as in the church

one day when she came out looking as if she had seen a ghost. Her conscience must have been troubling her.

(e) Katharine Eversleigh told the story about Clemency Jervis on board ship, flirting and showing off her clothes which had all been made for her by Lord and Taylor. If she was so extrovert then why did she become so quiet and nervous? Because she wasn't the same girl.

(f) Hetty's consternation when the green dress arrived from New York and it didn't exactly fit. It really didn't. Only I saw that. But I had written for it, and its unexpected arrival shocked and surprised Hetty.

(g) She kept having nightmares about the shipwreck, and there was Kitty's story about the badly wounded Canadian airman who had seemed to know her, but not as Clemency Jervis.

(h) Once she cried out the name Clemency in her sleep. Kitty told me Lionel had heard that and it had puzzled him. In view of all these things I thought it only right to clear up our suspicions for good and all by sending for Clemency's nearest relative, her Uncle Jonas. He was the only one who could identify her positively. I felt absolutely justified in doing this.

Hetty lifted her head.

"Well?" said Lady Flora.

"I don't think any of this would stand up in a court of law."

"Of course it wouldn't. But is it true?"

"Some of it. I did have nightmares. I still do. I get sudden attacks of terror. Of course I'm haunted by seeing all those people drowning, being nearly drowned myself." Suddenly she pressed her hands to her cheeks in her old defensive gesture. "What are you going to do?" she whispered.

"Me? Nothing. Except tear this regrettable confession up and throw it on the fire. I think a judge would rule that the witness's evidence was distorted by emotion."

She sighed. "Poor Julia."

"She – made me lose my baby."

"I know." Lady Flora was brisk and calm. "So we couldn't risk anything like that happening again."

"But, Lady Flora," Hetty seized the frail hands imploringly. "What do you yourself think?"

"Does it matter to you?"

"Oh, yes."

"Although I made you feel an alien for so long?"

"It does matter to me what you think. It does!"

"Well, then, I think you're a splendid wife for my son, and you'll be a charming mother for my grandchild. Not to mention your being a very nice human being. Now we don't need to say anything more. Not now, or ever."

"But –"

"I'm a very incurious old lady with a great desire to preserve the status quo."

"Like Uncle Jonas," Hetty said involuntarily.

Lady Flora gave a small burst of delighted laughter.

"Like Uncle Jonas. How nice to be compared to that worthy man."

Hetty didn't see Julia leave. She only knew that Hugo was relieved to have her gone.

"She'll be better in a place with horses," he said.

"A secretarial course, your mother said."

"Rubbish. She can't spell."

Two devious women, Hugo, and you're left with one of them. But she promises to be faithful and loving and kind . . .

In the early spring, and exactly to the day Hetty's labour began. She dreamed that she was Jacobina giving painful birth to a much-wanted but embarrassingly illegitimate child. What punishment would her husband have in store for her?

She heard the baby crying and opened her eyes.

"It's a girl," said Doctor Bailey. "Fine child. I hope you aren't disappointed about her sex."

Hetty roused herself. "Disappointed! Doctor! As long as she's alive and healthy. That's all Hugo and I ask for. Give her to me."

She was very tired. That seemed to have been a long speech she had made. She fell asleep cuddling the newly-washed damp-haired creature who was her daughter. When she awoke there was a familiar face at her bedside. It had been there once before on a much less happy occasion.

"Freddie! How did you get in here? Did the nurse say you could come?"

"No. I sneaked. They say your baby's a girl, Hetty. Can I see her?"

Hetty unfolded the shawl, and Freddie's earnest gaze was bent for a long time on the small crumpled face. Then he nodded vigorously, as if he had come to some decision.

"What will you call her, Hetty?"

"You name her, Freddie. That will be my gift to you."

Freddie's face lighted with pleasure.

"Truly, Hetty? Do you mean that? Then I'd like her called Jessy, and when she's grown up I'll marry her."

EPILOGUE

It was early spring in New York, the daffodils blowing in Central Park, the trees spiky with buds. The air was sharp and clear, the whole scene so invigorating that Jessy jumped with excitement.

"Oh, I belong here."

"No, you don't, you belong in England," Freddie answered.

"But this city pulls me. I seem to have memories. Freddie, supposing I wanted to do what Mother did in reverse, and live in an American house, a New York house."

"I wouldn't allow you to. But let's not get bewitched by the house until we see it. It may be cold and dusty and neglected and horrible."

"There's always been a caretaker, hasn't there?"

"Supposed to have been. The bank said there would be someone here."

"Oh, Freddie!" Jessy was almost dancing on the hard clean pavement bordering the park. "This is where Mother must have played with her hoop and taken her dolls out for an airing."

"Can't see your mother with dolls."

"No. She wasn't sentimental, was she? Very cool and practical and honest." Jessy's fingers tightened round her husband's. "I loved her very much."

"I know. So did I. She was always my favourite person at Loburn. Until you were born, of course."

"And you instantly said you would marry me, even

251

though I was bright pink and hideous. How horribly faithful you are." Jessy's gaze lingered on his face lovingly. "We're so lucky, it almost scares me. Having each other, having Loburn, and now a famous old mansion on Fifth Avenue as well."

"And I think we're almost there. Half way up the next block. No, it's nearer. Look!" Now Freddie's voice was excited, too. "This must be it."

"It isn't quite derelict," Jessy said, after a while, looking at the tall narrow house squeezed between a towering block of apartments on one side, and something in heavy grey concrete with an ostentatious forecourt and fountain on the other. "But it does need painting and tidying up. No wonder property developers have wanted to get their hands on it. Look at the company it's in. That's surely a Rockefeller next door. This looks like millionaires' row."

"I expect it always was, even when your grandparents lived here. They were rich enough. But you know how New Yorkers are always pulling down buildings and putting up bigger and better ones."

"They won't pull this one down," Jessy said emphatically. "I own the freehold. Mother was very definite about that."

"Don't decide until we get through the front door. The place may be full of unsympathetic ghosts. Not like Loburn's gentle ones. I'll try ringing the bell and hope someone answers it."

They stood there at the top of the steps, a nice-looking couple, the girl with blowing dark hair, greenish eyes, rosy colour in her cheeks, the man a bit professorial, with his intelligent, rather prominent, grey eyes behind horn-rimmed spectacles, a floppy lock of fair hair sliding over his forehead, his sober English clothes.

The old woman who opened the door must have thought them people of class, for she patted her clothes, as if feeling for a white apron, and then gave an old-fashioned bob.

"Good morning," Freddie said. "I'm Lord Hazzard, and this is my wife. The bank was to let you know we were coming."

"They did, sir, but they didn't give me time to have the place looking right. Not like it was in the old days, when there was plenty of servants. But come in, sir, come in, ma'am."

"You speak as if you have known the house for a long time," Jessy said in her pleasant warm voice. "My grandmother lived here, you know."

"Yes, and was drowned in that terrible shipwreck," the old lady said with suitable solemnity. "She was a fine strong-minded lady, Mrs Jervis was. She knew what she wanted, and so did Miss Clemency. You're right, I have known this house for a long time. I was cook in them times, when the old mistress and Miss Clemency was here. I'm Mrs Crampton."

Jessy put out a small well-bred hand.

"What fun to meet someone who knew my mother as a girl. Isn't it, Freddie?"

Freddie also held out his hand to shake the withered and none too clean one offered him.

"It's the greatest luck," he said amiably. "So you were cook in those days. The last days that the house was lived in, I believe. Will you show us over?"

"Of couse, sir. That's my instructions from the bank. But don't look too close for dust. I'm only one old woman, I can't keep all these rooms spick and span. This one here," she flung open doors to display an ornately carved high-ceilinged room, "was used for parties. Miss Clemency had a ball here, once. Not a big one, there wasn't room, but the double doors into Mrs Jervis's sitting room were opened that night. See, the windows look over the garden. But that's gone to rack and ruin. Those great buildings next door shut out the sun. Nothing grows. Faugh! Look at these curtains, frayed and torn. It's the ravages of time, ma'am."

Jessy was fingering the tattered blue silk curtains.

"Isn't it a strange coincidence, Freddie, that Mother found Loburn in much the same state as this house, badly needing repair and refurnishing. And now here we are in her house with the same thing to do."

"We're not staying for long, Jessy."

"A month at least, darling. And then we'll come over every spring. What fun."

The old lady was giving a tight smile.

"I can see you take after Miss Clemency, ma'am. She always wanted her own way. She weren't so polite about it, though. She were spoilt, we always said."

"My mother?" Jessy asked in surprise.

"Oh, yes, she could pout and have her tantrums. You've got her eyes, ma'am, sort of sea-green like hers were, but softer. And your smile's real nice. Must take after your daddy. He was handsome, wasn't he? We called him the sun god in the servants' hall. At least that was Hetty's name for him. She was quite smitten. Poor Hetty."

"Hetty?" said Jessy slowly.

"Yes, ma'am. She was my protégée, in a manner of speaking. Well, the mistress's to begin with, but then I took care of her. Poor little orphan."

"Poor little orphan? Hetty?" It was Freddie's turn to look mystified.

The old lady's faded blue eyes went from one to the other in puzzlement.

"You speak as if you know her. You can't. She was lost on that ship, probably weighed down with all the luggage the mistress would expect to be saved. I wrote to Miss Clemency in England once, to ask about her."

"Who was Hetty, Mrs Crampton?" asked Freddie, very gently.

"Never did know. Brought here one day, and left here. But she were part of the family if looks were anything to go by. She could have been Miss Clemency's sister. Her

254

twin sister at that. Wrong side of the blanket, I said. Her name was Harriet. I called her Hetty because she said she liked it. She was a good girl, honest and respectable. She deserved better than what she got, both in this house and in that cold drowning sea. Life's a queer old business, isn't it? Will you come down to my kitchen and have some coffee? I just made it. Then I can show you the upstairs."

The old lady waddled ahead of them, talking only half audibly.

"So you're planning to brighten up the old house. That will be nice. There's only me and my cat below stairs." Mrs Crampton looked backwards at Jessy, saying pleased, "You aren't a bit stuck-up, are you, ma'am, coming to have coffee in my kitchen?"

"I should hardly think I have any right to be stuck-up after what you have just told us," Jessy murmured. Her eyes were twinkling, the dimples beginning to show at the corners of her mouth. "Freddie! You know Granny always knew something she wouldn't talk about."

Freddie nodded. "My father did, too. He had heard something, once,"

"But not Daddy?"

"No. Although I'm sure he wouldn't have minded."

"Why should he?" Jessy cried. "If you ask me, he was jolly lucky it wasn't – the other one. So was I . . ."

Mrs Crampton, her hands on the coffee pot, turned to ask bewilderedly, "Are you talking about my Hetty? I didn't know you knew her."

"We believe we did," Freddie said carefully.

"I wouldn't know how you could, if she drowned off that ship."

Mrs Crampton poured steaming black coffee into cups. Her mind was going off at a tangent again. "Trust that Miss Clemency to save herself. She had a gift for doing what she set out to do."

"I don't think Hetty came far behind," Jessy murmured, the dimples breaking.

"You keep saying Hetty."

"That was the name of a lady my husband and I loved very much. If I could have all her qualities, my husband would love me for ever. Wouldn't you, darling?"

"But you have. And I will."

Mrs Crampton pushed the coffee cups across the table. She had given up trying to understand the conversation. The young English couple were lovely, but odd. She had always heard the English were odd.